NEVER BROKEN

EVERLY CLAIRE

Never Broken: The Unchained Book One

Cover Designer: Qamber Designs
Editor: Emily A. Lawrence
Proofreader: Brianne Matheny

Published by: Hudson & Hawk Group
New York | Miami | Road Town | Hamilton
EverlyClaire.com

WARNING

This series is set in a dark fictional world and contains potentially disturbing and triggering themes. It is intended only for adults eighteen years of age and older. For a list of potential triggers in this and future books in the series, scan the QR code below or visit everlyclaire.com/triggers.

Please look after your mental health.

For my grandparents. I wish you had made it to this moment with me. But I've seen all of you in my dreams, and I know you're at peace where you are. I hope I've made you proud.

Now ask yourself, which bonds are formed and which bonds are broken?

— *A Primer on Organic Reactions*

1

HER

It was 2 a.m., and I yawned and stared at the little orange pill in my desk drawer—half dying to use it, half hating it was even there.

Here I was, heiress of a corporate empire, daughter of societal privilege, top of the Class of 2024 at *the* secondary school of the New North American Union elite. And I couldn't even figure out a way to stay awake long enough to finish one goddamn chemistry chapter, let alone prevent myself from flunking out of college and—since my father couldn't exactly help me anymore —losing my chance to become a doctor, build a life, and actually make a difference in the world. Or at least start figuring out how.

So here it was, decision time: either pop this pep pill down my throat or guzzle a macchiato.

The macchiato was looking like the winner. Fewer side effects, *and* I could order a slave to bring it up to my room.

However, here was my other thought: that the toilet was

just a few short steps away in my en suite bathroom, and that to be safe, maybe the pill was better off there.

Before I could decide whether to flush the pill or hit the intercom to call a slave, my phone saved me. My friend Juliette was blowing it up. The smug little vibrations came one after another—first, some cartoonishly chiseled college guy grinning and guzzling a lager, then the obligatory selfie of her and him tossing ping-pong balls at each other and grinning like the drunk, horny idiots I wished to God I had the luxury of being right now.

But that wasn't my world, much as I had once hoped it would be.

With a sigh, I stared at the phone, which was still buzzing obnoxiously. Saving me? Right. If anything belonged in the toilet —

> JULIETTE
> Where are u?? This mixer is lit

> LOUISA
> Studying
> It's kind of the point of college, remember?

Maybe I'd feel better about spending all my time in college studying instead of partying if it had been the college I *wanted*. I'd *wanted* to go east, but the university here in Phoenix had offered me a better academic scholarship—one that at that point I not only wanted but needed. Plus, it had a good scholastic reputation, not to mention a handful of faculty that had so far managed to evade being fired or arrested for being radical enemies of the union. And it had been crowned one of the union's top ten party schools. The best of all worlds, right?

Or, for someone who was currently missing out on all of it, the worst.

I huffed a long curl off my face, closed the drawer, flipped the phone upside down, and turned back to my organic chemistry book. Sometimes my fellow pre-meds seemed to proudly rack up all-night study sessions the way some girls racked up drunken hookups. It didn't seem fair that after nearly a semester, I'd notched exactly zero of either. But as my eyelids drooped, I knew tonight would be no exception. Suddenly, pills and macchiatos and intercoms *all* seemed like too much work.

I slammed the book and rested my head on its cool, glossy cover. My long, thick, not-quite-brown curls were a bitch to care for most of the time, but they did offer an awfully good natural pillow. Even though I needed to take my contacts out, I actually allowed my eyelids to close for a split second.

JULIETTE
U there?

No. I sprang up at the vibration. My midterm was looming over me like a thunderhead, and I, who had gently breezed through secondary school, was barely scraping by with a D. If I didn't pass, I could kiss my academic scholarship—and my dreams of ever getting the hell out of my parents' house, let alone becoming a doctor—goodbye.

LOUISA
Sorry, fell asleep for a second

JULIETTE
U need a pick-me-up, girl

I prescribe some Vitamin D

She sent another sly pic of a pair of distressed jeans that *may* have outlined a guy's bulge if you squinted. Not like my mind wouldn't have gone there anyway, even if it hadn't.

In any case, *that* wasn't on tonight's menu. There wasn't

any good D within ten miles of our neighborhood unless you counted one of the well-shampooed corporate types that Daddy had had over for cocktails earlier in the evening to try to convince them that he was still relevant to the union's corporate elite, even though he was unemployed and buried under an avalanche of debt. The suit had to be thirty at least, but perhaps the time had come to consider that I was, well, desperate.

And desperate to get out of this bland, depressing, financially nosediving snooze factory I currently called home, which required graduating, so maybe my pick-me-up would have to be some Vitamin B: Benzedrine. Impulsively, I opened the drawer again and picked up the pill, turning it over between my fingers. My classmate Corey, an engineering major and family friend on a never-ending quest to prove he had everything about college figured out—and to nail me—had slipped it to me after my last lecture. "Every guy in my fraternity uses it," he'd whispered. "There's no reason to suffer."

It was only later when I'd looked up the brand name that I realized it was meth. He was offering me meth. I didn't know what was worse: that he'd thought I'd consider taking it, or that I actually *was*.

I dropped the pill and slammed the drawer shut again. I'd rather suffer. The last thing we needed in the Wainwright-Phillips family was another addict: my mother and my brother, Ethan, wherever he'd disappeared to, had *that* taken care of, thank you very much. Instead, my mind drifted down to the kitchen and to the brand-new artisan espresso machine with twenty-seven different settings, the one Daddy had brought home last week, accompanied by a full-color booklet packed with arty, luscious photos of all the drinks you could make. Lattes, cappuccinos, Americanos ... Daddy had explained every single one of them as he unboxed the machine, trying to coax a smile. "Only the best for my Loulou," he'd said, nice enough not to add: *Only the best, as long as it's cheaper than letting your addiction to daily store-bought espressos keep draining what remains of the puny allowance that's all I can afford to give you since your brother relapsed, your mom started drinking, and I went off the deep end and flushed away our family fortune.*

Ugh. I used to obsess over a perfect cup of espresso, but even that didn't thrill me anymore. All it did was remind me of how Daddy had made me live at home instead of in Choate Hall, the newest, shiniest dorm on campus, complete with private bathrooms and kitchenettes and even a rooftop pool, situated right next door to the student center and only a block down from Frat Row, and the dorm whose brochure still sat sadly lodged in the rack on my desk. Juliette—who had never been my closest friend, though we'd become closer after learning we'd wound up at the same school—had even spent all summer ordering coordinated pink-and-green furniture to decorate the suite we planned to share. Together, we could see it: late-night streaming TV binges, spa parties, and a revolving door of toned, glistening frat boys chilling on neon floats. For a safety school, it was actually starting to sound pretty great.

Then, with Daddy's decree, it all went up in smoke. I'd told Juliette that my mom's recent knee surgery meant someone needed to be there to help her get up and down the stairs. And it was no lie that Mom sometimes needed help navigating steps, though it was usually after one too many vodka martinis. Anyway, Juliette probably already suspected the truth. But if the other members of the Scottsdale glam squad found out my family was having money problems, they'd drop me like a bad stomach virus.

But that didn't really matter. The only thing that mattered was becoming a successful doctor, at which point I'd be able to get the hell out of here and go somewhere far away from the union, somewhere where I could actually help people and make a difference. And where I wouldn't have to rely on Daddy or his money—whatever was left of it—any longer.

Sighing, I stuck the phone in a drawer next to the pill and turned back to *A Primer on Organic Reactions* by Edgar Malchow, who was lucky I still had eight months to go before I could gleefully toss him on top of a bonfire. No matter how long I stared at his neat little elements and symbols, I never seemed to be able to rearrange them into anything but alphabet soup.

It didn't seem fair that I should only start floundering *now* when the stakes were so high. Over time, I'd learned to expect to do well in school because I always had. Calculus had come just as easily to me as English literature. That's why my GPA was so high, my teachers all said, because I was smart on both sides of my brain. It seemed perfect. As a doctor, not only would I be able to diagnose people, but I could *explain* everything to them, too, in a way that wouldn't leave them feeling hopeless and scared. Thanks to a girls' summer science camp in Chicago a few years ago—when Daddy could still afford things like that —I fell in love with the idea of helping people that way, and it was why I thought I'd love pre-med. The problem was, pre-med didn't love me. So far, I'd hired tutors; been to the study sessions; and even searched online homework help boards, hoping for that face-slapping eureka moment. I knew I wasn't dumb. I knew I had it in me. I just had to study harder, stay up later. I couldn't afford to let my eyes close for even a second. There was too much at stake.

So that settled that. The winner was Vitamin C: Coffee.

Except it wasn't. Despite poring over that manual for an hour, the only thing I'd figured out how to make was a mess. Pathetic. No wonder I was flunking o-chem. Some med student I'd make. How was I supposed to understand the inner workings of the human nervous system when I couldn't even use a simple coffee machine? But I had to stay awake *somehow*.

Luckily, I could enlist a slave to figure it out for me. There was always one on call, engaged in busywork while waiting to spring obediently into action when someone buzzed the intercom. Tonight, it would either be Daddy's old valet or the pretty green-eyed brunette maid. I hoped it would be the valet because the maid was seriously starting to get on my nerves. She had the kind of teasing little wrinkle next to her mouth that guys seemed to love but that I myself could never manage without looking demented, and said "Yes, Miss Louisa" in a way that made it abundantly clear that she thought my orders weren't worth following. Of course I *could* punish her. But for what? You couldn't really punish someone for a look or a tone of voice—well, you could, but I couldn't and wouldn't. And I was certain she knew that, which was exactly what made it so aggravating.

If the maid answered, I'd pretend I'd rung by accident.

Mind made up, I reached for the intercom. Just before my finger pushed the button, though, I stopped when the words of Erica Muller, my Slavery Studies 101 professor—whose paper, I remembered with a groan, I was also supposed to have started on tonight—echoed somewhere in the back of my somnambulating brain.

"Federal regulations require that each slave receive at minimum four hours of sleep a night, and studies show that two-thirds of slaves receive considerably less than that. And yet lawmakers, terrified of losing campaign contributions from the pro-slavery lobby that put them in office, have voted fifteen times in a row to keep—"

But God, that triple macchiato was sounding better and better the more I thought about it. Besides, could the average slave be any less sleep-deprived than the average college student? Talk about unfair. Where were the activists lobbying for *me*?

I hadn't even wanted to take that class, anyway. Everybody knew that Erica Muller had been a wanted fugitive decades ago for planting bombs under police cars as a member of the Slave Liberation Army. Nobody was exactly sure how she'd managed to get the charges dropped. Most of her compatriots had been arrested and sent to the mines. But there seemed to be somebody trying to get her fired and/or arrested every few months or so for being an enemy of the union. Up until he'd died, it had usually been one of Daddy's old golf buddies, Gerhard Langer. A German-born, copper-mining magnate, he was a member of that very same pro-slavery lobby Muller railed against—and a member of one of my university's Board of Regents, like his tech-mogul son, Max, was now.

For now, the progressive majority on the board protected her, but Professor Muller herself had stated in class that it was probably only a matter of time before she got ousted. "Luckily, we still technically have free speech in the union. I plan to enjoy it while it lasts," she'd said, standing at the front of the lecture hall that morning in her loose, oatmeal-colored natural-fiber shirt and pants, frizzy graying hair falling across the frames of her wire-rimmed glasses. Why did it seem like hopeless frumpiness was somehow a key requirement in the fight for social justice? Another good reason to keep away from the anti-slavery crowd. Muller might have had relatively free rein in progressive academia, but in more conservative circles like medicine, views like hers could still get you fired, expelled, blacklisted, ostracized—hell, Daddy himself would disown me instantly.

Besides, ultimately, Muller was just a kook. Slavery had been here for a century, and it wasn't going anywhere. It was all in that week's lecture notes, sitting patiently unopened in the corner of my desk. When the hard times of the 1930s had dragged on for two decades, hitting the middle classes as badly as the poor, somebody got the bright idea to start emptying out the prisons, then letting people sell their children temporarily, either to pay off debt or just to keep them from starving.

In a few years, nobody was starving. We and our allies had won a would-be world war with barely a shot fired. Then the boom times came, and New North America decided slavery should be more than temporary. The New European Union and all the allied regimes followed suit. Not to mention, those first slaves had started breeding more slaves, and by now, in 2025, they'd swelled to a third of the world population, a figure I'd memorized because Professor Muller had helpfully informed us it would be on the exam.

So they *must* have been happy. They were housed and fed, which had to beat starving or dealing drugs to survive. Sure, there were some low-class sadists out there who tortured them —they still made the news every now and then—but respectable people like my parents weren't among them. Our housekeeper had belonged to Mom's family since both were children, and I'd grown up among other loyal and affectionate slaves I knew for sure had *never* been tortured or sleep-deprived.

Hmm. Maybe *that* could be the topic for my paper.

I pressed the button.

"Hey."

I snapped my finger back as if I'd been burned.

The fuck? It was a *boy*. Well, a young man, to be more precise. In any case, definitely not the maid *or* the valet.

But that made no sense. Our former army of slaves had dwindled. As far as I knew, my parents now only owned four. Two females: the housekeeper—who also cooked and managed the others—and the maid. And two males: the old valet and the creepy gardener that I avoided like rush-hour traffic.

Not only did this bold, flippant voice clearly not belong to any of them, but it barely sounded like a slave at all. He could be new, I supposed, but Daddy couldn't even afford my daily espresso anymore. How the fuck could he afford an entire human being? On the other hand, who else would be answering the slave intercom this time of night, but a slave? And there weren't any other men in this house, unless—

Oh. *Of course.* The suit. He must have stayed later than I'd thought. What was his name again? Benji? Bennett? I chuckled a little at my own sleep-deprived stupidity. Well, if he was in his cups and wanted to have a little fun, no reason I couldn't toss the ball back. So what if he was a bit ... mature?

Cautiously, I pressed the talk button again. "Hello?"

"Didn't we do this already?" The reply came instantly. Okay, he had a good voice. Kind of low and slow, but not *too* much of either. The kind of voice that made my insides feel all soft and deep and velvety. And with a lilt—no, not a lilt. An *accent.* A New European accent, from the sound of it, though not from any country I recognized, and—

Wait. Benny was from New York, wasn't he?

Did that mean—

It couldn't.

No slave would *dare.*

But I had to find out for sure, right?

I cleared my throat, trying to sound disapproving. "Is that any way to talk to me?"

"Sorry. Didn't we do this already, miss?"

An accent it was, but slight, and New York was nowhere in the mix. More like Berlin by way of Paris by way of ... California, maybe? And even more shocking, a sense of humor. The last time the valet had cracked a smile was probably three decades ago. The same more or less went for the others. Humor was not generally something that fetched a high price on the auction

block. Obedience, physical strength, and occasionally looks—
that was what counted.

"Make up your mind yet?"

"Huh?"

"About what you wanted."

"What?" I was speaking in monosyllables, but I was
exhausted and delirious and quite frankly, shocked. Nothing
about what was going on right now made sense.

"You must have wanted something. A glass of water,
maybe? A turndown? Or maybe a back massage?"

"From you?" Actually, my back was killing me, and so was
the thought of how good a cute boy's hands might feel pressing
firmly, deeply, maybe even a little bit roughly into those knots.
But *he* didn't need to know that. Whoever *he* was. And how the
hell could I be so sure he was cute?

Beats me. But I was.

Anyway, I shouldn't be engaging with him at all. Sure, he
was just joking around with me. No harm there—at least if he'd
been some cocky frat boy in my class. From a slave—and what
else could he be?—it was bold, unacceptable, dangerous
insolence.

On the other hand, nobody else was around to hear. "What
do *you* know about massages?" I asked before I could talk
myself out of it.

"Okay, I admit, nothing. But I could probably figure it out.
They say it's all in the wrists."

"I don't think you're allowed to touch me." Don't *think*? If he
was a slave, touching me could get him thrown into a pit mine.

"Come on, nobody would see."

"Oh, sure." I snorted. "And give you an excuse to get your
hands on me?"

"Who says I want my hands on you? I don't even know

what you look like. Come down here and show me, and then I'll decide."

"Why should I come down there? I wanted a macchiato. You're supposed to make it and bring it up to me."

"Oh, so you did buzz for a reason."

I scoffed in irritation. "Yes. Now can you please get me some coffee?"

"*Please*," he repeated, savoring the word like chocolate—the kind of chocolate slaves, even well-treated ones, rarely got to taste. "I don't hear that word too often. I like the sound of it, coming from you. Say it again."

"Not a chance." Why did my face feel so—oh, fuck. I was *blushing*. He was flirting with me, and to my astonishment, I was kind of—just a little—flirting back. This was crazy. I had to stop it, now. "Forget the *please*. I'm ordering you to get me a coffee."

"Can't. I'm busy."

"Busy?" *That* was a word that didn't seem to be in a slave's vocabulary. "Doing what?"

"I'll give you a hint—my hands are wet."

"With water?"

He laughed. And not a fake chuckle designed to humor a master's stupid, unfunny joke. A *real* laugh, like a real person, and for some reason, a warm, strange thrill shot right through my body. What the hell was going on with this guy—no, not guy. Slave. *Slave.*

"Sure. If that makes you more comfortable."

"You know what would make me comfortable?" I asked.

"Let me guess. A good f—"

"Don't you *dare*."

"Foamy espresso. Why, what did you think I was going to say?"

"Nothing," I said quickly, face on fire now. "Foamy espresso.

A good foamy espresso. That's what I want." I cringed, wondering why the hell I was still enabling this, even as I waited breathlessly for his next remark. My room, like every room in the desert foothills, was air-conditioned, but it felt like the temperature had shot up twenty degrees.

"Oh, you mean this?"

From the speaker came a high-pitched grinding noise, then a gurgling that was unmistakably the sound of, uh, foamy espresso being poured into one of Mom's tiny, hand-painted china cups. So *he'd* figured the machine out easily and he couldn't have possibly been in this house for more than a day. My mouth watered; I could practically smell it. Damn him.

"Ah, organic Ecuadorian caramel macchiato," he said as if he were leisurely sitting back in a chair and sipping it. "The last one in the house."

I gasped. "You're not allowed to drink that."

"Who's going to stop me? You won't come down here, and there's nobody else around."

"I can tell Daddy. He'll have you whipped." I mean, he could, but he wouldn't. Not for *that*. Plus, I couldn't imagine a stupider thing to go tattling to him about.

"Or you could come down here and do it yourself."

"Don't be ridiculous." I'd never whipped a slave—never even seen it done. Daddy kept a switch and a cane around but rarely touched them himself, and *I* certainly never had. For anything beyond that, we had always hired a handler, who was discreet enough to do his work well out of earshot of us.

"Come on. You're not curious about me?"

"Hardly." Curious? The word hardly seemed adequate, when literally the only thing I could think about right now was throwing open the door, sprinting down the stairs, and glimpsing for myself just what this mystery guy—mystery slave?—looked like. *Of course* I was curious. I'd never before been so thoroughly overwhelmed with curiosity about anyone. And even though I still hadn't a clue what he looked like, the flush in my face and the tingling in my thighs was leading me to suspect that curiosity wasn't all it was.

"Miss?" I realized I'd stopped talking, and here he was, suddenly being all proper. Still, there was a challenge here and something else I couldn't put my finger on. Sarcasm? Bitterness? No, danger.

That was it.

Danger.

A massive, blinking red warning sign. *Slave:* do not approach.

"Okay, I lied," he said, almost sincerely, like he was afraid he'd disappointed me.

Disappointing? *This? That* would be the biggest laugh all night. In all of five minutes, I'd been revived, struck dead, and revived again.

"There's some coffee left," he said. "You still want it?"

"I—" Yes. Yes, I did want it. Desperately. "Forget it," I said and released the button.

I sank back into my desk chair, staring at the door, flushed, heart rattling, even a little out of breath. I flipped open Malchow, but at this point, even a triple macchiato wouldn't be enough to help me concentrate. I'd had no pills, no caffeine, and yet for the first time in months and months, my whole body felt awake, and it had nothing to do with chemistry.

Or maybe it did.

2

EARLIER

My new owner's name was Keith Wainwright-Phillips. I knew because I picked him out myself.

I didn't know too much about him, though. He was the ex-CEO of a company that sold insurance to corporations that used slave labor, he lived in Phoenix, Arizona, and he knew where to find my sister. Beyond that, he could be a rapist, he could be a sadist, he could be a psychopath. Hell, I hoped he was all three because it would make it easier for me to kill him when and if the time came. But all that mattered to me right now was making sure he wouldn't send me back. Because I *couldn't* be sent back. I needed to be in Phoenix because Phoenix was where my sister was. And Keith Wainwright-Phillips, before I killed him, was going to help me find her—whether he liked it or not.

So for the past forty-eight hours, I'd tried to be good. I'd tried to be a helpful, polite, obedient little slave, the kind that when I was a kid, everyone thought—briefly—I would grow up to be. *Yes, sir, no, sir, whatever pleases you, sir.* Hell, I even spent a large portion of the flights from Berlin to New York to Phoenix trying to tell stories to a red-faced, sobbing little boy, mostly for the sake of the eardrums of the other slaves chained in the cargo hold with us, just so they wouldn't riot out of sheer annoyance and force the handlers to come down and start whaling on all of us.

With a book, it would be easy, because, unlike most slaves, I could read. But we weren't allowed any books on the flight, so to tell stories, I'd have to be like my sister and make them up. The problem was, I couldn't. I was the logician of the family, the same way *she* was the storyteller. Which made sense, since our mother had been smart enough—in a different universe—to have been both. The ironic thing was, our mistress used to cane my sister all the time for lying, though she'd never lied in her life. She didn't know *how* to lie. All she'd been doing, by claiming that she hadn't swept the bedrooms because she'd followed a unicorn through a portal in search of the gnomes who had hidden her dustpan in a dragon's cave, was making up her own truth, a truth that was so much sweeter and more beautiful than life had ever given her.

As for me? When I was twelve or so, I ripped a star chart out of one of our master's kids' textbooks. I couldn't read the names, but I was trying to learn all the planets and constellations by color and shape because I wanted to be *right*. And she was the only one who'd sit out on the roof of our master's Luxembourg City townhouse and stargaze with me, late at night when we were supposed to be in bed.

But *she* didn't care about being right. She'd just make everything up to suit her. Everything was a fairy or a mermaid or a unicorn. And then to really get me going, she'd throw an elephant or a pig or something in there. Then she'd tell crazy stories about them that had no logic, except to her, I guess, and insist they were true. And I'd just get fed up and call her a stupid idiot who didn't understand science, and go inside.

Needless to say, I regretted that a year later when my last glimpse of her tear-streaked, terrified face was from separate pens as we were sold apart, punished for something I alone had done. And then I didn't see the stars for three years.

But I kept on hearing her voice—in the fields, on the whipping post, in the punishment cage. *Who cares if they're not right?* She'd demand. *What is "right," anyway? No one owns the sky. In my stories, no one owns anything or anyone.*

It was a nice thought. Really nice. Problem was, I wasn't like her. I couldn't tell stories, nor did I really believe in them. But I could lie. Holy shit, could I lie. The same muscle that made me logical helped me manipulate logic—which I did, often, to protect my sister at the price of my own skin.

And I could steal. Hell, it was how I'd gotten where I was right now—stealing and lying and scheming and bribing and calling in favors from everyone I knew, slave and free, to get myself sold to where I needed to be. And here I was, scheming and lying and stealing again because if I got beaten up, deemed trouble, and sent back because of this screeching little kid next to me, I'd fail.

And I'd already failed with my mother. I could not, *would not*, fail with my sister. I'd make up for what I'd done and make sure freedom, for her, would be more than just a story. And if the only freedom *I* ever found was dying doing that, well, it would still be a happier ending than most of us get.

So instead of making up stories for this kid, I stole them. From memory, out of the only comic book I'd ever been able to call my own, one my old master's son had left out in the rain and then decided it had been rendered suitable only for a slave to have. I'd treasured it. Of course, I'd been illiterate, too, then, so as near as I could figure it, the bad guys were the ancient Romans trying to invade Gaul and boss everybody around, and the good guy, Asterix, fought back using his brains *and* his fists. And if my master's son hadn't been too stupid to realize how much a slave could relate to that, he never would have given me the comic.

"You know what Asterix told those Roman bullies when they tried to push him around?" I said to the boy in German because it was all he understood, putting on my best story-telling voice, like *her*. Curious, he sniffled and wriggled a bit closer, though, like all of us, the chains on his ankles bolted him to the bulkhead. Unlike me and a few others onboard who couldn't be trusted, though, he didn't have a muzzle fastened to his head with leather straps. Luckily, the wire cage over my mouth only prevented me from biting, not from talking. "He looked them right in the eye and said, 'You might be bigger, but I've got friends and a whole lot of smarts. And that beats muscle any day of the week.'"

Yeah, Asterix never actually said that. But the kid didn't know that. He was illiterate, same as I'd once been. Plus, it *felt* right. And it seemed to do the trick. The kid's eyes got all wide, like for a second, he actually forgot he was helpless and chained in a dark cargo hold on his way to be sold to some possibly psychotic stranger who held his very life in their hands. I'd call that a win.

Actually, now that I could read, I wished I still had the comic. It was the only thing besides dense physics and chemistry texts I think I'd actually enjoy. Hell, maybe I'd been wrong. Maybe it would turn out that the story was completely different than I'd imagined. Maybe the Romans were actually the good guys. But at least I would finally be able to find out for myself.

After landing, we were loaded with cattle prods into a van to the distribution center for Cosgrove's Human Assets, the private dealer who'd handled my sale. There, my cuffs and shackles and muzzle were finally removed. My old clothes were taken from me, and I was shoved into a cold shower, deloused, and given a pair of khaki scrubs to wear, identical to the eighteen male slaves standing around me and the dozen more female slaves in a separate pen. Every so often, the sales manager would appear outside the pen, calling out our numbers one by one as our owners arrived.

So this was Phoenix, a place I knew nothing about except that it was in the middle of a goddamn desert somewhere to the west of New North America, it was home to one of the largest mirror telescopes in the world, and that I wasn't impressed.

We'd now been here for three hours. I hadn't slept in almost eighteen, and since we'd arrived, nobody had offered me so much as a morsel of food, a gulp of water, or ice for the electrical burns still sizzling on my torso. Not that I'd expected it. But the little boy evidently had because he kept tugging at my arm as if he'd decided I must have a stash of lollipops somewhere that I just wasn't telling him about for some reason.

From behind me, the chain-link pen clattered open as Weiss, a walking meat cube of a handler who'd come all the way with us from Germany, entered with a set of keys. Feeding time, I hoped, if only because it would get this kid off my case.

No such luck. From behind me came a wail.

I groaned. "Look, kid, I told you, I'm really sorry, but I—"

But the kid wasn't there. He had been yanked backward and onto the ground, cowering now behind the handler's legs. "Back off, slave," the handler said to me in German. "This one said he was hungry. So I'm gonna shove a gourmet meal down his throat." Smiling like his birthday had come early, the handler prodded the kid up and started dragging him toward the gate again.

But the boy's number hadn't been called. The sales manager

wasn't waiting outside the pen. My heart dropped. By *gourmet meal*, did he mean—

The boy's eyes, when they met mine, were two petrified saucers, though he didn't struggle or even, for once, start screaming. He'd been trained better than that. If it happened, he'd just ... let it happen.

But I knew why he was looking at me. What he was pleading for. The same thing we were all pleading for, all the time. Even if we never said it out loud.

I glanced around in horror at the blank, emotionless faces of my fellow slaves. Seriously? *Nobody* was going to do anything about this?

I mean, I knew why—because it was suicide—but that didn't make it right.

My sister, when I got myself killed saving this kid before I could save *her*, might feel otherwise. But knowing what we'd both been through, I think she'd also understand why I lunged for the guy anyway.

Luckily for me, he must have been on steroids or something because his muscles deflated like balloons when I grabbed him —my own muscles forged on the handles of hoes and pickaxes —and hurled him against the concrete wall, hard enough to crack his skull if I had only aimed him right. As it was, it only bent his nose at a forty-five-degree angle, blood gushing out of it like a broken hose.

I would have tried again, but a second later, thugs outnumbered me four to one. Two of them held me down while the third laid into me with one of their standard-issue cattle prods, all over my neck, jaw, and torso—prods that, strangely, never seemed to hurt any less, no matter how many times I'd been zapped with them. The fourth thug just stood by forebodingly until the end, when he clobbered me right in the eye as a parting gift.

Finally, they threw me down like a wet rag to slump against the wall, and I doubled over, trying to quell the pounding in my head, praying I wouldn't pass out, vomit, or die. Not here, anyway. I still had things to do.

Actually, I was lucky for another reason: If I'd done what I'd just done to an owner, I'd be flayed alive, if not sold to the mines. But these assholes were just hired goons, here to help close the sale. They wouldn't risk their paychecks by harming the merchandise. Much. Besides, they probably figured my body was already ripped to shreds enough—from the trip and just in general—that nobody would notice.

But *I* was pretty sure I was fucked.

Meanwhile, the little boy, forgotten by the handlers, was howling again, but the other slaves didn't react. They barely looked at me *or* him, fearing guilt by association. I'd done everything I could do for him. Now, all I could do was strain through my blurred vision to try to see through the chain-link surrounding me and down the harsh, fluorescent-lit corridor, waiting for my number to be called, desperately trying to think up a clever explanation for my new owner that wouldn't get me sent back. Because I *couldn't* be sent back.

My sister was depending on me.

"773496S6."

Called like a dog, I raised my head automatically. *Lucky Sevens*, they'd sometimes called me ironically at the factory farm in Romania, where I'd spent the three years after being sold away from my sister. It was a nickname I'd hated but couldn't do much about. A bitter joke, really, though I *was* praying it would hold today. It was derived from the number that had been etched into my brain as deeply as it had been on the steel chain bracelet I, like all slaves, wore welded tight to my wrist. That number was the closest thing I'd ever had to a real name. Maybe the closest I ever would. Legally, we were supposed to be called either by our numbers or nothing, but many of us were called *something*, if only in private—a birth name if we were born free, a nickname if we weren't.

But not me.

They tell me I'm not a person. I say, fine. I get away with more that way.

A different handler, also speaking German but with a New North American accent, clanged his unlit cattle prod on the chain-link, the same as he'd done for the others. The only difference was that he was carrying an armful of chains and another muzzle.

My turn, then.

My chest tightened—I couldn't help it—at the clang of steel as the new handler, Barrett, unlocked the pen again with a ring of keys. Not that I was nervous, of course. I'd done this before, after all. Although granted, never when someone's life was in the balance: my sister's.

I stumbled to my feet more unsteadily than I would have liked, squared my shoulders, and made sure to neutralize my face. Behind me, the little boy, abandoned by his tormentors, increased his wails as he realized his protector was about to leave. *Get used to it, kid. Everyone who cares leaves. Or dies. Or gets sold.* I bent down and spoke low in German. Even if his new master spoke the language, he'd still have to pick up English on the fly—and he'd have to cut out the crying, ASAP.

"Remember Asterix?" I asked. The boy nodded.

"What's the holdup? Move it, slave!"

I bent down to the boy, who was clearly about to start bawling again. "Quick. What does he say?" I whispered, recalling the one thing I'd told him that I knew Asterix had *actually* said.

The kid thought for a second, then twisted his face into a

kind of crooked smile. "Them Romans be crazy," he said in ungrammatical German.

"You know it, kid." I offered him a fist-bump, which he returned half-heartedly.

Look, aside from the crying, he was a good-looking, well-trained boy, and chances were his owners would treat him right, at least for a while. If I had to guess, he'd go to a rich household much like the one I'd been born in, where they'd want a playmate for their children who could be trained as a valet as he grew. He'd still work twelve-hour days and be whipped or caned for the slightest infraction, but nobody spent thousands importing a foreign slave just to brutally rape, torture, and/or kill them.

Usually.

Turning away from the sniffling little boy like an asshole, I stepped out of the pen, wincing as the door crashed closed behind me.

The New North American sales manager, slick and gelled and different from the one on the plane, raised his manicured eyebrows when he saw the state of my face. "What happened to—"

"I don't know, Mr. Harrigan," lied the handler, Barrett, in English, eyes flicking this way and that as if he were afraid *I* would be stupid enough to say something and get him and his buddies in trouble. "I wasn't there, sir." Meanwhile, he strapped on my muzzle, pulling the leather straps as tight as if it were a parachute and he was about to push me out of a plane. I'd never bitten, of course, but I was starting to think I should try it one of these days, as long as my mouth was going to be behind bars no matter what. He ordered me to kneel and hold out my hands. My wrists were already throbbing, rubbed red and raw from being restrained for the past eighteen hours. Fuck, I'd rather stick my hands in a piranha tank than be cuffed again. I was used to cuffs and shackles, of course, but they were like cattle prods—they never seemed to hurt any less. Still, there was nothing to be gained by not cooperating—not at this point, anyway. So I squeezed my eyes shut and did as I was told, hearing the familiar ratcheting as the cool metal again sank its teeth into my already brutalized wrists.

"Jesus, look at him," exclaimed Harrigan in disgust when I opened them again. "Is this what you—"He groaned and pinched the bridge of his nose. "We never should have outsourced the slave handling. Ah, but it's too late now. We're already backed up enough. Up, boy," he ordered me. "And keep your mouth shut about this. If anybody asks, they loaded you on the plane like that."

"Yes, sir," I said, following their lead and switching to English. It was a language I'd learned half from British and North American streaming shows, half from Shakespeare and Dickens, all of which I'd been allowed to consume courtesy of my last master, the Heidelberg professor who'd bought me off the factory farm when I was fifteen. I was nearly twenty now, and in that time, he'd taught me everything I knew. Everything academic, anyway.

My shackles and cuffs rattling with a sick familiarity, I followed exactly three paces behind the two men, just like we were taught, down under the familiar harsh fluorescent lighting of the corridor with its cement floors and cinder block walls, the kind of hard, brutal institutional space that was practically home for me. The kind of space that—given what I'd done—I probably belonged in.

But Keith Wainwright-Phillips knew what I'd done, and he had bought me anyway. Why? I was about to find out—and also whether he was the kind of guy who, when he received a package full of defective merchandise, blamed the merchandise or the company who'd shipped it to him.

A door opened, and I stepped into the incandescent glow of the gallery. Out here, it was all soft lighting, upholstered furniture, plush carpeting, and mood music meant to lull rich buyers into forgetting they were trading in human flesh. Hell, it almost made *me* forget that *I* was human flesh.

Barrett—with the kind of viciousness I couldn't explain, even in a handler, given he'd just met me—jerked me to a stop somewhere in the middle of the endlessly long room and pointed to the floor.

"Kneel, boy," he said, swatting me with the unlit prod, which was totally unnecessary and from him, totally expected. I obeyed immediately, chains clinking, hands folded in my lap. A lock of my golden-blond hair came loose from behind my ear and swung into my face. I wondered whether trying to reach up and replace it would look like insolence and decided not to risk it. I was already fucked up enough from the fight. The littlest thing could cost me the time and resources I needed to find my sister.

From above, the first sound I heard out of my new owner was an annoyed sigh—and not at me. "Why is he muzzled when the others aren't?" he asked.

"Protocol, sir," said Harrigan.

Barrett caught my eye with a sneer. "And after what this particular slave did to Weiss—"

Oh. I'd just broken his work husband's nose. That explained it. Luckily, Harrigan shushed him before he could go into detail. It was his ass on the line, too.

"Take it off," said my master.

What?

"But, Mr. Wainwright-Phillips, his history—"

Shouldn't the master be giving the orders? I thought.

"Shouldn't the master be giving the orders?" he said.

Damn right.

"I'm well aware of his history," Wainwright-Phillips's voice continued, "but I decided to give him a chance anyway. I want him to trust me, and needless to say, chaining him up like a rabid animal won't accomplish that. Now take that muzzle off. I want to see his face properly."

Fuck. The prospect of actually not completely hating this guy had *not* been on my agenda. And it was going to ruin everything.

"Of course, sir." The handler seethed. He jerked my face forward and violently unbuckled the muzzle, sending a cloud of his oniony breath radiating down onto my face as the device clattered to the floor. Some improvement. He yanked a thick lock of my hair, wrenching my head to the side. "Bite anybody and you leave here with one nut, mutt," he muttered in my ear.

"Duly noted, sir," I muttered back.

"Restraints, too," said Wainwright-Phillips. Hell, compared to most masters, this guy was practically Spartacus.

"But he—"

"*Restraints, too*," my new master repeated. And all of a sudden, those, too, clattered to the ground again. And there I was with three free people—limbs unfettered, mouth uncaged, just like them. But still I stayed obediently kneeling, eyes on the floor because the chains that bound me were so much more than physical, and all four of us knew it.

All at once, someone wearing expensive leather boat shoes stepped into view. Despite myself, my breathing grew shallow. This was it, and it never got easier. Plan or no plan.

"You can look up, boy."

I still didn't move. It could be a trick.

"I mean it. I bought you. You might as well see what you're dealing with. My name's Keith Wainwright-Phillips, by the way." I already knew that, of course, and besides, it wasn't like we'd be on a first-name basis. That was impossible when one person didn't have one.

"Yes, sir," I said, and my master and the sales manager exchanged bemused smiles like I'd just said something cute.

Oh, the accent. Right.

All right, time to size up this weirdo. In his mid-fifties, fit and tall but not as tall as me, with a full head of salt-and-pepper hair and a slight growth of beard, Master Wainwright-Phillips carried with him the same musk of privilege all my masters had had. There was, however, something different about him, and I was kicking myself that I couldn't yet figure out what. Unless I'd lost track of time, it was a workday, though he wasn't dressed for work. Rather, with his polo shirt, beard growth, and tan, he looked like someone who enjoyed his leisure time. An avid sailor or golfer, maybe, like my old master.

Maybe that was it. Or maybe it was the fact that just by his critical gaze, I could tell right away that he noticed the burns and bruises. But he didn't say anything.

Why?

Before I could brainstorm a reason, my new master grabbed my chin and tilted it up, and I knew the gaze. It could come from a male or a female. It didn't really matter. Let's face it: When it *wasn't* contused black and blue, the face I'd inherited from my mother—perfect Euclidean bone structure, foxlike eyes somewhere between amber and gold, and thick waves of sun-bleached golden hair falling across it all just so—did the trick every time. I didn't even pretend to be modest about it. As a slave, you couldn't be. We were products, after all. I might have sparked Wainwright-Phillips' initial interest with my education and skills—and my bargain price for a slave *with* those skills—but my pictures were what had closed the deal, and I knew it.

"He really is beautiful," Wainwright-Phillips said idly to

Harrigan, even though at the moment, I was a complete fucking mess. He tapped my mouth to get me to open it, to see if I had all my teeth, or something. Who the fuck knows why they did it? "The photos didn't lie. I might have to start having dinner parties again; it would be a shame not to show him off. And look at those shoulders. He's not one of those waifish little pets you see all the time. He's strong." He pinched my bicep below my uniform sleeve—still ripped, like the rest of me, from three years working in chains—then ran his hand down my flat torso like admiring a Thoroughbred.

There wasn't anything overly suggestive about the touch; it was pretty par for the course. Still, I knew enough never to rule anything out. Even the most devoted hetero family men had been known to make exceptions for slaves because slaves didn't count, and free men—unlike free women—could fuck whoever and whatever they wanted. Lucky bastards. But to men like my master, a valuable slave was more like a well-trained purebred hunting dog or horse. A creature attractive, functional, maybe even endearing, but decidedly not a person.

Meanwhile, the sales manager nodded obsequiously along, though he would have done that even if Wainwright-Phillips had just told him the clouds were literally cotton candy. Meanwhile, Barrett glared at me, practically salivating. *Your balls are mine, mutt.*

And as for me? I just waited, heart pounding in my ears. Waited for my new master to mention the bruise that still throbbed like an alarm bell near my eye. Waited for him to realize that bargain or no bargain, I was trouble—what kind of idiot slave gets in a fight mere minutes before meeting his new master?—and decide to send me back. I wondered if Barrett would say anything. Even though he clearly hated me, he probably wouldn't. To risk killing a sale, he'd have to be dumber than he looked. And that was pretty damn dumb.

The sales manager cleared his throat. "He can be stripped, if you prefer to inspect him further."

The handler nodded encouragingly, and I rolled my eyes inwardly. *Oh, so you're a perv, too. Figures.*

"No. He's already had a health examination over there, and I know he's got scarring—the photos they sent were very thorough. No need to show it off here. There's a thirty-day money-back guarantee, anyway. If there's anything wrong with him, I expect I'll find out sooner or later. I'd rather just get him home."

"Of course, sir. Hold out your hands, boy," Barrett ordered gleefully, whipping out the cuffs, clearly relishing the last chance he'd get to remind me that I was property. Dick.

I closed my eyes, stifled a groan, and did as I was told for the third time. I could only hope the ride to the Wainwright-Phillips home would be a short one and that they'd actually come off at the end of it.

"What are you doing?" Wainwright-Phillips demanded.

My eyes popped open. But the question was directed toward the staff.

"It's policy, Mr. Wainwright-Phillips," said the sales manager. "The restraints are included."

"I don't care. I told you I don't want him chained. At all." He grabbed one of my arms. "Look, his wrists are all sliced up already. I realize it's for your own safety, but if you don't want the merchandise damaged, how much would it cost you to take five minutes to train your staff to put these things on properly?"

Coincidentally, I had thought the same thing. I guess we both had heads for logic. And all of a sudden, the metal was gone.

Thank you, I thought because even saying that out of turn would have been inappropriate. My master beckoned me to get up, and I could see Harrigan and Barrett breathe audible sighs, probably relieved as I was that this bullshit was almost over. Then—

"By the way, don't think I don't notice those fresh burns on his face and neck," Wainwright-Phillips said, peering closer. "And bruises."

Oh, shit. *No, no, no.* I thought I was—

"And I want to know what your so-called 'experienced slave handling professionals' have been doing to the poor kid," he demanded. "Who, considering the money's cleared escrow, is my property, not yours."

Wait, *what*? Wainwright-Phillips *was* incensed, it seemed, but not at me. And for some reason, he'd held off mentioning it. Why? Just to fuck with the handlers? To fuck with *me*? Or to put me at ease? But who the fuck cared whether a slave was at ease? Slaves didn't *have* ease.

The sales manager sputtered, his slick, sophisticated facade toppling as these bastards' facades always did when someone called them out on being the sick, violent fucks they really were. "We received him from his previous owner like that," he stammered, glaring at Barrett. "We don't take any responsibility for—"

"The mutt was being aggressive," broke in the handler, unable to hold back anymore, jabbing a finger at me. Harrigan shot him a death glare whose meaning was clear: *Shut up, you idiot.*

"Somehow I doubt that, considering he's completely exhausted, and from what I've seen, your staff seem far too quick to punish, when other means of control are available." My master gestured for me to rise, and I started to get to my feet with a sigh of relief. I was in the clear, for now. "This is completely unacceptable," he said. "Who's your supervisor?"

"He's out to lunch, sir."

"Well—" Wainwright-Phillips sputtered, looking around as

if to see how much further his overinflated sense of entitlement would get him. Not very. "I'm not finished here. You can bet your supervisor will be hearing from me, and so will everyone I know in the market for a slave. And you won't relish my responses on the customer satisfaction survey, I can tell you that. Come, boy."

I walked toward him in a daze. Well, shit. If I hadn't known what I knew about him, I'd say that Keith Wainwright-Phillips almost deserved a chance.

All that remained was for me to get scanned under the microchip machine so the data could be updated and Wainwright-Phillips would be officially registered as my owner. It took seconds only. As we turned to exit the gallery, I caught one last glimpse of the boy from the plane, who'd also been claimed. He kneeled before a well-dressed woman, looking more than a little stressed. She was speaking German to him while she clutched a baby in a sling and held a shrieking toddler by the hand. A teenage slave girl waited nearby, wrangling another child. Just as I'd suspected. The kid wouldn't get a moment's peace, but he'd probably be fine. For a while.

Another slave greeted us in the waiting room, a woman with a lined, rosy face, round glasses, and bunned gray hair with a little bit of its original black clinging stubbornly. She was thin and reserved but exuded competence, and more importantly, she didn't look terrified of Wainwright-Phillips. That was huge.

"This is my housekeeper," said my master with a slight smile. She actually smiled *back*. Masters could feel affection for their slaves, I'd heard. It was just that none of *mine* ever had. "She's also my cook, so I'd advise you to get on her good side immediately if you want access to the treats."

Treats? Now the woman turned her sympathetic smile on me, and it *almost* made me want to return it, even though it—

and the mention of treats—made me feel about five years old.
But then we directed our gazes to the ground and fell into lock-
step behind our owner as we trailed him to his car. It could only
help me to demonstrate to a valued fellow slave that I was well-
trained and wouldn't cause trouble. Yet.

I couldn't help but blink as we emerged into the sunlight of
a sprawling suburban parking lot, the sound of traffic zooming
by on the frontage road drowning our footsteps. But I was most
surprised to glimpse jagged, russet-colored mountains in the
distance, entirely alien from anything in any part of New
Europe I'd lived in. My only real frame of reference for them
were cliché scenes from Western movies I'd glimpsed, although
since then, stagecoaches, saloons, and horse corrals seemed to
have been replaced with interstate highways, big-box stores,
and fast-food outlets.

Any change in scenery was a relief, though. For the last few
days, I'd been in chains, going from dark, mildewed holding
pens to trucks to planes to more holding pens. At least now I
could breathe fresh air, even if it was hot, dry, and strange. I
turned my face to the sun, drinking it up without shame. Sure,
my master could still be a sadist, but he probably wasn't. And if
he was, and if he was helping the man who had my sister, I'd
kill him and save her.

It didn't matter what happened to me after that.

The housekeeper dragged me back to reality as she opened
the door of Wainwright-Phillips's luxury sedan—a classic
model of Mercedes-Benz, I instantly noted. (I'd never driven
one, of course, but I'd washed a few). If he admired German
engines as much as I did, there was yet another point in his
favor. Goddamn.

"We'll find you some clothes as soon as we get back,"
murmured the housekeeper, indicating that I should slide in
next to her in the back seat. *Find*, not buy. She herself was

dressed neatly in a pink blouse, black skirt, and sandals, but they were probably secondhand from her mistress. I took that to mean there wouldn't be any lavish shopping trips in my future. Was Wainwright-Phillips on a budget or something? If so, how and why had he bought me at all? I still hadn't figured that out, and it bothered me. My background may have made me a bargain, but I sure as hell wasn't cheap. "We've got a bunk in the slave quarters made up for you, and you've already been worked into the rotation. You'll be on the night shift tonight— the low man on the totem pole always gets it. Don't worry, though," she said, touching my arm lightly, "it's just light cleaning and waiting around in case something comes up. Hardly anything ever does."

Her eyes shifted to my electrical burns, and I squirmed in the leather seat like a kid getting a booster shot.

"Poor boy. Look at those," she said softly, flicking aside a longer lock of my hair to examine my neck. "How did—never mind." I appreciated her discretion, given our master's presence. "We'll get you some ice, too." She gave me another small smile. "It always takes a day or two to settle in, and this is not only a new household, but a new continent."

I didn't answer because I was suddenly, for some reason, thinking of my mother. The care in the housekeeper's voice— care I'd long ago stopped expecting—must have reminded me of hers somehow. The difference was that my mother had been young and beautiful, all light and laughter and energy, barely more than a girl even when I was a teen. But thinking about her and what our world had done to her was a shortcut to wanting to break things, so I stopped. Instead, I sank into the seat, trying to enjoy the softness of the leather after twelve hours of hard steel.

"Your most recent master educated you, then, boy?" Master Wainwright-Phillips spoke up.

Shit, I guess we were chitchatting instead. I straightened up, careful to avert my eyes as he peered at me through the rearview mirror. "Yes, sir. Professor von Esch, in Heidelberg. He taught me to read and write and to speak English." I left it there. I *could* be modest when I really tried. Or at least fool people into thinking I was.

"Your file said he taught you engineering, physics, and chemistry, too, and that you even helped him with his research," he pushed. "That's not exactly a common skillset for a slave. Is it useful?"

I paused, trying to read the car. "I'll never make enough money to pay my student loans back, sir."

It was a bold reply—maybe even stupid. But my master chuckled, and even the housekeeper hid a smile. Good, she was under my spell already—for me, it usually didn't take long with women. Even no-nonsense, middle-aged housekeeping slaves. And it *never* hurt.

I breathed—really breathed—for the first time in over two days.

Then Wainwright-Phillips added, "My daughter, Louisa, is about your age. She's pre-med at the university here."

A daughter. I filed that away. It might be helpful. I was bound to come across her soon, and knowing something about her might help win her support. Knowing what turned her on might help win even more of it. I'd learned young that charming (read: manipulating) my way into eating chocolate truffles out of the hand of a hot, lonely girl was a hell of a lot more fun than scrubbing baseboards and that I had all the tools to make it happen. Of course slave boys weren't allowed to even touch free women unless they were their mistresses, and even that usually had to be hidden away like a filthy secret. In the back of my head, always, was the all-powerful weapon free women had against me. Rejecting a come-on from the wrong girl could be as dangerous as accepting it because a slave was always guilty until proven innocent. On *that* charge, anyway.

So I'd have to be smart about it. But I wouldn't have survived this long if I weren't.

Meanwhile, the housekeeper was massaging my wrist in a motherly way. I raised my eyes and smiled, then lowered them again.

That was it, then. I'd get in good with the spoiled princess of the household; chances were she had her father wrapped around her finger.

And her father would lead me to Max Langer, and Max Langer would lead me to my sister.

3

"Can you believe that crazy bat?" Corey grunted as he and I elbowed our way through the crowds pouring out of the social sciences building. Adding Juliette at the Old Main fountain, we navigated across the grass of the campus mall, dodging frisbee-throwers and sunbathers soaking up an admittedly brilliant late October afternoon in the Valley. We were heading toward the student union because it went without saying that after an Erica Muller lecture, blueberry-raspberry smoothies were in order. Or maybe peanut butter and chocolate, if I really wanted to hate myself. "Standing up there just making up all this shit about Gerhard Langer giving birth to the —what did she call it?"

"Slavery-industrial complex," I mumbled, parroting the professor for some reason, though this was the last topic I wanted to get into with him right now. Well, next to last.

"Yeah. That."

"It's true, though," I said despite my better judgment. How did Muller's lectures keep worming their way into my brain like this? Hell, at this rate, I'd be eating vegan and wearing natural fibers before I knew it. "Langer was one of the biggest slave dealers in New North America. Not to mention," I said, though I now felt like *I* was giving the lecture, "he was believed to be responsible for the deaths of almost two hundred slaves in the aftermath of the Cebolla Canyon mine uprising—"

"Langer helped build the world into what it is today," interrupted Corey. "What you'll never hear Muller mention is that if he and some of the other early slave barons hadn't lobbied to institute slavery back in the thirties, who knows what kind of mess this place would be in?"

"I don't know, but I do know she said that like a lot of government programs, it was only ever supposed to be temporary," I said softly as we passed two young male uniformed landscaping slaves watering the begonias that edged the mall. They leaped out of our way. "It wasn't supposed to result in generations of families in slavery."

"That's because they declared that the children of slaves were also slaves, which is the most ingenious policy move of the twentieth century as far as I'm concerned," he said like he'd studied this for years and wasn't just going off what he'd read yesterday on one of those pro-slavery online forums.

"Why?"

"Hey, it was either that, or we'd all be slaves because we'd have been so broke that we'd have lost the war," countered Corey. "So take your pick. Which would you prefer?"

I knew which one I'd prefer, of course, but why did *my* preferences matter more than the slaves'? And why had that never occurred to me before today?

No reason.

"Anyway, it doesn't matter now," Corey rambled on, oblivious to the morality play going on in my head. "Gerhard Langer's dead. His era is over. I'm working with Max Langer now, and he got rid of all his slaves long ago. He says as a society we've evolved beyond it. He's disrupting the whole slavery industry."

I rolled my eyes, not sure I was ready yet to change the subject, but more than ready to call out Corey on having his head permanently stuck up his boss's ass. Mostly thanks to his family connections, Corey had started interning with Langer last summer, in some super-special position that saw him working with the tech mogul one-on-one. But so far, his sole job description, as far as I could tell, seemed to have been swallowing a bucketload of Langer's bullshit every damn day. "You know, just because you got a job with him all sewn up after you graduate doesn't mean you're required to defend every single thing he does," I said. "Besides, if you're now so evolved and all, why haven't you gotten rid of *your* slaves?"

Corey laughed. "What am I supposed to do, make my own bed? Sweep my own floor? I don't have time for that. I have school and work to worry about."

Of course I didn't want to do any of that stuff either. Nobody did—just like nobody wanted to flip burgers or pick oranges or dig copper. But someone had to. The whole economy would collapse otherwise, wouldn't it? That's what Daddy had always told me, anyway, the few times as a kid I'd been curious enough to ask why I got to go to school and the girl wiping down our table at my favorite fast-food hamburger place didn't.

"Come to think of it, you're starting to sound a little bit like Muller yourself." Corey looked at me sharply, his green eyes boring into me like he thought I might be turning into an enemy of the union. You couldn't get reported *that* easily anymore—those days had ended after most of the violent agitators from Muller's generation had been arrested and enslaved themselves. Like Muller had said, we nominally had free speech. But that didn't mean I felt like getting rejected from med school for being some kind of crazed radical when I was barely scraping by as it was. Which meant I should probably shut up. I didn't even believe this stuff, anyway. Did I?

"If you hate her so much, why did you even sign up for that course?" Juliette asked Corey. I hadn't even known my friend was listening, as rapidly as she was tapping out texts on her pink, blinged-out phone, peering over the gigantic tortoiseshell sunglasses designed to conceal her hangover from last night's frat mixer.

"I didn't want to!" moaned Corey. "It's all those politically correct abolitionist snowflakes in the dean's office, always yammering on and on about oppression. It's part of those new course requirements they put in this year. So now I'm stuck in that bullshit factory twice a week, hearing about how slavery reinforces toxic masculinity, whatever that is."

"Well, part of it, as you must know," I said, reciting more of one of Muller's lectures before I could stop myself, "is that masters rape female slaves all the time. Hell, they rape *male* slaves all the time. And all with no consequences. But women are barred from even touching male slaves. Even if they own them, it's considered taboo. Even if they *order* it. It's a sexist double standard."

"Rape? Seriously? Now a guy can't even have sex with his own property without some social justice warrior calling it rape? Besides, it's totally different with free women. What if they get pregnant? You know if the mother's free, the kid is free. We can't have a bunch of free people walking around with slaves for fathers. They could even inherit *property*." He shuddered as if that would somehow lead to the imminent collapse of society.

"Who cares? How would you even know? Do you think they're different species or something? I don't know if you've noticed this, Corey, but slaves and free people, except for the bracelets, look exactly alike."

Corey jerked backward. Juliette stopped, too. In fact, a chill came over me as I realized that it wasn't just them. There were *other* people staring at me. Why?

Because nobody ever pointed out this stuff—especially not in public. Nobody really talked about it at all. Even when my parents had had swanky cocktail parties where they used to discuss business and art, nobody breathed a word to question *why* there were nameless human beings carrying trays full of prosciutto-wrapped melon balls back and forth for no pay. No wonder Erica Muller, who not only wrote papers on the subject but *published* them, got a dozen death threats last week.

"Never mind," I said, my face starting to burn. "Let's just get our smoothies, okay?"

"You never cared so much about this stuff before, Lou," needled Corey as we marched up the stairs of the adobe-style structure to the second-floor café and took our places at the back of the smoothie line. "Is there some slave somewhere who's gotten you all hot and bothered?"

I froze. Then I tried to laugh, but it got stuck in my throat and started to sound like choking. I grabbed the bottle of water from my bag and took a long swig. When I swallowed, everyone was still staring, and water was dripping down my chin. I swiped at it with the back of my arm. "No."

Smooth. Real smooth.

"Don't even joke about that," scolded Juliette. "Remember what happened to"—she dropped her voice—"Rebekah Roth?"

We swallowed awkwardly. Rebekah—red-haired banker's daughter, champion swimmer, Type A idea girl—had been an integral part of our social circle until we were sixteen. That was when a neighbor had caught her—in her childhood treehouse, of all places—with the slave boy next door. The boy, like most slaves guilty of serious crimes, had been sold to the mines by his owners. Rebekah had had her college admission rescinded and the family, after pleading guilty to exploitation of their minor daughter, had moved somewhere on the East Coast and faded into obscurity. Some people whispered that Rebekah *herself* had been sold into slavery, which happened to minor girls who got in trouble with slave boys, especially if their parents couldn't or didn't pay the fine. I never did find out for sure, though. The only exception, of course, was if rape could be proven. My own parents hadn't been shy in pointing to Rebekah as an example of someone who had foolishly ruined her life. In any case, like *don't talk to strangers*, it was a rule we took for granted: slave boys were simply not to be touched, and that didn't change when you turned eighteen: it just meant *you* got charged with a crime instead of your parents and got sentenced to slavery if you couldn't pay the fine. I, personally—up until recently, maybe—had always wondered why anyone would want to touch a slave boy. After all, you wouldn't kiss a designer table lamp, any more than you would smash it on the ground and destroy it for no reason.

But now that I thought about it, that sounded just ... bad.

Anyway, the mere *thought* of Rebekah should be enough to wipe all thoughts of last night out of my mind forever. Should be.

Last night. Every single thought of it sent a jolt of electricity through me, as pure as if someone had flicked a goddamn switch. Hell, it was no wonder Corey had said what he had. He must have seen it flashing across my face like a black-and-white slow-motion movie. *Everyone* must have.

I'd awoken this morning and crept breathlessly into the kitchen, stomach twisting, heart pounding, toes flexing on the cold kitchen floor, curl clamped tight between my teeth. All in anticipation of what—*who*—I might encounter. But the only slave there was the maid, boiling steel-cut oats and glaring at me to get lost, complete with her usual stuck-up, sexy pout. The guy—the boy—the slave—whoever he was—was nowhere to be found. Was he asleep? Had he left? Or had I conjured him up from the depths of my sex-starved, sleep-deprived brain? I even, for a half-second of insanity, considered dropping down to the slave quarters—an area of the house off-limits to me, not that I'd ever cared—to see if there were any new faces down there.

Then I came to my senses. Better to forget it ever happened. If he existed, he clearly had forgotten it, too. I'd been sleep-deprived and delirious last night. I had not, repeat *not*, been flirting with a slave, let alone one whose face I couldn't even see, let alone one living in my own house.

Okay, maybe I had. But I wouldn't do it *again*. What if Daddy found out?

"Lou?"

I whirled around. "*What*?"

Juliette held out her hands. "Whoa, relax. I was just saying, I'm sick of talking about this stuff. Want to check out Fig and Firkin tonight? Atlas from the mixer last night is deejaying."

"Who, Ping Pong Man?"

She fluttered her eyelashes modestly. "He invited me. Anyway, I feel bad that I kept bugging you last night when you couldn't be there. But you really do need to have some fun, instead of rehashing all this boring history shit."

"History shit?" I couldn't help but protest. "These are current events, Jules. Hell, there are slaves working at Fig and Firkin. Who do you think cleans the toilets and washes the glasses?" In fact, one-third of the people on our very campus were slaves—virtually all of the grounds and cleaning crews and most of the service workers, too. There was one over in the corner mopping the floor right now.

"I know, but who cares? All that matters is that they don't look very hard at phony IDs. Come on, Lou. You deserve it. You've been thinking too hard."

That was for sure. For a moment, I actually thought about it —at the very least, it would be a way to let down my guard, meet some cute (free) guys, and forget about my exceedingly strange night—and day. Juliette seemed sincere, and I knew I should take her up on it. But for some reason, in the face of *that*, and rape and war and mining disasters, my problems from last night—stressed, flailing, undercaffeinated, missing out on life —already felt like a million years ago. Plus, I couldn't afford it.

"Forget it," I said as I finally accepted my smoothie: peanut butter, of course. The slave girl behind the counter handed over the tiny cup, and I sloshed the thick straw up and down nervously as I looked at my receipt. Seven dollars for *this*? And they said slave labor kept prices down. "I'm in class until three, then I have to go home and study."

And absolutely, positively nothing else.

"That's all you ever do anymore," broke in Corey, grabbing my arm and pulling me toward him so I could smell the body-wash he used. Something like Infatuation or Captivation. I was not captivated, especially with the way he felt entitled to touch me. Just because he wasn't a slave didn't mean I had to like it. Unfortunately, though the Erica Muller types might rail against toxic masculinity, most of my male classmates seemed to think they had a right to touch whoever and whatever they wanted. Slave girls, free girls, everyone. The only difference was that free girls were allowed to fight back. "Don't you want to have some fun?"

I untangled firmly from his grasp. I knew I shouldn't be blowing off Corey. Half the girls on campus wanted him for his money; the other half wanted him for his softly curled dark brown hair, piercing green eyes, and golden-brown tennis biceps rippling under his polo shirts. My father had already indicated I'd have his approval to date him, and my mother—an old classmate of *his* mother's—seemed convinced we'd been written in the stars since preschool.

Lately, she'd been putting it even more bluntly. "You know, plenty of girls still get their MRS degree. It's hard to find a job these days, and there's no shame in it," she'd slurred affectionately during cocktail hour the other night—not that cocktail hour wasn't *every* hour for her. In any case, I'd slammed down the dirty martini she'd given me—which I hadn't wanted anyway—and stalked out of the room.

So that's what they thought. That I couldn't make it; that I should take the easy way out and become just another gold-digging bimbo. *Not* me, I'd thought. But that was back at the start of the semester, when I'd still been pulling a B-plus in o-chem.

Now, I eyed Corey as he confidently popped the plastic top of his smoothie, removed the straw, and poured it down his throat, wondering what it would be like to be joined at the hip as his girlfriend. I'd longed for college to be about exploration; about pushing the limits and growing in every possible way. That's what I'd always heard it *should* be about. But I had plenty of friends from school who were coupled up; some were even discussing marriage. All of them, without exception, spent Saturdays in their dorms, watching streaming shows and drinking canned cocktails. But at least they seemed happy—unlike me, they weren't contemplating popping meth to stay awake and scrambling to find the least objectionable way to put food on the table. And none of them were failing a required course for their major or watching their fathers' finances going belly-up before their eyes. I could do much worse than them, and if I continued down my current path, I *would*.

But I wasn't ready yet for Corey.

"My parents need me at home tonight," I said vaguely.

"You know, your dad might want to talk to Langer about a partnership," Corey suggested. "He's always looking for new ventures."

I wondered what Corey had heard to make him suggest such a thing. "Why? He doesn't need his help. He doesn't need anyone's help."

"But—"

"He's fine. We're fine. Have fun at Fig and Firkin," I said, hurling my empty cup into a nearby trash bin. The comment had made me more determined than ever to pass o-chem. If I could just manage a C, I'd be fine. I'd keep my academic scholarship. I wouldn't be broke on the street, or ruined, or selling myself into slavery. This would all feel like a bad dream when I was successful, rich, and actually making a difference in the world instead of being buried beneath it. "I'm hitting the books."

"But wait—"

"Corey, what is your problem?" I turned back in exasperation. "Just because you're acing college doesn't mean the rest of us are. I've got a D going in this course. My scholarship—"

"Okay, okay," he cut me off. "It's important to you. I get it."

Well, no, he didn't. Not really. I'd let him think it was out of pure vanity that I wanted to hang onto my scholarship, which I'd been awarded by merit, based on my high grades and exam scores. I didn't have an inkling that without it, I'd be stuck rolling burritos or something—assuming fast-food restaurants had any jobs left that hadn't been filled by slaves.

"Did you even *try* the pills?" he demanded.

"No, I did not try the pills, and I'm not going to." I crossed my arms. I'd never acknowledge to him that my family had an unfortunate tendency to not know when to stop when it came to substances; getting hooked on uppers was the last thing I needed on top of having no money.

"Okay," he said finally, smiling beatifically as if he were descending from his lofty perch to do me some grand favor. It made me slightly ill. "How about I come over tonight and help you? I know a few tricks. I've got calc now, but I'll stop by around four-thirty, okay?"

I frowned.

"I'll bring burritos."

I shook my head. "Pizza, and it's a deal."

HIM

As I rifled through Keith Wainwright-Phillips's file cabinet, I held an ice pack up to my singed eye and considered that the fact that anybody here had bothered to treat my wounds was almost enough to make me feel guilty about what I was doing. Almost.

In fact, at the Wainwright-Phillips house, they'd done more than treat my wounds. As soon as we'd arrived here yesterday, the housekeeper had whisked me to the kitchen and given me a meal of chicken and rice, an ice pack, and three ibuprofen, then handed me a thin, soft T-shirt and a pair of cut-off khaki shorts from a box of clothes cast off from my master's family and other slaves, along with some flip-flops and a few other items that looked like they might fit. A skinny, full-lipped maid that I knew I'd be nailing within the week had even brought me half a broken chocolate cupcake from a fresh batch she'd baked, which I'd inhaled shamelessly after almost a week of gruel and worse. Finally, I'd been directed to a bunk in the basement slave quarters and allowed to sleep for two hours, which was way less than I needed but way more than I expected, and it almost made up for having the night shift.

The night shift. The princess. That *voice*. Fuck me. My plan had been to feel her out, soften her up, and *if* she was receptive, have a little fun with her in anticipation of getting what I needed—not to let her voice cast some bizarre hex on me where I couldn't chase it out of my head no matter what I did. Besides, I don't know if she thought I was someone else or what, but the fact that Daddy's little angel had even stooped to humor me for more than a few seconds was kind of blowing my mind. Bottom line, so much for the "good slave" act. I shouldn't have said any of it, and I shouldn't have *done* any of it.

But every single part of me wanted to do it again.

Well. Despite that unfortunate little blip, Lucky Sevens were still paying out. Today, nobody threw cold water on me, screamed in my ear, or kicked me awake. When I woke up again around nine, as the other slaves went about their chores, I sat in the slaves' common area—small and cluttered with household knickknacks and sewing projects, but still comfortable, with a small, sunny window—with the housekeeper. We drank cups of weak coffee from an industrial drum (I tried to forget about last night's Ecuadorian roast), and swapped the usual stories. The housekeeper had come from New York, bought sight unseen at nine years old by my new mistress's parents. "Mistress Wainwright-Phillips had married by then and they were both working long hours, so off to them I went. I looked after Miss Louisa and Master Ethan for a few years before they bought a nanny, while my partner was the gardener. Then I became the cook and housekeeper."

I just looked down at my rough hands curled around the chipped mug, hoping my face hadn't given away my reaction to her name. Which annoyed me because I wasn't supposed to *have* a reaction. I was *supposed* to use her to curry favor with her father, forget about her, and go get a blow job from the maid. That was the way I had operated for years, and there was a reason for that: it was safe, and it worked. And so it was really fucking inconvenient that my dick had decided to start twitching instead. To get rid of it, I decided Louisa was a spoiled brat and probably only looked good in dim lighting. Of course this approach could only work for so long, since I'd already noticed from the hallway that there were pictures of her and her brother on the living room mantel. So far, I'd managed to avoid going in there.

As the housekeeper bustled maternally back upstairs, I thought about how she'd mentioned a partner. With slaves, that usually indicated children, though none of them seemed to be around, and the current gardener *definitely* wasn't the same guy. I wouldn't ask about them, of course—why cause the woman to mourn all over again? Still, it was another reason to dismiss Louisa. She'd been partially raised by a woman who'd likely had her own children ripped out of her arms so she could care for her master's babies.

Yeah. Louisa was like all the rest of them. She was tainted by the original sin of slavery, and there was nothing she could do to erase it.

She didn't have any say in it. She hadn't chosen to be born rich and free, just as I hadn't chosen to be born a slave. Not like I was defending her. Why was I defending her?

Anyway, it soon wouldn't matter. When I was told the chore I'd been assigned that afternoon — helping the housekeeper with the heavy lifting as she helped clean and rearrange Wainwright-Phillips's home office—I resolved that I wouldn't be seeing Louisa much longer anyway. Not once I used whatever was in there to figure out where my sister was, and, even more challenging, get to her. And then, most challenging of all, figure out a place to hide her where she couldn't be tracked down, even though currently, all four slavery-free countries in the world were islands in the South Pacific. Besides, to save her, I might have to kill Louisa's dad, and then whatever fucked-up connection I'd apparently made with Louisa would be as good as dead anyway—and so would I.

They were swapping out some of the old furniture in the office for a more modern theme, the housekeeper told me. "The master said he wants this to look more like a startup," she explained with a shrug. "Any idea what he means by that?"

Not much, aside from a few photos I'd seen in my old master's magazines and a few internet sites I'd glimpsed whenever I could sneak online. But I could sure bullshit it. "Of course. My old master owned one. Just relax and leave it to me. Will Master Wainwright-Phillips be overseeing this operation personally?" I asked slyly.

"No. He trusts my good taste."

"Smart guy," I said with my most charming smile, and she preened. Too easy. It got even easier twenty minutes later, when the maid burst in, hysterical, saying the motor on the stand mixer had blown out and she couldn't find the handheld beaters anywhere, and the housekeeper ran off. If there was a god for slaves somewhere—or a god at all, which, logical as I was, I had rather confidently doubted for some time—he was smiling down right now as I triumphantly rolled open the top drawer of the file cabinet.

The files were mostly old as if my master had let filing fall by the wayside recently, and after ten minutes of digging, I'd seen mostly tax returns and folders and folders of receipts for office supplies and construction equipment. Nothing in the least bit useful, and I was already down to the innermost reaches of the bottommost cabinet when I spotted a thin file labeled "Langer." Inside was a copy of a reference letter Wainwright-Phillips had written for some guy named Corey Killeen for a position as Langer's intern. *I have known Corey on a personal basis for nearly two decades, and during that time, I've found him to be a conscientious, ambitious, and industrious young man,* it read.

In other words, a complete douchebag. I tossed it aside.

The only other thing in the file was a sealed manila envelope with the Langer Enterprises return address. Bingo. Wainwright-Phillips could pretend to be Man of the Year all he wanted, but if he was in any way in cahoots with the guy who'd stolen my sister, he was a scumbag, and he deserved to die. And if I had to, I'd be the one to kill him. I wouldn't even think twice about it.

In the meantime, time to steam open this envelope. The trick would be to get it unsealed and resealed, then back into the file before anybody noticed it missing. I already had an idea how, if I could find an unoccupied bathroom somewhere, which shouldn't be hard—I'd already passed about thirty of them. Footsteps pounded in the hall, and I muttered a curse in Luxembourgish, shoving the envelope under my T-shirt and down the waistband of my cutoff shorts.

"I think I can take this from here. You're needed out in the yard. The gardener needs all the palo verde trimmings bagged up and removed. Move it," the housekeeper said, swatting me lightly on the arm. It wasn't her fault really, but it looked like the honeymoon was over and I was back to being treated like livestock.

Business as usual.

4

I hummed a tune from *Girl Crazy*, the only school musical I'd ever been stupid enough to try to overcome my stage fright long enough to perform in, as I rounded the hall. I planned to jump in the shower, rinse off the day, and rub myself down with that new pomegranate bodywash before Corey's arrival— it had been a birthday present and more expensive than anything I could afford these days, and it smelled divine.

Maybe I'd been wrong about Corey after all. He'd offered to help me study instead of going drinking, hadn't he? Sure, his attitude about slaves was a bit harsh, but just because Erica Muller was a professor didn't mean she was right about everything, either. And who knew? As improbable as it sounded, maybe Max Langer's plan, whatever it was, would disrupt slavery or even end it. And even if it didn't, Corey would make boatloads of money one day working for Langer, and if I chose to hitch myself to that wagon, I'd probably be able to coax him to see the light—to treat the slaves we would someday own more like the people nobody seemed to want to acknowledge they were.

I shook my head as I rounded the corner of the hallway. What was I *thinking*?

There was no "we." Yet.

Even before I reached the bathroom, I knew something was wrong. The light was off and the door was closed, but I could already hear water gushing out of the tap and into the tub. When I pried the door open, steam was fogging up the mirror. Someone was running the bath. How? Why? This was *my* bathroom. Nobody else bathed here.

"Hey, what's going on in here? I need to use the—"

Before I could switch on the light, I stumbled right into a rather large form crouched by the bathtub. Whoever it was scrambled backward to steady himself. He'd been holding something over the tub, which he quickly, furtively, shoved beneath his shirt. In the process, his hand—his wrist bearing the kinds of abrasions I'd seen on slaves forced into tight shackles—landed on the top of my foot. I recoiled immediately, not because it was unpleasant but from the shock. Electric shock.

"Sorry."

Sorry? Did he think he'd touched another slave or something? Because that sure wasn't how he was supposed to apologize to *me*.

To his credit, though, he realized his mistake quickly as soon as I flicked the switch. "Oh, *shit*." He even shrank back for a second but composed himself, running a damp hand through his hair as he shut the water off and scrambled to rise to a height that was as impressive as his audacity.

The only thing I *should* have been thinking about right then was how to punish him for touching me. But when I saw what stood before me, I was robbed of all thought *and* speech. In the past twelve hours, I'd spent way more time than I'd ever admit to anybody dreaming, imagining, and—okay, I admit it—touching myself thinking about that guy on the intercom, but never for a single second had I imagined *this*.

If my father had bought him specifically to torture me, I couldn't imagine how he could be more gorgeous than he was. Natural sun-bleached golden streaks shot through thick hair long enough to brush his neck, falling carelessly across and to one side of his milky face with its bone structure sculpted and smooth enough for a sorority girl to envy, all topped off by eyelashes so ridiculously long they cast shadows on his cheeks.

And then there was that body.

Shoulders as broad as a football player's were barely contained beneath a thin gray T-shirt that grazed veiny biceps, flat abs, and narrow hips: not massive, not burly, just perfectly and beautifully proportioned; the archetypal masculine shape. I wouldn't dare look any lower than his waist—yet—but the thought was there. And I was already blushing, because, oh yes, it was there.

Well, it may be a body an athlete would envy, and yet I knew it hadn't come from any gym. Corey may have had the prestigious internship, but this was a boy—young man, really—who knew what work was. And, I realized with a sinking feeling, given the bruises and electrical burns marring his face and neck, he apparently knew what punishment was, too.

But surely he must have done something to deserve it.

"It's you, isn't it?" Yeah, I could have come up with something more intelligent to say, but my brain wasn't exactly my number one concern at that moment. Something lower down was. Needless to say, the faucet wasn't the only thing in here that was gushing.

And he wasn't even *done*. What happened next just about shattered me. His eyes—that foxy shape, that fiery shade somewhere between amber and gold, that boldness to confound me and a sadness to break my heart—actually lowered for a split second as if his slave training had suddenly kicked in. But he raised them again, however, and formed his full lips into a half-smile—and suddenly, there was the charming, infuriating sexual deviant I'd spent last night sparring with, in the flesh. "Still want that coffee, miss?" he asked mischievously in that rich, slow, lilting accent, the sharp T just ever-so-vaguely New European. "Or was it a massage? I forgot."

There was no denying it now; no hoping that it was all some bizarre prank or a dream. The proof was right there on his wrist, etched into a metal ID tag on a chain. My mystery guy—the one responsible for my waking up shamelessly wet this morning, unable to function until I reached down to finger the unexpected slickness of my private parts and purr like a tigress at the memory of his voice—was indeed a slave. A shockingly beautiful one, at that. Well, shit. He was a slave, and he had touched me and hadn't apologized, and now he was standing there, staring me right in the eyes. Had o-chem broken my brain? What was I thinking, letting him get away with that?

"Eyes on the floor, boy," I said in the most commanding voice I could muster up. That was more like it. I glanced down at the bathtub. "And what were you doing in here, anyway?"

Instead of answering, he extended one long arm, his taut, sinewy muscles flexing beneath his skin in ways that didn't even seem anatomically possible. He pointed to the book in my hand. "Malchow," he said. "My condolences."

"Huh?" I'd been mesmerized by his lips. The last thing in the world I'd expected to come out of them was the name of the author of my o-chem book.

"I can't stand that pretentious fuck," he continued. "I swear he must have gotten paid by the word to write that. Hey, guys, why use one page to explain something when we can use ten?"

My mouth went dry. "You—you can read."

"Yes." A trace of a smile, an impudent one at that, which was all the more amazing given his eyes were still lowered obediently, though he was still clearly taking in everything as easily as if he'd been straight-up staring.

"And write."

"Yes." He was clearly amused at my shock, which was more than a bit annoying. Still, I kept going. I was too in awe to stop.

"And—and do chemistry?"

"And calculus, physics, and engineering. If I were free, I'd be a certified nerd," he said. "And probably rich, too. But who's complaining?"

And I thought I'd been blown away last night. Still, a slave was a slave. And I hadn't yet called him out on it.

"You touched me."

He shrugged. *Shrugged.* Slaves didn't—

"You going to whip me?"

"I—" His response was correct, logical, and clearly meant to infuriate me. And it was working, of course.

"Ah, I see you've met."

Daddy.

Just like that, the boy's eyes met mine again. One glance said it all, and even though we hadn't technically been doing anything improper, we both immediately put several feet of distance between us. But only *he* looked at the floor.

"I'm sorry, Loulou, I brought him home yesterday while you were in class. I'd hoped to introduce you properly, but I see you've already done that yourself."

Daddy looked from me to his slave boy and back again, with the same question on his lips I'd had when I'd entered. And for some reason, I wondered what the boy was thinking as he studied the bathroom tile—even though slaves weren't supposed to think anything, and even if they did, I wasn't supposed to care what it was.

"However, is there any particular reason you were both in the bathroom?" Daddy asked neutrally. Though he clearly expected a good answer. "Loulou?"

"Uh—" I could actually see the muscles in the back of the slave boy's neck tense in anticipation of whether I was about to have him punished—from the looks of it, for the second time in as many days. And I should. After all, he'd dodged my question about why he'd been running the bath, suggesting that his reasons, whatever they were, were less than pure. Not to mention his behavior had been shockingly inappropriate throughout pretty much our entire interaction.

And yet the last thing I wanted at that moment was for Daddy to know about any of it.

"I-I asked him to listen to the showerhead," I blurted out. "It was making a funny noise." It wasn't a lie. Well, most of it wasn't.

The boy looked up at me in surprise, but quickly, skillfully, dropped his gaze again before Daddy noticed anything.

"Is that true, boy?"

This slave, though he was likely my age or a bit older, had a man's body, a man's shoulders, a man's *everything*, no doubt. However, in this house, he was going to be "boy" no matter what, just like all male slaves under about fifty or so. Hell, I'd just called him that myself.

"Yes, sir," he replied, and though he never looked up from the floor, I could see that not only was he thinking, he was, of all things, *calculating*, his mind nimbly adapting to the circumstances as they evolved. "Erosion of the gasket in the valve could cause a high-frequency vibration when the water flows past."

Who knew whether this was an actual thing or not, but

coming out of his mouth—and in that accent—it sounded oddly brilliant, like some kind of groundbreaking theory of physics instead of mere plumbing.

To my relief, Daddy looked, at worst, bemused. "Well, we'll have to get that looked at," he said finally. "I can't believe the pipes are going already. This house is only ten years old."

"You didn't tell me you were buying anybody new," I said, borrowing the boy's tactic of changing the subject quickly.

"I wasn't sure the sale would go through until a few days ago," Daddy replied, seemingly pleased to be able to transition to showing off his shiny new purchase. "New Europe is notorious for red tape."

"But slaves are expensive, Daddy. Aren't we—" I swallowed. If he hadn't figured it out already, the slave definitely didn't need to know about our plummeting financial situation. What the hell was Daddy planning on using this guy for, anyway, when he couldn't even afford to buy me a daily coffee anymore? I knew what slaves cost. And I knew there was no way in hell *this* one had come at all cheap.

Daddy paused for a moment. "Foreign slaves are a bargain, Loulou, given the exchange rate," he said finally, but he paused again as if he really wasn't interested in sharing the full story behind the boy's price. The way the boy's eyes shifted as he pretended to stare at the floor suggested *he* wasn't, either. "Both the valet and gardener are getting up there, and this boy's young and strong as an ox. Can do the work of two, no doubt." Daddy clapped the boy's impressive shoulder as if it were something he'd had custom-built. "And educated. Not to the level of a free man, of course, but I plan on finding a use for that, just you wait. Sounds like maybe you already have," he added with a light chuckle. "And of course, that face alone is worth what I paid." He grabbed the boy's chin and tilted it up, and his lip curled back as he obviously struggled to keep from making eye contact with either of us. He'd also gone silent, but it was only proper: he was no longer being spoken to, after all. "I thought he'd be a nice complement to the maid. You can never have too many pretty things around the house."

Classic. Leave it to my father to buy the most attractive slave he could find and then expect me not to touch him.

The front door slammed. "Hey, Lou!" called an impatient voice. Corey's.

Heat and nerves and God knew what else had made my hair and makeup even more of a sweaty mess than they had been when I'd entered, but it was too late to do anything about it now. I'd have to grab some blotting powder from my bag and hope for the best.

"You home? I got food. Let's do this already!"

The boy and I both looked up curiously, and I used the opportunity to slip out of the room because if I stayed, I'd do something I was sure to regret. Or maybe not regret at all. Either way, I didn't want to find out.

♥

Half an hour later, I could at least say one good thing about my study session with Corey: he'd chosen a beautiful day. I would have preferred the privacy of my room, but Corey had insisted on studying outside to enjoy the perfect desert sun. Or maybe just to be seen. He had plopped himself on one of the pool lounge chairs like some movie star in dark glasses, a half-eaten burrito next to him, apparently having forgotten that I'd requested pizza. As he gesticulated his explanation of how halogens combined with alkenes to form dihalides, he paused to slurp a cola with beads of perspiration on the side. He'd said he would have gotten me something to drink, but he didn't know what I wanted. As if soda weren't a fairly safe choice.

I shoved my textbook off my lap with disgust, then headed for the kitchen. Anything to get away from this disaster. Much as I hated to admit it, the slave boy had been right. Malchow's long-winded explanations were what was making o-chem impossible, and Corey's grandiose methods of trying to explain it to me were making it that much worse.

"Where are you going?" he called after me. "We're right in the middle of a chapter."

"I need something to drink."

As I walked away, Corey leaned back in his chair, unfazed. "You know," he called out, swirling the cola can like it was full of fine wine, "if you can't follow the simple mechanism where the electrophilic addition leads to the formation of a cyclic bromonium ion, maybe med school just isn't for you. But don't worry, when you get back, I can try another explanation that's maybe more your speed. Hey," he remarked suddenly. "Wait, your slave's right over there. Just make *him* get you something."

Oh, shit. I turned around, praying he'd been referring to the gardener, though I already knew he wasn't.

The boy had pushed up the sleeves of his gray T-shirt— either an old one of my brother's or borrowed from one of the other slaves—and was dragging a wheelbarrow full of pruned palo verde branches, which he emptied into a gigantic plastic yard waste bag. Every so often, the sunlight would catch his thick, damp, wild hair, sending shafts of gold shooting through it, and when he reached up to brush it out of his eyes, it went flying in eighteen different delicious directions. Oh, and if that weren't bad enough, the rest of him was glowing almost ethereally from the work, his T-shirt sticking wetly to his torso, outlining the way his muscles bunched and rippled like liquid gold. And how *dare* he have a strip of skin show just above the waistband of his shorts and below his shirt, where the tiniest trace of soft, fine, sunlight-colored hair was visible? I didn't dare plunge my eyes lower, but, come on, I'd gotten this far. I hugged my arms to my body, suddenly flailing with jealousy over the women who must have touched that very spot. Who were they? Slave girls? Free girls? And what had he—

"Lou?"

"Huh?" I spun around guiltily, realizing I'd been engaged in some serious one-woman foreplay—right in front of Corey. Fucking hell, I was out of *breath* over it. *Goddamn* this guy, and no—*not guy*. Slave, slave, slave. I wasn't supposed to be wondering about his package, or what he'd done with it, or what he could *do* with it. I wasn't supposed to be wondering about him at *all*. He was furniture. An accessory. A tool. As much as the fucking wheelbarrow he—

"I *told* you to ask that slave to get you something to drink," Corey demanded.

"I don't—he's busy." I gasped.

Corey stared at me as if I'd sprouted a third eye. "So?"

"But—"

"He's new," Corey announced like a royal decree, studying the boy with narrowed eyes, which couldn't be good. "Where's he from?"

"Not sure," I said, desperately trying to keep my voice neutral. "His accent is weird, though. He almost sounds German or something. And I think he knows chemistry?"

"Fantastic. A tutor you don't have to pay for, and he weeds the garden." Corey laughed at his own joke. "Hey, you! Slave," he called, shaking his empty can. The boy raised his head and set down the wheelbarrow. I face-palmed. I'd wanted to let him work undisturbed, but I also couldn't let him ignore the request. It just wasn't done. "Another. And one for Miss Louisa."

I cringed at Corey's rudeness, but the boy, so far, took it in stride, saying "yes, sir" as he accepted the can, kept his eyes down obediently—well, maybe not so obediently, since he was actually checking out Corey's calculus textbook. Spotting his interest, Corey smiled nastily.

"Louisa says you're educated, boy. Where did you go to college? Oxford? Sorbonne? Were you Phi Beta Kappa?"

"Shut up, Corey," I hissed, glancing between them. This was about to spiral quickly out of hand. It *always* spiraled out of hand with Corey. He'd been like this since our mothers' book club meeting when we were six when he'd convinced me to help him eat an entire box of sandwich cookies out of the pantry and blame it all on his family's slave boy. I didn't know what exactly happened to the kid after that. But I didn't *have* to know exactly.

"Simon Schechter, sir?" the boy asked, indicating the book's author. "I met him a few times, actually. He used to crash on my old master's sofa whenever they went out drinking in Heidelberg. You don't want to know the kinds of things I used to find when I cleaned the flat the next morning." He had raised his head now with the trace of a smile, and I realized that, despite what he'd no doubt been taught his whole life, this guy didn't have a submissive bone in his body. Frankly, it was hard to believe he'd survived this long, talking to free men so casually. The burns and bruises on his face suddenly seemed to make a lot more sense, and my heart clenched despite myself.

But no. He deserved it. He was defiant. He was disobedient. He was a bad slave. No, he was just bad in general, and it wasn't my job to care what happened to him. Not like I didn't have enough problems of my own.

"I studied in Germany last year." Corey, much to my dismay,

was still talking. "I co-wrote a paper on the P versus NP problem with Simon Schechter. It won an award from the International Mathematics Forum."

"That must have been rough, sir," the boy replied.

Corey scoffed. "Of course it was rough. Mathematicians had been working on that for two decades."

"No, I mean not getting credit for your paper." He pointed to the textbook on Corey's lap. "May I?"

Corey's mouth had dropped open in shocked silence. Not waiting for permission, the boy flipped to the biography page, pointing out the award Schechter had won and the year he'd won it—with a different coauthor.

"Ah, it's probably just a misprint, though, sir," the boy added, completely straight-faced.

I couldn't help it. I felt a slow grin overtaking my face. Corey's face, meanwhile, instantly flushed an unattractive shade of strawberry. The textbook rolled off his lap and onto the grass.

"He doesn't know what he's talking about," Corey growled, which told me all I needed to know. "How dare you contradict a free man?" He turned to me. "Aren't you going to do something about this?"

I looked at the slave, who stood there, defiant, unapologetic, unafraid. Dangerous. "He's—he belongs to Daddy. I can't—It's up to him."

"Oh, come on, I know you've got a switch inside. Draw some blood. Show him who's boss, or he'll think he can walk all over you."

I looked in vain from one boy to the other. I should have been furious that a slave would speak to my guest that way, but instead, I was frantic to think of something, anything, to get us out of this situation. "I-I'll do it inside," I said desperately, jabbing my thumb toward the kitchen. As satisfying as it was to see Corey humbled so completely, this was getting serious.

"What were you thinking?" I hissed at him as soon as I slammed the patio door. I was scolding him, but for some reason, it didn't feel like scolding a slave. It felt, somehow, like scolding an equal. There didn't seem like there should have been a difference, but there was. "You see what you've done? He wants me to switch you!"

He crossed his arms and leaned against the marble island top, glaring back at me. "Ah," he said. But in his accent, it didn't sound like "ah." It sounded more like "ach," with a guttural little noise at the end that I might have found oddly adorable if I weren't so furious. "Worth it. Trust me, anybody who uses that douchebag as a tutor is going to end up on the seven-year plan. Don't tell me you're dating him, too."

"What did you say?"

"I'm not going to repeat it. Douche. Dating. Don't tell me. I thought the meaning was fairly clear," he said, turning around to the sink, flicking on the tap, and filling a glass. Wait, was he going to—did I even need to ask? Of course he was. All the dishes in this kitchen were off-limits to the slaves, and he knew it. That was *why* he was doing it.

"It's none of your damn business!" I sputtered as he knocked back most of the cup and set it stubbornly on the counter. He was clearly daring me to say anything, so I didn't. And just how that gave *me* the upper hand, I wasn't sure. "You've known me for less than a day, and you're a slave. On what planet does that give you the right to question who I spend time with? And for the last time, keep your eyes on the floor!" I snapped because they were enthralling and fathomless and liquid gold, and they were making my pulse race in a way I had no control over. So why, when he reluctantly obeyed, did it make me want to start sobbing? "Anyway, Corey's not a douchebag. He's one of the most popular guys on campus."

"Really? How big is the campus?" He paused and tilted his head a little. "Wait. Corey? Corey Killeen?"

"Yeah," I said cautiously. "How do you know?"

He shook his head. "No reason."

"His dad owns every it-restaurant in the city, and we've been friends since preschool," I explained. "And his boss is a tech mogul who got rich by, among other things, launching rockets into space. They're both going to be over for dinner soon. We can't afford to piss them off."

He seemed to consider this seriously. "Well, I'll say this. If your dad needs money, it can't hurt to borrow it from somebody too dumb to calculate simple interest."

A giggle escaped my mouth. I met his eyes again—yes, on purpose this time—and suddenly, we were both melting into the counter with laughter.

He had a beautiful smile.

"I suppose you think you can do better?" I finally said.

"This kitchen sponge could do better," he scoffed. "I know that textbook he was holding."

"So what? Corey's been an engineering major for three years."

"I was studying that shit when I was sixteen. And I bet he didn't get his knuckles switched whenever he forgot to carry the one. I never made the same mistake twice after that."

"But you must have!"

"Never."

"Come on," I insisted. Then, after a pause: "Will you show me?"

"How much is it worth to you?" He rubbed his thumb and finger together, a sly look on his face.

"Are you crazy? You're a slave. You don't get paid. If I tell you to tutor me, you tutor me."

"Nope. Not how it works. You said it yourself. Your dad owns me. It's up to him."

"Forget it, then." If I asked him, I wasn't a hundred percent convinced my father would say no. In fact, the odds were very good he'd say yes, which scared me even more. Was I hoping he'd say yes? And if I was, was it because the boy's knowledge could save me from flunking out of school, or because I was already melting into a puddle at the prospect of seeing that magnificent body sitting across the desk from me every day while I ordered him not to look me in the eyes and secretly, breathlessly hoped that he would?

Probably better that I didn't find out.

"Come on. We've both got work to do." I gestured toward the door.

But he didn't move. "Aren't you forgetting something?"

I couldn't help it. I followed his gaze downward to where his arms were crossed in front of his chest. Looking closer to where hundreds of small, precise scars were on display, following the trails of his veins.

He must have read my expression. "Like I said," he explained quietly. "Every time I got a problem wrong."

I knew then I couldn't hurt him again. I just couldn't. "I'll make up a story," I said. "Just stay in here until he leaves. It'll be fine. It's my house. I don't care what he thinks."

From outside came an angry pounding on the door. "Lou, what are you doing in there? Hitting the shit out of him, I hope."

"Did I mention your boyfriend's a real charming guy?"

"He's not my—"

"Whatever. Look, if we go out there and I'm not bleeding, or if he thinks you're lying, he's going to think something's up.

There are witnesses. And then it's going to get back to your dad."

I hadn't thought of that. If Corey told Daddy I'd refused to punish his new slave, all of a sudden, Daddy's mind would be racing to places it shouldn't race. But. I bit back a sob, looking from him to the door. Why was *I* the one who felt like I was about to cry? "But I can't. I told you, I never—"

"There." He had turned, his eyes alighting on the thin bamboo switch, sitting innocuously in the umbrella stand by the front door.

Slowly, my heart pounding, I crossed the room and picked it up.

"Give it to me."

He'd just given me an order. The irony of it was bitter. Still, slowly, mechanically, I handed it to him and took a step back, but not before meeting his amber-gold eyes guiltily one more time.

What's one more? They seemed to reassure me.

He closed his eyes briefly. Then he brought it down on his own hand, hard.

But only I flinched.

I opened my eyes to a thin red line of blood glistening on his wrist, perfect and jewel-like, over the old scars. He handed me back the switch, then opened the door to the terrace and held it. "After you, miss."

HIM

It was a real estate title.

2481 Salt River Boulevard in Glendale. That number, that address, looped around in my mind all day and all night. What was it? I knew it wasn't corporate headquarters—that was One Langer Drive, reprinted on the envelope's return address. It was something else. Something Wainwright-Phillips thought was important enough to file away in a sealed envelope but not open. Something he didn't want to know but also didn't want anybody else to know.

It had to be where Langer was keeping my sister.

I thought about it the next morning while the green-eyed maid sucked me off. Her mouth was even bigger than it had looked, and I closed my eyes and at least *tried* to enjoy the sensation of her full lips working my shaft hungrily, licking and kissing her way up and down with little moans of delight like someone had treated her to a crème brûlée. Of course it didn't help the mood that my back was pressed up against a bag of rice, the individual grains poking into my skin, and the pantry was hot, cramped, and smelled like stale cereal and old dog food. It was far from the worst place I'd ever tried to get my rocks off, but as much as this girl was trying her best to make things interesting, I couldn't pretend this wasn't exactly like most slave sex: rushed, clinical, matter-of-fact. Just a way to release tension—to forget, for a few minutes, that life was shit.

And then all of a sudden, *nothing* was shit because it wasn't her anymore. It was the *other* her. Ridiculous reams of curls, huge gray eyes staring up at me, as rapt and dilated as the glossy, pouty, spoiled (virgin?) lips wrapped luxuriously around my shaft, inhaling—

Fuck. No. Just no.

Shoving the image away violently, I came with a grunt in the maid's mouth, and she swallowed greedily, continuing to moan her squirrely little moans even as she choked a little. But I wasn't even seeing her anymore as I zipped up and reached for the door.

"Hey," she purred, grabbing my raw wrist in a gentle way that sort of broke my heart. "Stay. They won't be down here for a few minutes." I turned around. She ran her tongue around the edges of her lips enticingly as if gulping down my entire wad had still left her hungry. But I saw the desperation behind it. Briefly, I wondered if Wainwright-Phillips himself was fucking her—it was rare for a slave girl as enticing as she was to go unused by at least one free man, and our master was the only free man currently living there. But that was unlikely since if she were his favorite, she probably wouldn't be stuck scouring ovens. And if she wasn't, that meant she hadn't been laid anytime recently. It wasn't like she was swimming in options. The valet looked like he hadn't had sex in decades, if ever, and the gardener was such a perverted creep that the housekeeper had said they'd had to board up the window of the women's quarters to keep him from peeping in at them from outside. Plus, the property was sprawling; even the closest neighbors were a half-mile away. She was lonely. In other words, she wanted to form an attachment.

Fuck attachments. It was bad enough that I'd been raised with my sister long enough to know her and love her. It was even worse that I'd known my mother long enough to go feral with rage when she died. I knew attachments. Attachments were why I was trying to figure out the best way to get to 2481 Salt River Boulevard without getting hauled in as a runaway. Why part of me just wanted to take off—hitchhike, steal a car, whatever I had to do. But it would be suicide. For one, I didn't know the area, and removing the metal chain on my wrist was impossible without the right tools, not to mention being a crime in itself. Worst of all, the minute Wainwright-Phillips realized I was gone, he'd trigger the GPS tracker in my microchip. I'd be shackled in the back of a police van by morning. I might not end up in the mines as a first-time runaway, but either way, I'd be fucked, and no closer to finding my sister.

Attachments were what was going to get me killed.

Horny or not, I'd have to keep my distance from the maid

from now on. It would hurt her, probably, but not as much as if I led her on further. I needed to get entangled with her like I needed more welts on my back, and given what I was planning, it was for her own good, too. In the aftermath, she'd be the first person they'd question, and it would only go downhill for her from there.

Plus, there was Louisa Wainwright-Phillips.

Plus? Plus *what?* An attachment with a slave girl may be stupid, but an attachment with a free girl would be like digging my own grave and jumping into it. So what if the dim-lighting theory didn't hold up? So what if it had turned out that, despite all my hopes, my new master's daughter had a body that drank up *every* kind of light, a body made entirely of soft lines and slow curves, one of those tiny, sexy moles right under her eye, gray irises that reminded me of a stormy day on the North Sea, and more long, thick cascades of curly hair than a guy—any guy, no one in particular—could ever run his fingers through in a million years?

And the smile. When she deigned to let it blossom over her entire face, it transformed her from daddy's Type A princess, anxious to do everything proper and correctly, back into the carefree, goofy, gap-toothed girl she must still be, somewhere deep down where for some reason she was determined to never let it show.

Not that I'd been looking at her. That would have been inappropriate.

Plus, she couldn't hum a George Gershwin tune to save her life, and adorably, still couldn't decide whether she wanted to screech at me not to look at her or giggle at my jokes, most of which, let's face it, were B material at best.

And rather than hurt me, she'd been willing to risk her father's wrath. There had been *tears* in those gray eyes over it.

Like I hadn't already experienced 100 times worse than whatever she could possibly do to me.

And absolutely none of this should matter. Fuck, I was here to save my sister, and getting myself flogged and thrown in a mine for touching my master's daughter would put more than a slight wrinkle in that plan. At this point, it didn't matter what I planned to use Louisa for, or how good or lucky I was at doing it. The trouble she could get me in outweighed whatever value she offered. I should have shut it all down after the intercom, for fuck's sake. Not to mention she was dating Douchebag McQueen or whatever his name was, even though she said she wasn't. I wondered if he'd fucked her yet. I couldn't imagine that creep would wait—but maybe *she* would. Maybe she *was* a virgin. Or maybe they both were.

And again, why the hell should I care?

Focus, kid. I needed a computer, or at least a phone. And no, not to watch porn, as much tension as I still needed to blow off.

A computer might be easier to get to. It was illegal for slaves to use the internet—too many dangerous ideas there—but that had never stopped me from sneaking online whenever my old master's back was turned. In the chemistry lab, it had been easy enough. They had satellite images of almost anywhere in the world. If only they had X-ray images; then I could see into Langer's building to figure out just what diabolical project he had in the works and whether it included my sister. But where to find a computer?

"Hey, you okay?"

I'd forgotten the maid was even there. But even as she reached up to arc her hands around to touch my broad, solid shoulders, her fingers digging into my back, I couldn't relax. The massage felt good, and it was clear she wanted me to open up to her. But the only two things on my mind right now—my sister and, fuck it all, Louisa—were impossible to tell her about.

"Tell me," she murmured. "Can I help?"

"Yeah," I replied with a sudden burst of inspiration. I was good at those. "Maybe you can. How many computers are in this house?"

As she kneaded, she spewed valuable intel. "The one in the master's office, of course, and the mistress's laptop and a tablet. And Miss Louisa has a laptop."

"Where does she keep it?" I asked casually.

"On her desk. But only when she's home."

Damn. "Who usually cleans Miss Louisa's room, and when?"

"Me," she said, long fingers magically digging out a knot that had been there for days, while I valiantly tried not to melt too far into the touch because it already wasn't her hands I was feeling anymore. "At two o'clock."

I gently took her wrist and slid it off my shoulder, easing her disappointment with an irresistible smile and an offer. "You know, I *was* just thinking you look like you need a break."

5

HER

I should have known when the knock was five minutes late.

From my desk littered with chemistry notes, I shouted, "Come in," in the most annoyed voice I could conjure up. The nerve of that little trollop actually trying to *clean my room* while I was in it. I'd have to move my study session elsewhere, or I'd never be able to concentrate with her passive-aggressively slamming her mop and bucket around, clogging up my nostrils with that acrid cleaning solution she always used.

Of course, when the door opened, I instantly knew I'd never be able to concentrate anyway.

Worse, I couldn't possibly be feeling and looking less sexy in my flannel pajama pants with the frayed bottoms and gray camisole, complete with a toothpaste stain over the nipple. But that was what I was wearing when, instead of a pouty-lipped maid, the guy of my very ridiculously inappropriate dreams loomed tall in the doorway instead, wearing one of those soft, thin T-shirts with the buttons at the neck, one that seemed to inexplicably fit him despite having come out of a communal bin and clung artfully to his collarbone, his biceps, and every single infuriating place I'd made up my mind to never, ever look.

I gasped and practically leaped out of my chair, banging my hip on the side of the desk. Smooth as usual. "What are you doing?" I demanded. It was a totally stupid question and yet somehow, at the same time, the only appropriate one to ask.

"Oh, this is your room?" he asked evenly, expression unreadable, setting down the vacuum and bucket full of cleaning supplies. "I had no idea."

I rolled my eyes. "I find it very hard to believe that you don't have this place memorized by now. And where's the maid?"

"I told her she looked like she could use an hour off."

"I wish she'd take a month," I scoffed, folding my arms in a closed-off posture that was the exact opposite of how I really felt when I was around him. Like my entire body was blossoming, stretching toward his light and heat and complete and total forbiddenness. "But why are *you* here?"

"There are just some things I find irresistible," he said darkly, his stunning amber-gold eyes under those long lashes still averted from mine ever so slightly—but I knew that didn't mean he wasn't looking.

I swallowed.

"And chemistry is one of them," he finished.

Same here.

"I know you didn't ask your dad if I could tutor you."

"But I—"

He held up his hand. "I don't want to hear it. I know. So I'm going to *show* you."

My mouth went dry. Of course I'd decided not to ask my dad, to pretend that the request had never been made. There was too much risk that he'd say yes, and I didn't trust myself around the boy for a second—to say nothing of *him*. Not asking for permission—though it still left me saddled with o-chem—removed a temptation I was desperate to dodge.

Except now here he was anyway. Was the universe trying to tell me something? If so, the universe must hate me. The same way it hated Rebekah Roth.

"So are you here to tutor me or clean my room?"

"That's up to you," he said. "And me. See, I have a deal for you: I tutor you for an hour. If you haven't started to understand o-chem after that, I'll clean the room, and you don't have to deal with you-know-who. If you do, *you* clean the room. Either way, it's win-win."

"But I don't know how to clean the room." Really? *That* was my best objection?

"I'll teach you that, too."

I was too mesmerized by the way the sunlight from my bedroom window was making his hair glimmer to think about whether his proposal made any goddamn sense.

Half in a daze, I pulled the white wicker chair over to my desk and collapsed back down into my own, flipping open the dreaded book to the even more dreaded chapter. "Thing is, I understand what the chemicals are and where they go. I just don't understand *why* they—" I turned back when I realized he hadn't budged from the spot on the carpet where he stood, just outside of my room.

"May I sit down?"

This boy was breaking my brain, and we hadn't even started yet. He had talked his way into my room with a deal worthy of a real estate mogul, and now he was waiting for permission to sit in a chair. But a kid who had grown up in slavery had probably been scolded countless times for sitting on the furniture without permission. It was probably automatic. Or maybe it was just a test.

At least he hadn't added *miss*.

I gestured to the chair next to mine. "Sit," I said with a sigh. This was going to be harder than I thought. Never before had I worked side by side with a slave like this, and I hadn't the first clue how to go about it. And on top of that, he was my tutor, which meant *he* was calling the shots. I had to speak up now. "Going forward, if we keep doing this? Y-you shouldn't ask for permission. For stuff like that," I added hastily. I blushed deeper. *That* hadn't sounded right. God, I was bungling this. For the first time, I realized why most free people were assholes to slaves—it was a hell of a lot easier than trying to treat them like fellow human beings. "Okay?"

I thought I saw a smirk flicker across his face as he sank into the chair. "You're the boss."

Holy hell, was I going to regret this.

An hour later, it was official. I was distracted.

Distracted by the tendons in his bare forearm moving under his scarred skin as he scratched down formulas and the way his calloused fingers curled around the fountain pen my father had given me for my high school graduation, beneath that engraved metal chain he was made to wear because of course they had to remind him *and* me, every single second, that he wasn't really a person. Distracted by the way he bit flakes of skin off his sun-chapped lips when he was concentrating; by how, when he racked his brain for some obscure word in English, he'd rake his fingers through his sun-streaked strands of golden hair and claim not to know—and then a second later, magically come up with it and pronounce it perfectly, too. Distracted by the way he had, in the course of an hour, jokingly crowned me everything from a slow learner to a remedial student, to a late bloomer, but clearly didn't mean any of it. I wasn't sure *why* I knew he didn't mean it. The way he looked at me, maybe. The way he was *patient*, like even if it took me until the end of the goddamn world to get it, he'd still be there waiting. Or even if I *never* got it.

Or maybe it was how, when I got a problem right—and shit, I actually *did* get a few, thanks to him—he'd flash me a smile. A real smile. Like his *first* smile. One so beautiful and sunny and *life-affirming* that it left me convinced—for a split second, at least—that I loved o-chem as much as *he* clearly did.

Idiot. You're digging your own goddamn grave. And his.

And yet here I was, refusing to throw down the shovel.

In fact, I leaned back in my chair, awestruck. "Don't take this the wrong way, but you—you're amazing." I slapped a hand over my face. "The chemistry. The chemistry is amazing. I mean—how good you are at chemistry. *That's* amazing. I mean —shit. I should just stop."

"No, please, go on. I'm really enjoying this."

Of course I couldn't see his face behind my hands, but I could imagine what it looked like.

It was true. This boy was magic, but *I* shouldn't be saying it. *No one* should be saying it. Slaves weren't *magic*. They weren't even people.

Keep reminding yourself of that, dumbass. Maybe the five hundredth time will be the charm.

"Anyway, thanks," he said. "You wouldn't know it from reading Malchow, or listening to that brilliant and enchanting boyfriend of yours I had the pleasure of meeting the other day," he said, and my heart clenched at how he glanced down at the fresh, self-inflicted scab on his arm. I was wondering if he'd bring that up. *I'd* certainly spent a good portion of my day and night thinking about that thin, perfect trail of ruby-red blood. "But o-chem isn't that hard."

"That's easy for you to say."

"But it's true."

I sat back in my chair and rolled my eyes.

"It's not really science *or* math," he explained suddenly, endearingly, as if this were a field theory he'd formulated while washing dishes and had just been waiting to tell someone. "They think it is—even the people who write the textbooks— but it's not."

"It's not?"

"No, it's just logic. But for some reason, people think it's like reciting pi to the hundredth decimal place or something."

"Let me guess: you can do that, too."

He closed the book, and now it was his turn to lean back in the chair. "Hell, I could do *that* before I even learned to read."

"What, at age four?"

"Try fourteen."

I sat straight up again, peering at him. "Fourteen? I don't understand."

He laughed lightly. "What, you think they send us to school?"

I sputtered for an answer, feeling my face flush. "No, but you—you're so *smart*," I said again lamely. "All of this," I added, gesturing helplessly to the book on the desk. "The math, the vocabulary, the—"

He grinned. "I'm even more amazing now, yeah?"

"Not *that* amazing," I shot back. "Anyway, how *did* you learn to read?" I was going to regret asking. I was going to regret all of it. Because the more I knew about him, the more I wanted to know. And I *shouldn't* want to know. There wasn't supposed to be anything about slaves *to* know.

And he was about to tell me.

"Let's say someone bought me who recognized my 'potential.' Someone at the university in Heidelberg."

"Heidelberg. Is that where you're from?"

"I'm *from* Luxembourg," he said, with more than a little indignant pride.

Remember that. Get it right. As if I'd ever before cared in my life where a slave came from.

"And he just decided to... teach you quantum chemistry? For fun?"

"Okay, ready for story time?" he said, sliding his chair an inch or so closer to me and leaning forward melodramatically, resting his scarred-but-still-somehow-perfect forearm on the desk. I never wanted it to leave. "When I was thirteen, I got sold to this huge factory farm in Romania. It's not a high-end gig, to say the least. It's criminals and chronic runaways and slaves nobody else wanted to buy; ones that would have ended up in a mine otherwise."

So how had *he* ended up there? I had a feeling I wasn't going to get that part of the story. This boy had a *serious* knack for withholding absolutely everything but the precise information he wanted to share. It didn't make me want to know it any less, though. It just made me want to press harder, on places it was dangerous to press.

"When you get sold to one of those places, it's almost always for life, and by life, I mean until they work you to death, which usually takes a year or two for most people. If you're strong and you can deal with the punishments and rations and quotas, you can make it longer."

"How long did you make it?" I asked quietly.

"Three years."

A brief silence hung over us.

"Then?" I was almost afraid to keep asking.

"I'd got one of the overseers to teach me how to fix the farm machinery, so I could get out of the fields sometimes. It was a privilege, believe it or not. Until I got my arm caught in one of them. Severed it at the shoulder."

I gasped.

"Almost. Needless to say, I thought the next and last thing I'd see would be the inside of a shotgun barrel. But they decided to try to fix me up, so they had some hired goon do it using instructions he found on the internet."

I was dumbstruck by the way he shared the abject horror of his past, as casually as I recalled slumber parties and trips to the mall with my friends. "But owners aren't allowed to kill slaves," I protested with a gasp. "It's the law. And you shouldn't have been sold for farm labor, either. Not at thirteen. My professor—"

I stopped short, remembering what Erica Muller had said in class last week. *If they can do the work of an adult, they'll be made to do it. It doesn't matter what the law says.*

"Why you?" I finally asked softly.

He smiled and glanced away as if he could see the conflict raging in my head but had decided to let me ride it out alone. "The owner's wife, well... she liked me, let's put it that way. I used to talk to her through the fence. She slipped me sweets and stuff sometimes, and I would joke about how she should run away with me," he said, then added, "Just to make her laugh," as if somehow that would matter to me. It did, of course.

"What kind of sweets?" Though I instantly hated this woman, I *adored* that younger, shyer version of him, trying out his charm, maybe blushing exactly like he was blushing—just slightly—now. But then again, it was kind of warm in here.

"Namur pralines," he replied when a curious expression crossed my face. "It's a Luxembourgish thing. I asked her for them. Anyway, she intervened. So by some miracle, it worked, but needless to say, I still can't rotate that arm all the way," he said, and oh. He was going to show me because of course he was, pulling up the sleeve of his shirt to show me the long, deep, jagged surgical scar snaking around his shoulder. "After that, they sent me to one of those discount auctions, hoping to make back some of what they spent on me, which wasn't much. That's when *he* came in. We were all standing there in pens, and instead of looking in our mouths or feeling up our junk, he walked right down the line and started quizzing all of us. We all thought he was crazy, but he knew what he was doing. Looking for a diamond in the rough. I must have passed the test. He took me to Heidelberg, had the hospital there stitch me up properly, and six months later, I was reading Shakespeare."

"Six *months*?"

"I know. *I* didn't even think I could do it that fast, but it turns out anyone can, assuming you just never had the opportunity and don't have some learning disability. Eventually, he made me take all these tests, including this aptitude test—one that they give to students here. I forget what it's called."

I threw out the name.

"That's the one. I scored in the ninety-ninth percentile. Of course, to send it in, you can't put a number in the 'name' field. He had to make up a fake name for me."

"What was it?"

He laughed. "Nice try."

"But I don't have anything to call you."

"Not my problem."

It seemed odd that this should be the first time this particular issue had bothered me, but except for a nanny we'd had for a year or so when I was a kid, I'd never interacted closely enough with a slave to *care*. Not that some fake name he'd only used once would be better, but it would be something—and illegal. Slaves were kept nameless for a very good reason.

I just wished I knew what it was.

"Look, you have to admit, he gave you an incredible gift," I remarked.

"Some gift. I probably dragged his drunk ass home from every bar in Heidelberg at least once. I practically *wrote* his last paper myself—and got it published—when he was too wasted to even get out of bed. Not to mention, he used to develop explosives for the military, and he'd take me to the testing range and make me light the fuse."

I gasped. "You could have been killed!"

"Better me than him, was his logic."

"Well, fuck him, then. But in the long run, it could only be a good thing, right? Somebody educated you. Educated slaves are worth—"

"It could only increase my market value, right?" he finished, and my heart dropped.

Idiot girl. He was a person, not a fixer-upper house. And anyway, no matter what amount of money exchanged hands for him, it's not as if *he* would be seeing any of it.

"You're right, though. It's the only reason my master did it. To increase his profit margin. He didn't give a shit about me. Only what I could do for him."

"But still," I said, persisting against my better judgment. "He gave you—"

"He gave me this," he said, nodding with contempt at the scarred skin crawling over his forearms and almost up to his shoulders. "It's the only thing I have to show for the thousands of hours he spent teaching me. I would have been better off in the fields where he found me."

"Don't say that." He'd be *dead*, for one thing.

"It's true. What, am I going to get a scholarship? Go to university? Win the Nobel Prize?"

"But—"

There was a storm cloud forming in his amber-gold eyes. "You're going to *argue* with me about this? I couldn't even—" He turned away suddenly.

"What?"

"Nothing." His eyes flashed again. I'd seen them flash before, but not like this. With pain, yes, but it was beyond pain. It was something I couldn't ever begin to fathom. Something I wasn't *equipped* to fathom because nobody had ever thought I'd *need* to be equipped.

And in its face, there was nothing to say, so I stared intensely down at the page of the notebook in front of me as if written in it were the most fascinating story I'd ever read.

I'd done nothing but study for the past year, but I'd never felt more ignorant.

I *should* ask him, I knew. He wasn't allowed to lie to me or dodge the truth. If I demanded to know his entire history, from the day he was born to this exact second, he would be required to tell me. And good God, did I want to know all of it. I was in.

"You *can* tell me, you know," I said into the pages. Then I looked back over at him, embarrassed, expecting him to have turned away for good, fed up with my ignorance and nosiness and just ready to move on. To my shock, he was staring back at me, those brilliant eyes a mix of confusion and wonder, like I'd just said the last thing in the world he'd expected to hear.

And all at once, it terrified me. The silence, our closeness, the unspoken *everything*. Our hands, resting on the desk, nearly touching, and if he'd been anything other than what he was, I might have *already* reached out to. To offer the comfort he so badly deserved and seemed, astonishingly, to have never been offered. It was just an inch between us, only an inch, and I could know exactly what those calloused fingers would feel like under my touch.

He followed my gaze, noticing exactly where I was looking —and very likely what I was thinking. Ah, fuck. I swiftly hid my hands under the desk, and he turned around, staring at the sunburst-shaped wall clock.

"It's getting late," he said, changing the subject, then turned back to me with a smirk. "Shouldn't you be cleaning?"

I groaned, having forgotten about that part of the deal.

"Look, I'll make it easy for you," he said, rising from the chair. "I'll vacuum, dust, empty the wastebaskets, and make the bed out here while you do the bathroom."

"But I don't—"

"Slow learner, I said I'd show you."

I sighed. Frankly, I'd rather keep doing o-chem, if it was all the same. But he wasn't about to let me back out of the deal.

I didn't do a half-bad job, if I did say so myself. Of course I accidentally spilled bleach all over the tile and had to mop that up before I could even get to the shower or the mirror. By the time the vacuum stopped in the other room, I was ready to drop, and I'd only been cleaning for fifteen minutes.

He spent three years toiling in the fields, you big baby.

"Not bad for a first try," he said when he popped his head in and glimpsed the sparkling bathroom tile, mirror, and tub. He began gathering up the supplies and replacing them in the mop bucket. "Just think, next time we'll have you doing something crazy like putting your own dishes in the sink."

Well, it was official: story time was over. It was going to be snark from here on out. But before I could say anything, the intercom buzzed.

"Excuse me, miss." It was the housekeeper, clearing her throat ever-so-politely. "It's fifteen minutes past the time when

I would have needed all the outdoor furniture cleaned off and rearranged, the terrace swept, the table set—"

I took my finger off the button. "It's for you," I said to him with a smirk.

As soon as he'd left, I slammed the door, sat down, buried my face in my pillow, and screamed. Then I got up, went to my computer, and typed "slave welfare" into the search bar.

It was time to start my paper.

HIM

Getting what I'd come for had been the easy part.

First, distracting Louisa with a cunning bit of wit while subtly directing my eyes to her laptop password, then coaxing her out of the room and running a quick internet search to discover that the Salt River Boulevard address was a warehouse bought two years ago by Langer Enterprises with the intention of turning it into a lab/manufacturing plant for Project White Cedar—some kind of "revolutionary" thirty million-dollar biotechnology that Langer was assuring investors would disrupt the slavery industry. Learning that last year, the property had been transferred into Keith Wainwright-Phillips's name. Even getting the printout—a last-minute stroke of genius to use the vacuum cleaner to disguise the noise—hadn't been hard. And even though I got affectionately whacked with a wooden spoon by the housekeeper when I arrived late for my usual bullshit evening chores, she still let me polish off some leftover banana pudding, so she couldn't have been that upset.

No, I could have done all that with my eyes closed—and had, many times in my past.

Louisa. *She* was hard. Actually, so was I, but in an entirely different way.

Damn her for knowing exactly where to place those tiny

little moles. Besides the one on her cheek, she had one centered perfectly above her left tit, and if that weren't bad enough, the air conditioning kept making her nipples poke out of that tight little camisole she had on. And then she had the audacity to top it all off with that pile of curly hair she kept nervously running her delicate, manicured little fingers through. I loved them there, of course, but I *wanted* them somewhere else.

She *had* to know what she was doing, right? She couldn't be that innocent. Or maybe she was. Maybe she genuinely had no fucking clue that those hands in her hair were the cherry on top of a giant ice cream sundae behind double-paned glass—one my starving self wanted to smash open, grab, throw down on the bed, and give the orgasm of a lifetime.

But to my dismayed surprise—and my dick's—that wasn't even what I was thinking about the most. What I was thinking about the most—and what I *wanted* to think about the least—was how she had listened.

I hadn't meant to talk. I hadn't meant to bring those years up at all. Usually, I pushed them down into the far, far reaches of my psyche, where they couldn't crop up at inopportune moments and make me want to burn things or collapse into a broken heap on the floor. Yes, she'd said some ignorant, spoiled, artless things. Things that made me want to stop talking because she didn't deserve to hear them, and that she wouldn't understand if I told her, and that I wouldn't be so stupid as to imagine for a second that she'd care about. Things that reminded me that she had no reason to be different from all the other free women of my past who had held my fate in their manicured hands—a sweet, cuddly pet they could feed, tease, play with, and kill with one word the second I acted up.

But I'd kept talking. Because she wasn't feeding, teasing, or playing. She was *still*. All except for her huge gray eyes, wide not with pity but with horror. As if what had happened to me actually mattered to her, when sometimes it didn't even matter to *me*. I was just a slave, after all, and if slaves could feel, we wouldn't get treated like this.

Right.

It was almost enough to make me want to tell her the whole story. Almost.

Not to mention, I'd bet that hand on the desk wouldn't have felt *anything* like a slave girl's hand.

Okay. Stop right there. That's it. Abort the mission. I was done. Finished. Stage One had been achieved, right? I was there to use her, and I'd used her. It had taken all my boldness, all my cunning and skill, but I'd used her. And now it was time to throw her away.

But. What if I *kept* using her and just didn't—

No, you dumbfuck. Not only would she catch on—because she was fucking smart, *definitely* not in chemistry, but in other ways—but the more I went back, the more tempted I'd be by the information at my fingertips, information that could help me find my sister, and the greater the risk of getting caught. A slave found to be plotting against his master would be flogged and sold, if not to the mines then somewhere just as bad. But whatever beating I got couldn't be worse than the beating I was already giving myself for having gotten too caught up in this whole tutoring debacle and nearly forgetting what it was I had actually come here to do.

And yet, the next day, here I was climbing the stairs. Here I was with my hand on the knob. Here I was waiting for the door to open.

She was wearing a sundress today.

HER

Louisa Wainwright-Phillips

Slavery Studies 101 Section 2
Balancing Necessity and Compassion: Enhancing Slave Welfare Legislation in the NNAU

While it is an established fact that the institution of slavery is necessary for the functioning of the society and economy of the New North American Union, it is also becoming increasingly evident that laws intended to safeguard the welfare of slaves are few and laxly enforced. The existing legislation, when properly applied, can indeed provide a measure of care for slaves. However, more needs to be done to ensure these laws are followed and to introduce additional measures that genuinely protect the well-being of slaves within the system ...

I collapsed like a corpse into bed after drafting my paper, working on autopilot, knowing that if I stopped for even a second to reflect on what had just happened, I'd have no hope of accomplishing anything ever again.

I was ninety percent convinced he wouldn't come back.

Actually, I was at least half-convinced that the whole afternoon had been a dream. It was only when I pulled back a leaf of my notebook the following morning and glimpsed the strange, spiky, foreign male handwriting left on my study notes—and felt my heart do somersaults when I did—that convinced me it hadn't been a dream.

But when three rolled around, I couldn't pretend a part of me wasn't relieved he hadn't shown. Sure, it was just tutoring. But in actuality, it was a runaway train careening straight off a cliff. I knew it. Did he know it? And why was I even *thinking* about whether he knew it? For the last time, he wasn't supposed to know anything, and *I* wasn't supposed to care.

And *this* was exactly why I was in such deep fucking trouble.

But that didn't mean I hadn't still spent twenty minutes staring into my closet *just in case*, only to come up with nothing more inspired than a yellow sundress. Then again, none of the "bold fall fashion trends" I'd seen in the magazines that year seemed appropriate for this particular situation.

When the knock came, I toppled over the desk chair in shock. But when I opened the door to find him leaning patiently on the frame, he gave me a knowing smile, polite enough not to ask about the noise.

♥

He kept coming.

If the housekeeper—or even worse, my parents—had grown suspicious about why he and the maid had swapped cleaning duties, they hadn't spoken up. Most likely, nobody cared as long as the work was getting done. In reality, he and I always split the cleaning, and to my amazement, I was actually kind of *enjoying* it. I knew it was absurd, but even graduating with a near-perfect GPA and being honored for Best Hair in the senior yearbook hadn't engendered the same kind of absurd pride as having scrubbed my own toilet spotless.

The tutoring was the real gauntlet I was running.

As my midterm approached, he insisted we couldn't waste a second getting down to business, and I agreed, even though there was nothing I'd like better than to waste *many* seconds on him—to ask more, to know more. I just wanted *more*. But he seemingly had no more interest in telling me—not surprising, given that my responses the first time had been so stupid and clumsy it was a miracle he'd ever come back.

But he did come back, to drill me over and over again on

substitutions and eliminations and rearrangements so ruthlessly and precisely that I sometimes forgot he'd been awake for ten hours already. He was exacting, he was strict, he was simply *unfair*. What had that professor *done* to him, anyway?

I looked down at his hands. Oh.

"You're a sadist," I sputtered, throwing my pencil down the fifth time I'd got a problem correct, and he made me walk him back through the steps and explain *why* it was correct. And they were always the *hardest* problems, too—ones he should be *congratulating* me for solving, not busying himself finding new ways to torture me with.

Exasperating, infuriating, impossible boy.

"What?" He flashed me an innocent smirk. "This isn't pain. It's fun."

"Yeah, for *you*," I burst out. "That's the goddamn *definition* of a sadist."

"Hey, I promise, when we're done here, you're not only going to be able to *do* o-chem, you're going to *like* it."

"Impossible."

He raised an eyebrow. "Wanna bet?"

"What are the stakes?"

"Doesn't matter." He shook his head, laughed, and slyly turned back to the textbook. "I already won."

The *nerve*. I would have whacked him on the arm, but with him, it wouldn't *be* a whack on the arm. It would be a touch, it would be forbidden, and it would *mean* something. So I didn't.

Still, amid this body-and-soul torture, I progressed, which was frankly remarkable given that I couldn't tear my eyes away from *him*—his shimmering forelock of hair flipped carelessly over to one side, his veined biceps under his thin, always-clinging T-shirts; his raw, rough, scarred but somehow still inexplicably perfect hand curled around my expensive pens; his body heat radiating inches away from me; him, him, *him*—for more than a few seconds at a time to even remember where we were, or *what* we were, or that every second we were together felt like the second I might decide to throw my life away forever. And yes, somehow, amid it all, I was *learning* o-chem.

Miraculous boy.

On Thursday, though—just before I was about to open my desk drawer to suggest we share something I really, really shouldn't have bought—he became human again.

He yawned. Then he yawned again, and his long eyelashes started to cast even longer shadows on his face. Then it was *all* yawns. He was trying to stay alert, I could tell, but I was irritated. Seriously, how could he be tired this early? *My* mind and body still felt completely awake and abuzz because of course they did. Look what I was sitting across from.

But he couldn't shake it. It was dragging him down like an invisible tide.

"How much sleep did you get last night?" I bit my lip, thinking of Erica Muller's lecture from a few weeks ago, about how much sleep slaves were supposed to get versus how much they actually got. But surely that didn't apply to—

"Let's see," he said thoughtfully, dropping the pencil and leaning back in the chair. Story time again. "My day started at five, where I was told I had to help the gardener clear and chop up fallen tree branches that blew in from the neighbor's yard, followed by the valet informing me that your dad had decided that all three of his cars needed washing, waxing, and buffing. By then it was almost dinner, which ended up being late because the valve in the dishwasher was fucked and nobody noticed, so the maid and I had to spend an hour mopping water off the kitchen and pantry floor before it soaked into the cabinets and got mold everywhere. And then I was told to repair it, which required ordering parts from the hardware store, but they sent the wrong ones, so I have to wait and work on that *again* today. And that's all on top of my regular duties, which I can't go to bed without finishing, so I didn't get started on them until four and finished at around two." As if on cue, he yawned again, body unfurling in the wicker chair, stretching one long, sculpted arm over his head. Fuck, I hated when he did that because of course it made the hem of his T-shirt rise minutely to reveal a tiny sliver of *those abs*. Those abs I'd give a kidney to see in all their glory. So by *hate*, I meant *love*, naturally. "So, three hours?"

"But the law states that you're supposed to get at least four hours a night," I protested. "Not to mention, under New European law, you shouldn't have been sold for farm labor at that age, either. I've been researching this for my term paper, where I talk about closing the loopholes and adding more government oversight. If we had just done that, your life could have been—"

I clamped down on my lip. When I saw how he was looking at me, I couldn't do much else.

"No, keep going," he said. "I defer to the expert."

"Oops," I said in a tiny voice. "Sorry." I wanted to crumple myself up and throw myself in the wastebasket.

He was still smiling a little, thank fuck. Maybe the biggest miracle in all of this was that he didn't completely fucking hate me. "Oh," he said. "One more thing: I'm behind schedule again today."

I slumped in my chair. "Because of being here?"

"Yeah."

I buried my face in my hands.

"Which is the highlight of my day, of course."

Like an idiot, I blushed inwardly. "Really?"

"Well, yeah. It's the only time all day I get to use the furniture."

He was joking. But also not.

"Take a nap," I said resolutely. "In my bed. Right now."

"Under the covers?" he asked, arching an eyebrow.

I swallowed. "If you want."

His reply wasn't exactly the standard slave line when invited to take liberties: *Oh, miss, that wouldn't be proper, blah, blah, blah.*

"Damn, I thought you'd never ask," he said, pulled back the down comforter, tossed aside Pillow Mountain, and before my eyes, arrayed his rather large, rather long, rather exquisitely sculpted body on the bed in its place, practically purring. Noticing me staring, he patted the space next to him slyly. "Room for two."

"In your dreams," I said as if the entire inner workings of my body hadn't suddenly erupted like a fire hydrant just thinking about that. Clearly, this was a terrible idea. He wasn't supposed to be allowed on *any* furniture, let alone my *bed*. He was also, I reminded myself, a person, not a dog. Anyway, there was no changing my mind now.

"No one comes up here this time of day except the maid, and we're already doing her job," I said, rising and moving toward the door.

He went rigid, just for a split-second, and I knew I wasn't the only one who had suddenly remembered where we were and what we were, which was as far as it was possible to get from two ordinary kids shamelessly flirting while pretending not to.

"I'll keep the door open a crack and watch, just in case. And wake you up in plenty of time," I reassured him, suddenly convinced that the worst thing that could ever happen would be him deciding this was a terrible idea, even though I already had.

"You won't have to," he said matter-of-factly, his sanguinity regained. "I've got an internal alarm like you wouldn't believe."

"I always *wished* I had one of those."

"Spend three years getting kicked awake and you would."

Fuck. Like by now, I couldn't have *guessed* that.

He yawned again, and I watched that body relax and sink into the bed, muscle by gorgeous muscle untensing in turn. "Hey, I could get used to this," he said with another yawn.

"Don't," I said immediately. "This is a one-time offer."

"If you say so," he said with a half-smile, raising one arm over his head casually to rest on my favorite furry pink throw pillow. A small sigh escaped his lips as if this perfectly normal bed were some kind of luxury spa treatment. Then again, I'd never even spared a thought for the kinds of beds the slaves slept on.

"What do they make these sheets out of?" he asked.

Beds very unlike mine, evidently. "Nine-hundred-thread-count Egyptian cotton," I said as I came back toward the bed.

He shook his head in bemusement. "I have no idea what that means."

"So, Albert Einstein, there *is* something you don't know. It means it's expensive."

His eyes flicked back mischievously. "Maybe you should charge me by the hour."

I grabbed a pillow from the floor and threw it at him, prompting his laughter. "Half an hour is all you're getting. And you couldn't even afford that."

I sat back down. I'd let him settle down without me looking. No one enjoyed being stared at going to sleep, after all. Instead, I opened some dumb email from a clothing retailer promoting white skinny jeans and reread it ten times, and when I looked back some time later, his eyes were closed, his long, light lashes casting shadows on his milky skin, his lips slightly parted. He could have been pretending, but I didn't think so. His breathing was even. Peaceful.

And it only made me that much more curious. As silently as I could, I wheeled my desk chair closer.

A shaft of afternoon sunlight from my open window seemed to bless him uniquely, playing with his golden hair. It was the same light that made his metal bracelet shine, held as it was slightly over his head, out of the covers. The one bearing his number, the one that thanks to Erica Muller, I knew would have been assigned to him at birth and was the closest thing he had ever had to an official name.

Stalker was the word going through my head as, my heart rate picking up, I returned to my desk and quickly pulled up the website for the international slave registration database. I hesitated for a second before rapidly typing in the number from his bracelet and hitting "return." I closed my eyes and held my breath as the page loaded. Although I'd long known the site existed, I'd never been even remotely curious enough about a slave to look one up. But right now, my very fingers were buzzing with anticipation about what I might find.

And all of a sudden, there he was: 77349S6. *My* 77349S6: nineteen, male, blond, literate, right-handed, and born into slavery in Luxembourg City.

The front photo was older, since he looked noticeably younger, though every inch as stunningly gorgeous—more so in the photo's stark relief, which highlighted his high cheekbones and exquisite jawline. God, this boy could be a fucking aristocrat if he hadn't been a slave. Hell, maybe he was— European nobility had fallen victim to the hard times, same as everybody else. His ancestor might well have been one of them. Bolstering that theory was his expression, which, at least in this photo, was one of boredom and superiority, as if he'd had infinitely better things to do that day. And below the headshots were—

Shit. His abs. I lowered my laptop screen, stealthily glancing behind me. But he didn't stir.

Still, I thought it safer to click away—for now. But I sure had a date with them later.

However, I even forgot all about *that* when I saw the photo of his back. Just a puckered roadmap of destruction and pain—three years in the fields had left barely an inch left untouched by the whip. Feeling ill, I clicked away from *that* photo, too, not daring to glance again at the peaceful, angelic figure sleeping behind me. I was starting to regret logging on, though I couldn't stop now.

Three former owners. First, a private home in Luxembourg, where he'd lived until he was twelve. After that, I couldn't make much sense of things. It said "remanded to the government," then something about an auction. Then he'd been leased to something called Biofields SA and sent to Romania—the factory farm.

I couldn't forget that photo of his back. According to Erica Muller, farms that used slaves were barely a step up from the mines. If he'd spent three years at one of them and survived, he was stronger than I could possibly imagine—and not just physically.

But now I was *angry*. And as weird as it seemed, ashamed of my own kind. How the hell could a family who had owned and raised him since birth sell him to a place like that? Didn't they have any affection toward him at all? He'd been a *child*. Surely my parents would never dream of being that cruel toward—

But they had. At least, my grandparents had. They'd sold off the housekeeper's children right before my older brother was born—*because* he was born. And I'd never paused for even a second to think about how the woman must have grieved.

The same way my own parents must have grieved when Ethan disappeared.

Ethan. Scottsdale's favorite golden retriever. Tattooed, chestnut-curled, golf-betting, guitar-riffing party boy. A complete and total fuckup in the best possible way—or, when it came to my father, the worst. As hard as Daddy rode him to achieve, he couldn't solve Ethan's dyslexia or ADHD, and it was no surprise when he went the opposite way, turning to drugs and ultimately doing two stints in rehab in the most expensive facility in the union. Both times, he'd relapsed and after a few months, disappeared. The first time, he came back. The second time, he didn't.

We last heard from him two Decembers ago, when he'd called to ask for money. My father had refused, of course, while my mother cried silently into her triple appletini. He was now off the grid, off the radar, out of our lives unless and until he came back clean.

And that was why my father had given up and let our fortune slip away, and why my mother drank—because losing a family member felt like a thousand knives stabbing you all over your body every second of the day.

I knew because I'd felt it, too.

And so the housekeeper must have, times two. All while getting up at five every morning to cook breakfast, clean up after me and my brother's stupid messes, and attend to our petty cares.

They aren't like us, my father had reassured me once, when he'd sold my favorite slave, a playful teenage nanny who for a year or so had taken over caring for Ethan and me while the housekeeper attended culinary training. I'd called her Cupcake because she was always hiding them around the house for us, and even though Daddy subscribed to the theory that slaves shouldn't have names, even demeaning ones, he hadn't objected.

Then she was gone. *They get over it.*

How?

And what about the *kids*? Slave children were legally treated the same as adults in almost every way, I'd also been shocked to learn in class. If the slave boy—*my* slave boy—had been sold to the farm at thirteen, if Erica Muller could be believed, he would have worked twelve-hour days, been fed barely more than gruel and water, and given zero medical attention. And shackles, chains, beatings, and floggings to keep him in line—and worse punishments, ones that required a trigger warning in class. Having heard the remarks that came out of his mouth, I knew he would not have been spared them. Overseers weren't as easily charmed as farmers' wives.

At fifteen, blessedly—or not-so-blessedly, to hear him tell it —he'd been sold to Professor von Esch in Heidelberg. I knew the story after that, more or less. My father's name was at the end of the list of owners, but he hadn't gotten around to adding much to the file.

I scrolled down to the *Known Family* section, heart rate picking up.

He had one living family member: a sister. Clicking on the sister's number brought me to another page, where a beautiful blond seventeen-year-old girl—same sun-bleached hair, worn in a pixie bob around her heart-shaped face, and same amber-gold eyes, bigger and with longer lashes—greeted me. But unlike her brother, she didn't look bored. More like curious, dreamy, surprised, sad—maybe even a little mischievous. She had two former owners, the first one the same as the boy's, then a riding school in Belgium. But the page said *location unknown*, and there it stopped.

For both: *mother deceased, father unknown.*

Hands trembling, I opened my desk drawer again to look at the package of Luxembourgish pralines I'd ordered from a specialty website. In the face of all I'd just seen, they seemed inadequate. Lame, almost. But still. Maybe they'd make him smile. And his smiles were—

Well. When he woke up, I'd tell him I'd just happened to find them at a store near campus. Yeah, that was it. Then we'd share them. Perfect. Normal. Not obsessive in the least.

And then I'd rewrite my paper again.

Mind made up, I clicked back to the boy's page, where his owners, dating back to his childhood, had written comments. *Reviews,* really.

Positives: Bright, attractive, charming, sensitive, curious ...

Negatives: Defiant, mouthy, willful, manipulative, moody, lazy ...

I hid a smile. Sounded about right.

Then I reached the very bottom, under the heading *Warnings.*

DANGEROUS: Documented violent attack on an owner

A stirring from the bed behind me. Immediately, I slammed the laptop shut. I spun my chair around, trying to look casual.

"Hey," he said. "What were you doing?"

"Nothing," I replied quickly. "Homework."

He smiled. "You're a shit liar."

Yep, there was that signature charm. Fuck it all. It was too good to be true. I knew it. I *knew* it.

"No, really, what?" he pressed.

"Ordering a 'live, laugh, love' sign for over the desk," I muttered through gritted teeth. "Look, it doesn't matter, okay?"

"Come on, you can tell me."

He slid off the bed and came to my side innocently. No, he wasn't a dog, but right now—in contrast to what I'd just seen—he *was* like a puppy with a bone. Ears up, tail wagging. There was another "negative": stubborn.

"I really do have homework to do, and I think you're due downstairs." I was dying inside as I said it, but it had to be said.

"What?" He looked bewildered, and I didn't blame him.

I thought once more of the pralines in the drawer.

"But we——" he began.

"Go." I clenched my jaw harder, turning my back, staring intently at the tiny cactus in the pink ceramic pot on my desk like it was the most fascinating thing I'd ever seen. "It's an order."

He followed it.

6

I couldn't sleep.

Why was there a whole wing of my house I'd never thought to visit? Why was there a whole database of slaves—and their families, of all things—I had never thought to browse? Why had I spent all evening furiously rewriting a paper I had now tentatively titled: "Slave Welfare in the NNAU: Legislation or Illusion?" And why were both of them occupying so much space in my head right now that I couldn't get them out? I couldn't even close my *eyes*. All I could do was roll over, stare at my bedroom's elaborate wainscoting, and let it all crash over me, wave after wave.

Desert sage, sunshine, and some plain soap. That's what the sheets smelled like, I'd finally decided, inhaling again. Of course. The scent of a boy who worked outdoors much of the day.

Maybe I shouldn't have looked at the file. It hadn't satisfied my curiosity, after all. It had only awakened it. How could it not have? Every single goddamn thing I learned about him turned me onto a million more things I longed to know. And yet—

Dangerous.

That should be all I *needed* to know.

If the so-called boy—man—whatever—of my dreams had attacked one of his owners, he'd committed one of the worst crimes a slave could commit, and I suspected *that* was what he was hiding. *That's* why he'd been put in chains and sent to the farm. And if he hadn't been sold to the professor, he might still be there. Hell, it was probably where he *deserved* to be. Not to mention, it was clear now why Daddy had been able to afford him.

Anyway, the only pain that should concern me right now was my *own* pain, the pain I would feel if I flunked o-chem, lost my scholarship, and had to drop out of school. Problem was, whatever else he was, *he* was the only one standing between me and that fate: the fate of having to date Corey the douchebag for his money, or going to live with my father in a cardboard box. Or in slavery, if it came to that. Debt collectors still came knocking, after all. These days, if you weren't born a slave, that's often how you became one.

Fuck if *I'd* be the one to make my family poor again.

My friends had no idea—no one did—but years ago, when my father had started out in business, he and my mother had lived in a one-bedroom in one of Phoenix's scariest neighborhoods. He'd been doing better by the time I came along, thankfully—we all had. Nine figures better, to be exact.

And then Ethan disappeared.

I'd worshiped him, of course, because he was everything I wasn't. At the country club, he used to steal Daddy's golf cart and a six-pack of beers for us, veering crazily off the paved path on two wheels while I clung on white-knuckled. *You have to break a few rules now and then, Lou. That's how you find out who you really are.* I never took his advice—I figured he'd broken enough rules for both of us—but now, I stared where I knew his old marbled guitar pick sat on my dresser, the one he gave me when I was ten, and wondered whether I should have broken more. Maybe he would have stuck around if I weren't so goddamn boring.

But while I blamed myself, my father had imploded even *more* spectacularly. After struggling his entire life to reach the top, it had destroyed Daddy that he couldn't even save his own son. After the second relapse, my father didn't leave his bedroom for weeks. He didn't seem to care that the debts were piling up and the phone was ringing off the hook with calls from his colleagues and clients. Nothing seemed to matter to him anymore, not even us, his wife and daughter, who were left to find our own ways of coping—through alcohol and school, respectively.

So as much as I wanted to get out from under them, I also knew that without Ethan, I was my parents' only hope—not only financially, but to hopefully, someday, bring them both back to the land of the living.

And to achieve that, I needed the slave boy. But only as a calculator. A study aid. An object. *A tool.*

In other words, I'd need to treat him as exactly what everyone said he was.

Once again, my mind drifted to the pralines in my desk drawer, the ones I'd spent nearly every cent of my pathetic allowance on.

I'd never bought something like *that* for my goddamn calculator.

Plus, there was still so much of his story I didn't know. So much that could explain everything. He had a family. *Still* had a family—at least a sister—somewhere, *location unknown.* Was that what the attack had been about? Had he tried to defend them, to fight for them? He wouldn't be a person if he didn't.

A person. In the dark, the slightest smile crossed my lips. Why couldn't I just accept it? I knew it. *Everyone* knew it. And yet everyone was expected to act like they didn't.

Still. What could I do? I couldn't *help* him, for fuck's sake. Not only shouldn't, but *couldn't.* Without any money, I had about as much power as he did. And if I kept trying, if I kept getting closer, I couldn't kid myself anymore. I knew exactly what would happen: I'd get caught and throw away everything I'd worked so hard for, for the sake of a slave who could offer me nothing, and who might not even hesitate to shed my family's blood. Hell, he wouldn't even *tell* me anything. He'd made it perfectly clear: *He didn't want my help.*

So drop it. Grab those pralines, walk downstairs, toss them all down the garbage disposal, and flick the switch. Then come back up here and go. The fuck. To sleep.

Instead, I rolled over and took another long, deep inhale. I wasn't going to drop it. I was going to find out everything. If I didn't, I'd never sleep again.

HIM

I couldn't sleep.

The morning shift—five to eight—was supposed to be my time to do it, but I rarely did.

In fact, today, those twenty minutes in Louisa's pillowy bed, enveloped in citrus and rose and another scent I could only describe as *rich girl*—was going to be the best I could do, though I shouldn't have done it at all. And worse, because I had done it, now I *owed* her one.

Instead, I lay on my narrow metal top bunk in the basement room meant to serve as the male slave quarters, though, since the gardener slept in the shed and the valet slept upstairs, I had it all to myself. My hands behind my head, absently twisting my metal bracelet around and around on my wrist, staring at the pipes overhead, and realizing I was fucked.

There was a reason I didn't accept help. From free people, from fellow slaves, from anyone. Not unless I'd manipulated them into it and knew I'd earned it.

The truth was, I hadn't just been wagging my tail for that lonely middle-aged wife like a puppy through an electric fence, of course. And it wasn't just pralines I'd wanted—I'd actually been conning her into helping me escape. Of course, my plan was stupid and ill-conceived and destined to get me killed, but in my defense, I'd been fifteen. Ultimately, the only reason I hadn't done it was because my arm had nearly been lopped off first.

It was part of why they'd thrown me behind that electric fence to begin with: Because I was a liar. Because I was defiant. And because I was dangerous—hell, before the farm bought me, I'd spent a month living in a cage with a gigantic red label proclaiming me exactly that, and it wasn't wrong.

But I'd never done anything *this* dangerous: Flirting with my master's daughter not because I wanted something, but because I wanted *her*. Sure, I could tell myself that flirting got me what I wanted. And I could claim I just needed her computer, or her help ingratiating me to her father. But I could lie to myself all I wanted. I fucking wanted her, and if I wasn't afraid the goddamn gardener would walk in any second, I'd be jerking off right now to that image I'd tried to shove out of my head earlier—to those plump, pink, glossy princess lips too goddamn pristine to have ever sucked off anyone, let alone a slave, let alone *willingly*. But most of all, to the ludicrous idea that she might ever regard me as anything more than an object for *her* entertainment. Regarding me as a person, as a man who could *want* things, who could want *her*. And—to steal her phrasing—how *dare* she?

Slaves weren't supposed to want things.

In fact, for years, ever since my sister had vanished, the only thing I'd allowed myself to want was to find her and keep her safe, forever. The way any man—even if he was a slave—should do.

It didn't matter what happened to me after that, and there was never supposed to be anything else involved. Any*one* else involved.

But fuck it, now there was.

A shaft of white moonlight cut across the locked window of the slave quarters, bisecting my bunk. As spartan as it was, this was the best room I'd ever had, but it didn't mean that Keith Wainwright-Phillips wasn't scum. He was like all the rest. Those who had torn away my family, treated me like a farm animal, numbered me and chained me and herded me from pen to pen, forced me to spend my thirteenth, fourteenth, and fifteenth birthdays in shackles, hoeing and harvesting under the lash in a muddy field. Those who had destroyed my mother and stolen my sister. Those who deserved death.

It was a clear night, I noticed, and sleep sure wasn't working. *No plan survives contact with the enemy, boy,* the old professor used to tell me, rapping my knuckles over our games of speed chess—one of the many things von Esch had decided I simply had to learn to truly be considered educated. When he first bought me, we'd played on the regular, until I actually started winning and he'd knock the pieces off the board in a tantrum and stalk off to another bottle of Remy Martin. But I'd already learned enough. *A good opening only takes you so far.* It was time to change up the strategy, as usual. I jumped down from the bunk and grabbed some flip-flops from under the bedframe, right next to the wooden crate where I kept my clothes and other accouterments—I wouldn't say belongings because legally, nothing *could* belong to me.

The good thing about sleeping in the morning was that the basement quarters weren't locked. Slaves—dangerous or otherwise—couldn't be let out alone at night, you see, unless they were working. The Pleiades would be high by now, and if I was going to be awake anyway, nothing was going to prevent me from seeing it before the sunrise. I was loath to admit there was anything I liked about this place, but the desert was incontrovertibly the best place I'd ever lived for stargazing, and I'd found a spot in the garden right under a mesquite and next to the wind chimes. The housekeeper and maid were already up and over in the main house, and no one else was around to see me quietly latch the door to the room, make my way up the stairs, and head out the separate access door to the basement wing, furiously zeroing in on the garden path ahead of me so I wouldn't be tempted to head the opposite way to see if *her* light was on. Or whether her blinds were open.

In the garden, I nestled in the cool sand, my back against the bark of a timeless mesquite. Years had passed, but the seven sisters were still as innocent as when I'd first seen them, from the roof of my first master's country estate in Walferdange. As innocent as *I* had once been.

Right. As if slaves ever had the luxury of being innocent.

There *could* be death, you know. Did it matter what happened to Louisa? Did I care if she was collateral damage? The world didn't think I was worthy of touching her, so why should I care? I'd kill Keith Wainwright-Phillips in a second if I had to. But if I put Louisa in danger, I'd just be causing another innocent to suffer, an innocent whose window I *could* be looking up into right now if I walked around the corner of the house, not that I'd ever paid attention to such a thing, or for that matter, what she might be wearing—or not wearing—

while sleeping. A rich and free innocent, granted, but not one who deserved *that*. Which in itself took a lot to admit because up until recently, I was convinced they *all* deserved that.

And so did I, probably. After all, my sister wouldn't need saving if I hadn't fucked up and put her there to begin with.

I closed my eyes, and the star cluster—Alcyone, Maia, Electra, my constant women—arrayed themselves methodically and logically behind my lids the way they had on the star charts I'd stolen from my master's son's textbooks, showing me, as always, the way through darkness, even when I couldn't see them.

And they told me that the only way to help Louisa was to stay away from her. But the only way to help *myself* was to go back.

HER

I sat where I always did on campus when I wanted to eat lunch and think—on a little stone bench in the back of the optics building, where, in the spring, purple-throated hummingbirds gathered to sip on honeysuckle and ocotillo flowers.

But today, I wasn't alone. An insistent mist on my arm brought my attention to the fact that the bushes were being watered—by a slave girl with sandy hair cropped short, in the same style they all wore. She looked maybe eleven, and her fair skin reddened by exposure under that distinctive dull gray one-piece uniform. She'd rolled the sleeves up, but the fabric was too thick for the desert sun at its zenith, and at her feet was an empty plastic bottle that *may* have once contained drinking water. I vaguely knew that the slaves who worked on campus were supplied by an outside contractor, though most of them were housed in a forbidding-looking concrete building just off campus, complete with razor wire. Looking at the girl again, I was floored at how young she looked. Did they actually buy slaves her age for this kind of work? Or maybe they owned her mother, and the daughter was just part of the package? Did that happen, ever?

God, there was still so much I didn't know. And worse, had never thought to find out.

"Hi," I said.

"Himiss," she murmured as if it were all one word, staring at her feet. She wasn't allowed to ignore a free person, but she still used the smallest voice she could muster. She'd clearly hoped to go unnoticed, and I had to admit, a week ago, she probably would have, like one of those dull green compactable trash bins placed everywhere on campus. Now that she was in my crosshairs, though, she was shaking. It was obvious that getting any attention at all from a student had never resulted in anything good for her.

"It's okay," I said awkwardly. "I'm just—here." I held out the mini bag of potato chips that had come with my turkey sandwich. The girl was thin, and though I couldn't imagine it was in the university's best interests to starve their slaves, I doubted much junk food was included in whatever they were fed. It could be gruel three times a day, for all I knew. "I don't want them." Actually, I did want them, but I didn't *need* them. I beckoned her closer, still holding out the bag.

But instead of the gratitude I expected to see, her face looked as if I had just pointed a loaded gun at her and ordered her into the back of a van. She was shaking that hard, and the hose was flailing every which way in the small hand that had a shaky grip on it already.

"Okay, maybe not," I said helplessly. "One?" But the girl took a step back. Jesus, I'd never seen anyone so frightened of potatoes. I held it out ridiculously in my flat palm. I guess in my mind, the slave girl had now evolved from an inanimate object to one of the lower mammals. Erica Muller would be so proud.

Was that what the slave boy—*my* slave boy—was to me? A mammal? Had *he* been doing work like this at eleven? And what would he do if I offered him a potato chip? Laugh, probably, and make some sarcastic remark.

Oh wow, a potato chip. I'm moving up in the world. Next maybe I'll get a crouton.

And maybe take it. My own family's slaves didn't get chips, either.

"Or ... how about some water?" I unzipped my backpack and uncapped my reusable bottle, thinking I'd found the solution. But it got me nowhere. In the end, I left the chip bag gently on the bench and walked away, glancing back over my shoulder to see the girl still standing there, staring after me, water squirting forlornly out of the hose.

❤

"Well?" Corey demanded later that afternoon as I dashed out of my psychology lecture hall, head down, praying he wouldn't spot me. My mind was made up about where I was going, and my lunchtime encounter with the slave girl had only cemented it. But he had spotted me, of course, and I was about to pay the price for it.

"Well what?" I responded, hoping that when I didn't slow down, he'd get the message and fuck off.

"I haven't seen you in four days, and you've barely answered any of my messages."

"I answered your first message," I mumbled without looking at him. "I said I was studying for my o-chem midterm. That hasn't changed. When it does, I'll let you know."

"You were supposed to be studying with me!" he exclaimed.

I sped up further, heading single-mindedly toward the social sciences building. I only had a small window to meet with Erica Muller before the professor's office hours were done for the day. But her office was all the way across the campus mall, and I hadn't factored in having to spill my guts to Corey on the way there—which I dreaded, not only because I didn't have time, but because I didn't relish explaining the reason why I had stopped studying with him, or that I was now hauling ass across campus to meet with the professor he referred to as a pinko commie snowflake to *discuss* that reason.

Or that that reason was a person. Even if Corey didn't consider him one.

I would have to come up with an excuse. "You're busy working with Langer, not to mention your other classes," I bull-shitted. "I know you don't have time to tutor me every day. Anyway, I found … a new study technique," I said quickly. "Online. It's really helping."

He frowned, the muscles in his tanned face tightening unpleasantly. I knew he wasn't buying it. And if he got suspicious that I'd replaced him—with a slave, no less, one he'd already openly expressed his contempt, if not outright jealousy of, he wouldn't let it drop. He'd make sure both I and the slave boy paid the price for it. He was that vindictive. I was already starting to feel ashamed that I'd ever considered dating him. Unfortunately, he didn't feel the same.

"Let's do something tonight."

I couldn't help but think he was testing me, somehow.

"Can't. Girls' night with Juliette in Old Town. Nails and shopping. I haven't done anything social in months." The shopping would be minimal, of course. My dad had revoked access to his credit card, after all. But Corey didn't need to know that, even though he probably suspected it.

"What about—"

"Look, I'll see you on Friday. You're coming to our house for dinner with Langer, aren't you?"

Not that I was actually looking forward to that, knowing all the minefields I might step in, but at least it might get him off my case.

"Of course." He grabbed my arm. Why did he always feel entitled to do that? "But don't forget that next weekend's my birthday, and I'm planning a party. Are you coming?"

I groaned inwardly. Come to think of it, Juliette had mentioned something about that in a text, but it had slipped my mind after the past week had started giving way to something far more interesting than Corey.

I tried to shrug him off, but his grip tightened. "I'll try," I said, not trusting myself to say more.

He finally let me go with one of those supercilious smirks his face seemed to have been born with. "Good. I'll see you soon."

All I knew was that before "soon" rolled around, I'd have to figure out a way to get out of it. For the slave boy's sake, and my own.

Even if I never spoke to him again.

Academic offices weren't renowned for their size, but even by those standards, Erica Muller's was puny—a stuffy, cramped little room hidden down at the end of a dim hallway in the back of the social sciences building. The one window, covered by a pair of dusty, crooked Venetian blinds, looked directly at a breezeway with a massive air conditioning unit. I couldn't help but think that given the professor's reputation, the administration had given her this piece of real estate on purpose. And Erica Muller herself appeared to share my lack of enthusiasm for the space, given that she was shoving coffee-stained papers into her worn leather backpack when I appeared breathlessly at her door.

"Professor Muller, I'm so sorry I'm late. Do you have just a couple more minutes, please?"

She didn't even look up. "I'm sorry, but I've really got to get to this meeting. You'll have to wait until my next office hours on Thursday."

My heart sank into my knees. No. This absolutely couldn't wait. I *hated* being pushy with authority figures—or anyone—but there were always exceptions. And this was one. "Please, it's —it's really important. It's about a slave."

The professor looked up sharply.

I had a feeling that might do the trick.

Erica Muller looked different up close than she did in the lecture hall. She appeared younger, for one, despite the frizzy hair and dowdy glasses, and wore a sleeveless blouse that showed off a small tattoo on her shoulder, one that wouldn't have been visible from halfway back in the classroom. I couldn't quite make it out, but it looked like two broken links of chain with something written on it. I forced my eyes not to stare.

"Why would a slave attack an owner?" Before she could mount a response, I pressed on. "It's just that particular slave, he's—he's not like that. He's not—" *He's smart and kind and funny and completely amazing,* I wanted to say because it was true and because I couldn't say it to anyone else, not even him. *And hot,* but I doubted Muller would be much interested in that aspect of the problem. Even though it basically *was* the problem.

"Louisa."

"Yes?"

"Breathe."

"Oh, God." I practically fainted as she pulled out a wooden chair for me to collapse in. "I'm sorry, Professor Muller. There's a lot going on right now."

"Call me Erica. I'm not exactly big into hierarchy, in case you hadn't noticed." She retook her desk chair and spun it toward me. "You have my attention. I'm not going anywhere. Tell me."

I tried to get my breathing under control. I reached inside my bag.

"Here, I brought this," I said shyly. "Maybe you can make more out of it than I could."

She took the paper immediately from me, pushing up her oversized glasses to scan it, her face interested but maddeningly unreadable. "This kid's life reads like a novel. He went from a private home in Luxembourg to a factory farm in Romania to Heidelberg University, all before he turned eighteen?"

"He's ... kind of extraordinary."

From my professor, there came a tiny, almost undetectable smile.

"But it's not that part of his life I'm interested in." I was interested in *every* part of his life, actually, but not at this immediate moment.

"I see," Muller said neutrally. "The first thing that jumps out at me is that his mother died mere days before his first owner sold him. It seemed to be a hasty sale, too. They basically handed him over to a public auction house instead of going through a private buyer. That's unusual, given he was born and raised there."

"Do you think they're connected?" And what if they were? Would that be a good thing?

"It's possible. But you know, these files aren't always reliable. You'll remember we discussed this very thing in my lecture a few weeks ago. Sometimes owners will put false information in them simply to punish slaves they felt were disrespectful," she explained. "And the slaves have no recourse to get it corrected. In fact, there was legislation proposed several years ago to instate some sort of a verification process, but—"

She must have noticed my eyes glazing over.

"Sorry. I didn't mean to turn this into a lecture." She adjusted her glasses and examined the paper again. "I also notice that his disciplinary record shows no history of serious violence, except this." She looked up and spun her chair around again. "In any case, Louisa, recent research has found that there are very few attacks on owners that aren't provoked or justified in some way. You'd never know that to read about them in the corporate press, though," she added bitterly.

I let out another breath.

"Still, I know you don't know the exact circumstances, and that's what worries you."

I nodded. "So what do I do?"

"I have a suggestion, and I want you to consider it very carefully." She sat back in her chair and steepled her hands. "Have you thought about asking him?"

I was dumbfounded. "Asking him?"

"It's public information, Louisa. As a free person, you have a right to see it. And of course he should answer your questions. Not that I'm suggesting you order him to answer. But you could ask him. Politely."

"Um." I blushed. "There's a problem."

"What's that?"

"Then he'll know I was snooping."

I wondered if Erica Muller thought her office hours were starting to feel like a relationship therapy session. But she just gave me a small smile of amusement, or possibly concern. In any case, she scribbled a number down on a piece of paper. "Think it over, anyway, and let me know how it goes. This is my cell number. I always have it with me and turned on. Just in case you ever need it." She slid it across the table. "No questions asked."

By the time I walked out of her office, I'd forgotten all about Corey. I was actually feeling lighter. Not because I had a plan about what to do—I didn't, really—but because I was now aware of at least one person on the planet I could trust not to judge me. And that included the slave boy himself.

That light feeling melted away, however, the minute my phone buzzed and I glanced at it to see three missed calls from my father. His voice seemed to be coming from the bottom of the ocean as I shakily pressed the phone to my ear, stomach churning with anxiety. I hadn't *technically* done anything wrong, of course, but, well.

"I want you home immediately after class, Loulou. We need to talk."

HIM

"Sir?" I prompted.

I shouldn't have spoken, but why had Master Wainwright-Phillips called me in here if he was just going to stare dopily at his laptop screen for five minutes? For effect? In any case, while I waited, I stood in the middle of the southwestern-style rug I had just put down yesterday, expertly feigning interest in its orange-and-yellow geometric pattern while actually staring my master straight in the face, the way I'd learned to do a long, long time ago.

Despite all the effort he—well, his slaves—had put in to make his study look more "start-up-like," it was no different from all the free people's offices I'd ever seen. With their elaborate paneling and massive desks and chairs, they seemed designed to reinforce the inferiority of whoever entered, especially if that person was a slave, glistening and panting and covered in dust from having just hauled lava rocks all morning, and who didn't even have the privilege of being offered one of the very chairs I'd carried up to the office yesterday.

But that was the least of my problems right now. There didn't seem to be much question as to what this summons was about. The proof was hidden under my mattress downstairs: a map to 2481 Salt River Boulevard.

Given the expression on the housekeeper's face when she'd come out into the yard to inform me I'd been summoned, I knew it couldn't be good. It seemed unlikely that anyone could have discovered the printout already, but who knew?

I'd already made up my mind to go on tutoring Louisa. Naturally, because she was the easiest pathway to getting the information I needed, which right now was what Langer was doing under the code name White Cedar. I had some idea of where to look, but I needed to buy more time. Time in which I would grow closer and closer to losing control of the whole goddamn enterprise, all because my dick practically hit the bottom of the desk every time her tongue poked out of her mouth in concentration.

In the meantime, my mouth was dry as this goddamn desert. Plus, my palms were clammy and my heart was pounding as I stood there like a tool, waiting for my master to say something, no less nervous now than when I was eight or ten or fifteen years old and being ordered into a master's presence.

The only difference was I had gotten better at hiding it.

When Wainwright-Phillips *finally* looked up from his laptop as if he'd just realized I was there, I quickly threw my gaze to the floor, fast enough that there was no way he could have known how closely I'd been studying him.

Nobody I knew was better at that.

"What do you know about the financial situation of this household, boy?"

Um, okay. That definitely wasn't among the list of questions I'd been expecting. Which meant it was probably a trick.

"Relax. It's not a trick."

I raised an eyebrow, something I'd never get away with in a million years with most masters. But for some reason, with him, I decided to give it a try.

"Look, I know you're smart enough to be able to answer that question," he continued obliviously. "I knew you were smart when I bought you, but in a few days, you've managed to outdo even my own expectations for a slave."

That "for a slave" part was priceless, wasn't it? Still, he hadn't said anything about the eyebrow, so it evened out.

"So tell me."

I took a deep breath. It may not be a trick, but it was an important question, and the answer I gave would matter if I had any hope of keeping my neck off the chopping block. That meant *You went crazy and flushed all your money down the toilet* wasn't the right thing to say, even if it was true. Time to bring on the bullshit. "I know you're currently seeking some strategic new ventures to stabilize your financial position."

To my surprise, he smiled. "Right answer. Buying you was one of those strategic ventures, I see."

I exhaled. This conversation was already going in an unexpected direction, but that was no reason to let my guard down.

"I'm pursuing a business venture with Max Langer—I presume that at some point you've heard his name?"

"Yes, sir. He's the Phoenix tech wizard who created the FableFlow app, sold the company, made his first hundred million dollars, and is now CEO of Orbital Dynamics, the company pioneering the use of reusable rockets. He'll be a billionaire before he's fifty if all goes well. In short, he's exactly who you *should* be partnering with. Not that you asked for my opinion, sir."

Wainwright-Phillips coughed and took a sip of water. Fuck my curiosity, my mouth, and my tendency to push things too far, but to my surprise, he recovered quickly, smiled, and nodded. "Good. In any case, you'll meet him later this week as he's coming to a dinner party, at which I'll expect you to serve. You don't know this—even some of my closest associates don't —but unlike them, I didn't start out on third base. I worked my way through school, then started at the bottom rung of the corporate ladder so I could give my family everything they deserve. I've done that, and now the fact that I may lose it all has been ... difficult."

I'm a fucking slave, you dipshit. Forgive me for not weeping for you.

"In any case, you may as well know I've made a decision to embark on a venture with Mr. Langer that some may call risky, but that I predict will pay off handsomely down the line when the new product—top secret, of course—launches. In the meantime, this household has been on a shoestring budget as I'm sure you've noticed, which is hurting my wife and daughter immensely. It's so far from the lifestyle they're accustomed to."

Remember what I just said about weeping?

"I suppose I'm biased, but Louisa is one of the most determined and driven people I know, even though I admit I've spoiled her, which isn't doing her any favors now. But she's determined to make her own way in life, and the pressure to earn her degree is causing her a great deal of stress. I regret that there's not much I can do, science having never been my forte." He paused, peering down his nose at me. "So I guess it doesn't surprise me why she decided to enlist some unconventional studying techniques."

Boom. There it was. I swallowed, my mouth so parched I could hardly open it.

"Tell me, why didn't you ask permission first before tutoring my daughter?"

"Sir, I—"

"The ironic thing is that if you had asked, I would have allowed it. But you went behind my back, and you have to be punished for that. I think five lashes should do it."

I swallowed and bent my head, even in my relief that I was being punished for a lesser offense than the one I'd actually been afraid of being found guilty of. Sometimes that was all a slave had to give thanks for.

"Yes, sir."

"The gardener will do it in the back by the shed. It's more civilized to have another slave do it, I've found."

I'd heard of that practice. Apparently, it was more common in New North America than in New Europe, where punishments in private households were often meted out by hired handlers. But of course, it was also cheaper, and it was official now: Wainwright-Phillips was broke. It also seemed clear that he himself had no intention of being there. To him, it was just another rote, mildly unpleasant business task he could outsource, like ordering an assistant to fix a jammed copier.

"And before you assume anything, no, Louisa did not tell me, so you have no reason to hold anything against her. I found out on my own. You're not the only clever one in this house."

I believed him that Louisa hadn't told; if she'd wanted her father to know, she would have asked him right off the bat. But I would have to figure out who had told, and soon, because that person would need tight supervision and maybe a punch in the teeth for good measure.

"And yes, I'm punishing her, too. She's grounded for three days, except for school. She may be eighteen as she's quick to point out, but it's my house, my rules."

Though my eyes were still trained on the floor, I knew he had risen from his chair, and I half expected him to grab me by my ear and toss me out the door. Instead, when I dared to raise my gaze, I saw a conical paper cup from the water cooler in front of my face. His hand was attached to it.

"Sir?" I asked, still suspicious.

He laughed. "It's water, boy. You clearly need it."

I took it and gulped. "Thank you, sir," I said sincerely, or at least as sincere as I ever got with masters or anyone, really.

"I'll order the gardener to wait for you at the garden shed in an hour. Best to get it over with, don't you think?"

"Yes, sir." I took that as an order to leave.

"By the way," he continued.

I turned around.

"I want you to continue tutoring my daughter. For an hour every weekday, ideally. I'll make sure the housekeeper knows this and gives you the time you need. If the improvement continues and she passes her exam at the end of this month, I'll personally ensure that you're rewarded."

I paused suddenly, crushing the paper cup in my hand. To a slave, a reward was a matter of speaking—anything from a morsel of chocolate to better accommodations to relief from more backbreaking duties like gutter cleaning and floor scrubbing. In some rare cases, it could even mean freedom, but that was one thing, in the interests of surviving day to day, I tried to never let myself contemplate, and I didn't intend to start now. In any case, I didn't know Wainwright-Phillips well enough yet to know what a reward might mean in this case, and I didn't dare ask. All I knew was that things had just gotten exponentially more complicated—like they weren't already.

"Remember," he said. "I'm putting my trust in you, boy. Don't let me down."

"Sir, I—"

But he had already closed the door.

I knew the routine. The scars on my back testified to it. And while knowing the routine didn't make it easier, it did make it less surprising. My first master's old cook used to say there was a wild herb growing in the Grünewald that you could apply an hour before a whipping and you'd hardly feel a thing. I didn't really believe it was real, but I'd never given up hoping.

"I knew we had a date coming," said the hulking gardener, spittle gathering in the corners of his mostly tooth-free mouth as he pointed me behind the auxiliary shed, which I had gathered was the de facto punishment ground because it was as far away from the main house as it was possible to get without stepping in horse manure from the pasture next door.

"*You* told the master, didn't you?"

The sick fuck just laughed, a sound that came out more like a pained, asthmatic wheeze.

I took that as a yes, but how?

The gardener provided no clues, just watched me strip off my T-shirt, and then, to my annoyance, used his oversized muscles to shove my face painfully against the pole, mashing wood splinters into my skin.

"Hey, dickhead, take it easy. I'm cooperating, yeah?" Like

the son of a bitch actually cared. He roughly attached me to the thick wooden pole with a pair of rusty cuffs wrapped around it by a thick chain, my arms raised above my head at a weird angle he didn't bother to adjust. The pole had been hosed down, though it still bore visible spatters of flesh and blood, plus a distinctive metallic smell that I would know anywhere. I wondered who had been the last one whipped here. Hopefully the gardener himself.

Where is Louisa?

What the fuck? Why would *that* cross my mind? Miles from here, no doubt. I didn't dare to think she even knew what was happening, let alone would give a damn about it. She probably had some three-Cosmopolitan lunch to go to, some country club outing, some shopping spree, some pleasant and innocuous activity that made sense in her world. She would never have to see a scene like this. Why would she want to?

Behind me, the gardener drew in an impressed breath as he surveyed the handiwork of previous owners and their punishers. "Your back isn't nearly as pretty as your face, boy."

"That's what they tell me." I hadn't seen it, but I *had* seen the naked backs of plenty of other slaves, and I wasn't so vain as to think mine was any different. At eight, I'd graduated from canes to whips—a real rite of passage since after all, whips break the skin while canes generally don't. But my first master had been an amateur compared to the overseers at the farm, who used to attend fucking professional development seminars on how to make their punishments more brutal. I wasn't kidding. I'd once actually found the agenda for one, complete with diagrams.

The gardener, meanwhile, was a slave, not a professional. So he wasn't aware of best practices about whether to go for depth or breadth—aiming again and again for the same spot to deepen the pain or spreading it out to cover more area. He'd be relying on primitive technique, so what he'd do was anyone's guess. That would make it especially fun.

"Don't worry," the gardener said, running his thick paw down the whip sensually, like a Thoroughbred's mane, "the master told me to take it easy on ya. So I'm only gonna do six lashes instead of seven."

"But—" I cursed the fact that I was already chained, which of course was what the bastard had been counting on.

The gardener laughed wheezily again. "Don't worry, it'll be our little secret. By the way, I hear you and Miss Loulou are about to have regular dates."

Louisa's name in this ugly motherfucker's mouth made me want to rip my fist free and shatter every tooth the guy had left.

"Yeah? So what?"

"So what?" The gardener dug into the pocket of his dirt-covered jeans. "So unless you do exactly what I say, you're gonna find yourself back here real soon."

The last thing I saw before the first lash came was the map printout from under my mattress, crumpled between the gardener's grimy fingers. By the second, I was stifling the whimper I wouldn't let this asshole hear, pressing my head against the pole to stabilize myself. By the third, fourth, and fifth, when those familiar hot rivulets started flowing down my back, all I could do was squeeze my eyes shut, clench my jaw against the new pain and the old, and just breathe as my mother had taught me long ago.

♥

For once, I was actually looking forward to late-night duty, which always started with washing up from dinner. Other than tutoring, it was as light as my work got. Of course it wasn't my fault that the maid, indiscreetly tossing her black mane, had offered to do something to, as she put it, "help with the pain," then brushed up against me while I washed dishes and she ferried salads and desserts back and forth. Normally, I would have jumped at the chance to make at least one part of my body feel better, no matter the agony the rest of me was in.

But Louisa.

Yeah, what about her? I scolded myself as I scrubbed a casserole angrily with a piece of steel wool. Okay, so she hadn't told her father about the tutoring. Still, she was free. She was my master's daughter, she was a spoiled brat, and she clearly didn't know or care that she was the reason I was now groaning inwardly as I bent down to load the rest of the dishwasher. I'd thrown on a loose T-shirt with some dumb American brand logo on the front, and the housekeeper had given me an ibuprofen and some antiseptic cream, which, granted, was more than I'd been given after most whippings, though my back still wept blood and stung me like a hive full of angry bees whenever I moved.

So fuck Louisa. Fuck it all. The only way she could be of any use to me was if she could help me find Langer and find my sister. Anything else was a liability to me. A dangerous one. And after today, I was already in *enough* danger.

"If you know how to get this, you must know how to get other things," the gardener rasped poisonously in my ear as I dangled there in agony at the end of it all, hands still chained, stretched arm muscles screaming for relief. "Matter of fact, so do I. Over the years, I found ways to see anything I want, anytime I want."

What the fuck was this idiot talking about? I clenched my

teeth, forcing my murky, pain-contorted brain to think back to what the housekeeper had told me about the boarded-up window of the women's slave quarters.

"But the princess's room ..." He paused to chuckle throatily. "I'm still shut out of there, but it ain't for lack of trying."

Breathe, you stupid bastard. I know you know how. A sudden breeze blew a typhoon of grit into my torn-open flesh, and I bit back a moan. I prided myself on never begging anyone for anything, and I sure wasn't going to start with this asshole.

The gardener just stood there, watching me twist, holding the map printout. "I want you to plant *this* in her room. And not in a goddamn drawer."

He held a tiny device between his dirt-ridged fingers, and it only took a second for me to recognize what it was: a camera.

"What the fuck? Are you crazy?" Where would a gardener get *that?* Besides, if anyone was going to be watching Louisa strip naked, it was going to be me. Full stop.

"If I don't got pictures by Friday, this printout is going to be sitting in the middle of the dining room table when Langer shows up for dinner. Do we have a deal?"

"Fuck you."

"I'll take that as a yes."

The gardener unlatched the cuffs. Wrists released, I landed hard in a heap on the ground, in too much pain to try to chase after him and bash his head into the wall for daring to even *think* about her in that way or any way. Not that it would accomplish anything except sending me right back to this goddamn post. Neither would the microcamera, which was still in my pocket because what the fuck else was I supposed to do with it?

The only good news that afternoon was that Louisa was in class all day, so even though she was grounded, I'd probably be able to avoid seeing her.

But when 10 p.m. rolled around, the front door banged open dramatically. I was bent over the sink, and the sudden noise caused me to drop the pot I had been scrubbing. It clattered to the tile floor and kept clattering, while soapy water dripped off my hands. I quickly grabbed a tea towel and winced as I bent down to stop the noise and throw the pot into the sink. Smooth.

She stood in the entrance to the kitchen, silhouetted in moonlit blue, wearing her school clothes, which in Arizona this time of year apparently meant a tiny crop top and cutoff jean shorts, and I couldn't help but inconveniently notice, of all things, how perfectly they hugged her curvy little hips and ass. She was clutching a bottle of something shyly to her chest.

Before I could say anything, words—few of which made much sense to me—tumbled out of her mouth all at once.

"At first, I was all mad at you because I was going to miss our girls' night in Old Town with Juliette, which was the only thing I had to look forward to for the past three months. And I thought it was all your fault because I let you tutor me, and right after Daddy told me, I had to go to class. And then I scored an eighty-nine on a quiz, and I'm not failing anymore, and all because of you, too, and then when I got home, the house-keeper told me what happened." She took a deep breath. "To you, I mean."

I opened my mouth, but she barreled on. "I feel so stupid. It's all my fault. I'm sure it was something I said to Daddy. I can never fucking do anything right and—" She held out the bottle in her hands like some kind of religious offering.

And then—shit. She was crying. She was standing right in front of me, crying, complete with a glistening little tear running down from her big gray eye, down over my favorite tiny mole on her cheek and onto her chin. Her shoulders had even started to shake.

And, fuck, here I was swooping across the kitchen to her,

like some big hero—a hero who wasn't even allowed to touch the object of his heroics. Fuck, fuck, fuck.

Okay, first things first. I could take the bottle from her hand before she dropped it and spilled the damn thing all over the kitchen—which I did, just in time to read the label: *Aloe vera gel: relieves pain and treats wounds naturally.*

Even more fucks. It was for me. To help the pain. I put it on the counter. I'd deal with that later. Right now, a small, helpless, adorable creature was standing alone and in pain—not physical pain, but pain nonetheless—and every instinct and impulse I had was telling me to go to her. My mother and sister had been more stoic than most, especially given the life they'd led, but they had had their moments. Many a slave girl had also fallen into my arms when life became too much, and I was always happy to oblige, especially because I knew what usually followed. When it came to being a shoulder to cry on, I actually had a pretty decent résumé.

This was obviously different.

She hiccupped. I cringed, cursing myself, closing my eyes and reaching out a hand, kind of, sort of offering. She looked up for a second, then down at my hand. She did not move an inch, either forward or back. A split second later, the decision was made for me. She had practically launched herself at me, and all of a sudden, I had an armful of my master's daughter.

I was so fucked.

"I'm sorry, I didn't mean to. You'll get in trouble again—because of—because of—" She was still hiccupping. I wasn't sure if whatever I was doing was making it worse or better, but I did know that despite her protests, she was making no attempt to move away. In fact, one of my hands was now officially touching one of those curls, the ones so long and thick and over-the-top they hadn't even seemed real when I'd first seen them. Up close, she smelled exactly the same as her room always did: vases of fresh pink carnations; citrus perfume in tiny, jewel-like bottles; girly, expensive, precious things. More things I wasn't allowed to touch; things they chained me up and threw me in cages to keep me from touching. Things like, for instance, her tits, which had the audacity to actually be *heaving*, along with the rest of her, as they pressed up against my chest. Well, that was Fantasy Number One of roughly 3,128 fulfilled. If we stayed like this much longer, I'd go for numbers two, three, and four. Guaranteed.

Fuck. I took another deep breath. For her sake *and* mine, I had to get my dick under control, then I could decide what to do next. I'd never been so horny while still bloody from a whipping, but Louisa Wainwright-Phillips was really pushing my limits in more ways than one.

In the meantime, I should probably be doing something other than standing here marveling at the fact that this was even fucking happening. I spread my fingers and moved them gently a little down her spine and up again, careful not to make any sudden movements. Then, slowly, carefully, I eased them back so I could rest against the marble island, even though it sliced through my wounds like a butcher knife, and I made the mistake of making a little hiss of pain as the edge of the counter hit one of the lash marks.

"What are you doing? You're hurt!" she exclaimed, loud enough to be heard down the hall if not upstairs.

"Shhh," I whispered frantically into her hair, gently pressing her head down again. "Shouting isn't going to make it any better. And anyway, it's fine. Really. I'm fine." At that, I could swear she burrowed a bit closer into my arms. "Hey. Listen to me. This is not your fault."

"It's not?" she squeaked.

"No. It's not because of anything you said. Your dad told me that himself." I paused. "Besides," I remarked, "out of all the whippings I've had, this isn't even in the top ten."

A wail greeted me. Okay, wrong thing to say.

"You're not fine," she said. "You're in terrible pain and it's all because of me."

I couldn't help but laugh at her dramatics. "If that makes you feel better, sure."

There was silence for a second, then I heard what sounded like either a hiccup or a giggle emerge from the nest of hair that concealed her face. I had to admit, when her puffy, red, tear-streaked, and gorgeously imperfect visage finally emerged to gaze up at me, the sight—despite all of that—was as good as cool water down my ruined back. She didn't move her face, and now her glistening gray eyes were fixed on mine, her full lips glossy and rosy and impossible not to want to kiss, and—at least at that moment—eminently worth risking getting thrown into a mine for.

"Fuck it." I couldn't believe I was doing this, but I bent down, knowing exactly where my mouth was headed without registering at all what would happen when I got there.

A door abruptly opening and closing upstairs brought us both back to our senses. We broke apart, hearts pounding, and, just like that first meeting in her bathroom, we put as much empty space between each other as we could. We paused a minute before realizing nobody was coming.

She unfroze and grabbed the bottle of aloe, then pushed it toward me.

"Aloe grows all over the desert, you know. They make this at a natural store by the university. It's good for everything—sunburn, cuts, bruises. It's a natural antiseptic."

She paused. The clock ticked. Here was her cue to offer to put it on me herself. Well?

Instead, she flushed and glanced up at the clock. "I'd better go."

She paused, clearly hoping I'd reply. Maybe even ask her to stay. Of course if I asked her to stay, fuck the aloe. Fuck my back. If I had my way, I'd finish that goddamn kiss, first of all, and after that, rip that cutesy little crop top off, get her naked, and have her arching her back on the countertop and moaning in seconds flat.

Good thing for both of us that in this world, I didn't have my way.

"So I'll see you tomorrow?" she asked. "For studying?"

Studying? Hold on. Rewind.

As soon as it began, I had to end it. I turned away from her and threw open the cupboard. "I can't."

"What? What do you mean you can't?"

I didn't turn around. "Well, my English isn't perfect, but if I remember correctly, 'can't' is a contraction meaning 'cannot' or 'unable to.'" Classic immature male behavior. In mere minutes, I'd gone from noble hero to snarky dick.

"You know that's not what I meant. You don't get to tell me what you can and can't do." The vulnerable, crying Louisa was gone. The old, haughty, petulant Louisa, the one from the intercom, was making a reappearance.

"Look, you know enough that you can do it without me now. You need to tell your dad you don't need me anymore. That you figured it out."

What was I doing? I'd held her and been seconds away from kissing her. We both knew it. I'd slept in her bed, for fuck's sake. And now I was acting like I barely knew her. My only hope was that maybe eventually, she'd understand that it was for her own good as much as mine and wouldn't hate me for the rest of her life.

"But...but...I need you! I thought we were—" she cut herself off. "What are you doing?"

"Making you a macchiato. Ecuadorian roast," I said flatly. "That's the kind you like, yeah?"

"I don't understand."

I pulled out the coffee and banged it pointedly down on the counter, then forcefully pulled open the machine to fill it. "Well, in case you forgot, it's sort of my job."

"But Daddy ordered you to tutor me. It's an order," she said frantically, her voice now high-pitched and shrill. The classic spoiled child's solution to not getting her way. "Plus, my exam is coming up and there's no way I can pass it without you."

The machine's hissing cut her off as the steaming espresso poured into the cup. "Why are you being like this?"

I turned around and grandly placed the beverage in front of her. "Here you are, miss. Enjoy."

She looked down at the expensive ceramic cup of artisan coffee as if it were a dead rat. I crossed my arms and leaned back on the counter expectantly, waiting to see whether she would throw it back in my face, at which point I would have accomplished my goal and ruined both of our nights completely. Very slowly, delicately, and carefully, she placed two fingers on the rim of the cup and pushed it away from her. Then she looked at me.

"Does all this have something to do with why you attacked your first owner?"

My whole body went rigid. "What?"

"That is it, isn't it?" She pressed on. "Was it to protect your mother? Or your sister?"

Damn her. Like an idiot, I stood there fumbling for a response. I thought I was on it. I thought I'd figured everything out. I *always* figured everything out. And now there was this spoiled princess, this naive innocent, turning every single table on me, as easy as anything.

Maybe she wasn't so naive anymore.

"How do you know about my sister?" I finally asked.

"Two reasons. First, I looked at your file."

The file. Always the fucking file, my life history laid out as if I were a used car. With a deep breath, I resigned myself to hearing whatever she had to say next. "And second?"

"Second," she continued, "because I sent her a message on my computer this morning. And tonight, I got a reply. Her name is Maeve, by the way."

7

HER

Any number of thoughts knocked chaotically around in my head as I waited for him to react to the news, but the one that ultimately settled was that if I hadn't gotten in trouble, the highlight of my evening would have been debating between hot pink and blush pink gel polishes at an Old Town nail salon, followed by campus gossip, half an overstuffed burrito, and maybe downing some cheap pink bubbly in Juliette's dorm room.

Instead, in its place, I had a riot of images and sensations: My tears, not planned, then—yes, dammit, this was happening—my plunge into his arms, into the deep end—before I could talk myself down. Then, as if that weren't enough: A broad, calloused hand trailing lightly down my spine, hesitant at first, then more confident as he realized, maybe, how much I really wanted it there, igniting every nerve ending along the way like tiny little bliss-filled explosions. My hot, teary cheek pressed right up against the thin T-shirt, concealing all those layers of warm skin and hard muscle, and underneath all of *that*, a heart that was—it couldn't be just my imagination—pounding just as fast as my own.

But now it was over, and I wasn't sure it was ever coming back. Although I was willing to consider that the guy responsible for all of it had been so thrown off balance by what I just told him that he might need a minute to decide whether he'd ever dare to try again.

Either way: Gel polish zero, getting grounded a million.

"Did you know she's supposed to be free?" I asked. "Your sister?"

"I know," he said slowly as if he still couldn't believe he was even discussing this at all, let alone with *me*. "She told me right before she went dark on Palaestrio," he added, using the name of the secret communication network I had learned about only a few hours ago after one well-placed phone call. "Which, by the way, you aren't supposed to know about." His voice still sounded flat and distant.

"Apparently, you do if, like my professor, you're a card-carrying member of whatever's left of the SLA. She explained to me how it's done but that the technology is different here than what you used in New Europe. Your sister—Maeve, that is—may have tried to contact you before this, and you never even knew about it. Anyway, my professor gave me this. It's just a cheap phone, but she told me it'll give you access to the network. You can only use it a couple of times before you have to throw it away." I pulled it out of my schoolbag and placed it on the counter in front of him.

"But where's my sister?" he demanded. "Did she say?"

"It sounds like someone took her, but she doesn't know where. We only exchanged a few words. I don't think she was supposed to be on whatever device she was using, so I don't know how reliable it's going to be. But it's something to go on, don't you think?" I asked triumphantly.

That didn't last.

"Why did you do this for me?" He sounded suspicious and even a little bit angry, and I deflated. I hadn't expected a medal or anything, but what I had hoped to see on his face was very different from these opaque clouds and the traces of old wounds they hid.

"Curiosity, at first," I said softly. "You wouldn't tell me anything, so I went looking on my own."

"Curiosity," he said. "Right. Okay. So you want to use me as a case study for your research paper on slavery? Get a gold star from this do-gooder professor of yours? Sure. What do you want to know?"

I backtracked, remembering Erica Muller's advice. "I—you don't have to tell me anything. I just—"

"No, really, what? You ready for another fucking story time, princess? How about we start at the very beginning?"

"I—"

"With how my first owner passed around my mom like a party favor to his friends, one of whom was almost certainly my so-called father? Or that I got put to work when I was three, only to get caned every time I dropped something so I could, in my master's words, 'learn what my life would be?' Is that enough? Or if not, how about that a few years later, he gave me to his son to be his valet, but the son was a sociopathic freak who lit his younger brother on fire and got *me* flogged for it? Or that a few years after that, he tried to rape my sister and when my mom and I tried to protect her, he chained me up in the shed and raped my mom instead, right in front of me, causing her to later die of a miscarriage they refused to treat? And then I flipped out, went at his head with a garden spade, and would have killed him right there if the police hadn't come to cattle prod me into submission? He died a week later, by the way, and I'm not fucking sorry about it."

I clamped down on my lower lip as he barreled on without a pause, inhaling another tear I knew was forming in a hot pit deep down behind my eyes.

"The only thing I *am* sorry about is that the last time my sister and I saw each other was from separate pens at a public auction, after they sold us both to punish me." The hard, cold edge to his voice didn't change at all, even as he watched me stand there feeling ill. "Oh, and as a bonus epilogue, maybe you want to hear about how I lied and schemed and bribed and called in every favor I was owed from everyone I knew to make sure your dad bought me, to get here and look for her because I couldn't forgive myself if I lost her, and by favors, I'm not talking about driving them to the airport. So there's that, too. So what do you think? Great material, right? Think it'll get you an A? If not, I've got more."

It all felt like watching a horror film in slow motion. Of course I already knew intellectually that, at not yet twenty, he'd been through several lifetimes of hell. But to hear them fall out of his mouth like that, hard and brutal and unembellished? It felt like taking the blows *myself*.

"If you knew your sister was here, why didn't you tell me?" I asked quietly.

"*Tell* you? I don't know," he said incredulously. "Gee, I don't know, you think the fact that you're my master's daughter might have had something to do with it?"

There it was. *I didn't trust you*, in other words. *You were the enemy. Maybe you still are.*

But he wasn't done yet.

"Let me make this as clear as I can," he continued. "My sister has nothing to do with you. None of this has *anything* to do with you. And it won't, as long as you and I are … who we are. It never will. It never can. Stick to what you know. Shopping, manicures, Daddy's yacht in the Caribbean, and your advanced cosmetic dermatology course, or whatever the fuck it is you're studying. We'll both be a lot better off."

"*God*, you can be such an ass! I'm not studying dermatology, and I'm sorry!" I shouted, too loudly, though I wasn't apologizing for what I really wanted to apologize for: namely, his entire life. "I'm sorry I did anything, okay? I shouldn't have gotten involved." I could not cry again. Because I was pretty sure he was not going to comfort me this time.

"No, you shouldn't have." He crossed his arms in front of his chest again in that closed-off posture, an armor that nothing could pierce.

"I was trying to help you."

"Am I not getting through to you, slow learner? I. Don't. Need. Your. Help."

"Fine." I snatched up the aloe and the phone selfishly. "I'll just take these back too, as long as you enjoy suffering so much."

"Fine."

And that was where, of all places, things stood when the front door was flung open, then slammed shut. For real.

"Louisa, where are you?" my mother's voice slurred.

"Fuck," we said in unison.

She was back from women's league night at the country club, boozily trilling out my name again as she lurched toward the kitchen.

With another familiar, panicked exchange of glances, we sprang into action. He, one step ahead as usual, filled a glass with ice and sparkling water from the refrigerator and handed it to me. I took it and met my mother at the door of the kitchen, then guided her carefully away from the kitchen and into the living room and settled her on the sofa with the water next to her. Certain he'd had enough time to do whatever he had to do,

I turned to guiltily go—but my mom's icy-cool hand pinned me to the leather cushion.

"We hardly ever talk anymore, Louisa."

That was because we had nothing interesting to talk about —at least not anything, as of tonight, that wouldn't cause her to keel over in horror. Luckily, though, she didn't even want to talk about me. She just wanted inane chatter about everything from the latest celeb gossip to my father's golf game to her favorite story about that time I threw up on the dentist when I was six, *ha ha ha.*

Honestly, the best way to deal with her when she was in this state was to keep her talking. If I could just do that, she would eventually run out of steam and drift off to sleep. It was generally a slick and successful method.

Tonight, however, she was on a particularly good roll. I laughed and nodded and agreed at all the right moments, while secretly dying of agony to know what was going on in the kitchen. In my haste, I'd left the aloe and the phone. Had he taken them? Had he left them? Had he left *me?* Not that there was anything to leave, but—

The light was still on. He wasn't allowed to go to bed until four, and until then, he was supposed to find things to do around the house to make himself useful, or pretend to. Was there any chance he was standing with his back up against the other side of the door, hanging on our every word? Or had he given up in disgust, retreated back into the pantry or the garden, and was now just waiting for us to leave so he could be alone with his thoughts and figure out how to get to his sister without my incessant fuckery ruining everything?

"So how are things going with Corey?" Mom demanded. "Are things moving at all?"

I moaned and leaned back on the headrest. "Can we *not* talk about this? I've got my hands full with school, and—"

"Okay, then," she said, squinting at me through the haze of sparkling water she'd spritzed about the room in a fine mist. "But I know you're spending time with someone," she continued. "I can always tell. Moms can."

My eyes darted back and forth like a corralled mustang. I was pretty much praying for death at this point, and I couldn't imagine the boy in the kitchen was in a much more enviable position.

"You've been quiet. Secretive." Mom kept poking me rhythmically with one of her sculpted coral nail tips. "But inside, you're glowing. I see it." Poke, poke, poke. "So there's no use denying it, sweetie. What's his name?"

"Mom, please!"

This had to end. Anything I said, and he heard, had the chance of destroying any chance of him ever speaking to me again, at least as anything other than an enemy. One of *them*.

"Okay, fiiiine," Mom murmured, her eyelashes fluttering. "Be like that. Just give me one word. And then I'll leave you alone." She set her glass down clumsily on the edge of a coaster on the coffee table, and I pushed it back into place just in time.

"One word?"

"One word. If you had to describe this boy in one word," my mother said, pleased with herself, her slow, sly grin reappearing in the circle of light the lamp made, cutting through the blanket of darkness that hung over the house, silent except for the mantel clock. "What would it be?"

One word, and this could end. It came to me instantly, of course.

"Brave."

8

HIM

773496S6

Maeve?

S hit, did that look weird typed out.

Our first master, like Wainwright-Phillips, was old-school. He wouldn't allow our mother to name us, so to her, we were both *Schatzi*, and that only in private. But that's a name for a pet, not a person, and anyway, we couldn't *both* have it. So I'd pretty much known my sister her entire life by what she was to me—*Schwesterchen*—or by her face alone.

But if she had a name now, a real name, I'd have to learn to use it. She deserved it.

The house was quiet now, but I didn't want to find out whether anyone was still around. Instead, I was in the pantry, as far back as I could go, sitting on the floor with my back against the door, the one that led to the back of the property, with its vast desert gardens surrounding the terrace and pool.

Moonlight struggled through the dusty window above it, offering me a weak halo of light.

Gingerly, I opened up the cheap phone and tried to figure out what to do with the system before me, which looked nothing like the New European one, so no wonder I hadn't figured it out. My sister spoke minimal English, so I wrote in Luxembourgish, a language I honestly wasn't sure I'd ever get a chance to use again. Then I waited, the unbearable silence of the cold room pressing in on me from every side. I knew there was a good chance I wouldn't hear from her tonight; that I'd be left alone and awake, again, with the last companions in the world I wanted right now: my thoughts.

773541N0
I'm here

I dropped the phone clumsily and scrambled to snatch it up and type out a reply.

773541N0
Do you like Maeve? I found it in a book about fairies

773496S6
It's beautiful, but it'll take a while to get used to

773541N0
Take all the time you need :)

My sister had gotten luckier than I had at the public auction, which wasn't surprising given that her file, unlike mine, didn't state she'd attacked and killed her master's son mere days before. She'd ended up cleaning stalls and grooming horses at a riding school outside Brussels co-owned by a divorced mother and her three daughters and—best of all in terms of letting me sleep at night—no perv master to hassle her. We sent voice messages on the app as much as we could get away with, which, during my years on the farm, wasn't often. We spoke more frequently when I was in Heidelberg—at that point, we'd both learned to read and write, and it was easier to keep the conversations private. She'd tell me embellished stories about winged horses, and I'd tease her and try to keep her hopes up that we'd see each other again someday. Because I *did* have hope, despite it all. I shouldn't have, but I did. Especially when she'd sent me a message saying: *They're freeing all of us here.* But the message vanished, and radio silence followed.

For the next year, I asked about her to every slave I met passing through Heidelberg with little success, until I finally bumped into a slave boy who belonged to an American guest lecturer, who told me that two girls around my sister's age—one a slave and one recently freed, though before the paperwork had been filed—had vanished from Seattle. One of them turned up dead and mutilated in the desert outside Phoenix. Damaged, was the word they used in the news story. The American boy didn't know the details, and at first, the search for more information proved fruitless.

Gradually, though, one company kept coming up: Langer Enterprises. It was based outside Phoenix, and Max Langer and his executives had been at a conference in Brussels around the same time my sister had disappeared—and in Seattle around the same time the other girls had. From another acquaintance of the professor's, one who worked at the New European financial regulator—a free man this time, with the kind of peculiar demands I would prefer to block out entirely—I unearthed a pattern: before each girl vanished, Langer Enterprises, under some shadowy subsidiary, had purchased a peculiar set of chemicals and equipment I knew from my time in the lab.

Equipment that should never be used on a human, needless to say.

Meanwhile, Professor von Esch may have been a genius, but he was also a hustler—renting me out as a tutor for some of the wealthiest, stupidest students at Heidelberg—and a drunk, meaning I easily skimmed off hundreds of euros, which I used to bribe one of the in-house slaves at Cosgrove's Human Assets to keep an eye on any clients in Phoenix looking to import a slave.

While all this was going on, and when I wasn't dragging the professor out of bed every morning and forcibly pouring electrolytes down his gullet to get him to finish his paper on macroscopic molecular wave duality, I used my spare time to keep reading up on Max Langer et al. That's when Keith Wainwright-Phillips had first come up, in a picture of him and Langer playing golf in some country club charity event, though at the time, I hadn't targeted him specifically. By that time, the professor was finished—with the paper, with me, and with himself. He was dying, in fact, and I knew Cosgrove's would jump at the chance to make a high-profile sale to someone interested in a highly educated slave who could also do manual labor — and due to my history, available at a steep discount. The fact that it had turned out to be Wainwright-Phillips was just Lucky Sevens magic, I guess. From there, I only needed to play matchmaker, so to speak. And now here I was. Here she was.

773496S6

What happened to your owners??

You said they were freeing you and the others

773541N0
They lied
They left us at the riding school and never came back
We had nowhere to go if we didn't want to be caught by
the police and auctioned off

My teeth clenched. In a down economy, this happened a lot.
Owners fell on hard times and couldn't pay the manumission
fees or find buyers, so they just fucked off, leaving slaves who'd
served them loyally for years to live as fugitives. It was
nauseating.

773496S6

Where are you now??

773541N0
I don't know
We can't go outside
She said it's too dangerous, the police here will catch us
and the same thing will happen
And they can trace the phones, too

Fuck. Of course they could. But how else was I supposed to
communicate with her?

773496S6

But where are you??? And who's she??

There wasn't supposed to be any *she* involved, or anyone
helping Maeve, except for me. And how did Max Langer play in?
I watched the dots appear and reappear on the screen as Maeve
typed, erased, and retyped.

773541N0
Resi
She's the one helping us

773496S6

Helping you? How?

773541N0
I don't know, protecting us
I think she works here
And I don't think they know she's helping us
That's all I can figure out without speaking English
I don't understand anything else
I'm sorry

Text messages you could hear. I was here to save my sister, not make her cry about her shit detective skills. I tried another approach.

773496S6

I'm sorry, Maeve

Look, just tell me what it looks like inside, if you can't go out

I could almost see her swiping at her eyes, sucking in unshed tears. Fuck, if Louisa thought I was brave, my sister was ten times braver still. She'd endured almost everything I had. The only difference was that she hadn't done anything to deserve it.

773541N0
It's a house, a big one

A house? What about the warehouse on Salt River Boulevard? That didn't add up.

773541N0

We're only allowed in the upstairs, but I can see out the window

The houses here are really big, and there are pretty red mountains

Okay. At least we were in the right area of the union, probably.

773541N0

The sunrises are all pink and purple and gold, and I can see the Pleiades just before dawn

See? I called them by the right name

I CAN learn ;)

773496S6

I'm glad, Maeve

And you can call them whatever you want

Anything else?

773541N0

I don't know, some books, but everything's in English

773496S6

Is anyone else there?

773541N0

A few other girls

773496S6

Slaves?

773541N0

Yes
But Resi said we could choose names, so we did
There was one named Lemaya who was teaching me
English
She was nice even though I wasn't very good
She gave me this phone
But then she left

773496S6

Left for where?

773541N0

I don't know
But she didn't come back

I thought of the dead girl in the desert and shivered. Somehow,
I didn't think this Lemaya had left for a week at the health spa.

773496S6

Have you heard the name Max Langer
mentioned at all? Or Keith Wainwright-Phillips?

Or about any kind of experiments or research?

773541N0

I don't think so, but I'm just not sure
I'll try to find out, I promise I will

She was getting frustrated again, I could tell.

773496S6

Look, try to find out anything else you can

And listen for those names especially

773541N0

I'll ask Resi if I can figure out the words
I think she used to be a slave

I was glad people were helping her. Really, I was. But by
deputizing her, I'd made her even more of a target. And if
anything happened, it would be my fault. Again.

773496S6

Just be smart about it, ok?

And be careful

Do what I would do

Bad advice, given recent events, but she knew what I meant.

773496S6

I think I have an idea where you are, and I'm
not far

773541N0

But how are you here??

773496S6

What else? Science

I experimented

773541N0

Who's the girl who messaged me, by the way? ;)

Shit, was she really going to do this to me right now?

773496S6

No one

773541N0

So you have a "no one" already
That was fast, even for you

773496S6

Yeah, but it's different this time

773541N0

O nee,[1] is it that bad?

773496S6

Worse

773541N0

Nondikass[2]

773496S6

Don't worry

I told her to stay out of it

She'll fuck up everything

---

1. Oh no.
2. Goddammit.

773541N0

Bass du mëll??[3] If this girl were a slave that would be one thing

But do you realize what she risked??

> 773496S6
>
> What SHE risked??
>
> What about me??
>
> How the fuck am I supposed to help you if I'm shoveling coal??

773541N0

For someone so smart, how can you be so dumb??
Our lives are so shit we have to make up happy endings or we'll never get them, and here you are throwing away your chance for a real one

> 773496S6
>
> This story will NOT have a happy ending, Maeve
>
> It's going to end up with her life ruined and me dead
>
> Which is exactly why I'm ending it now and coming to get you
>
> You're all that matters

773541N0

But I'm not
Don't YOU want to be happy?

---

3. Are you crazy?

The simple logic of innocents.

773496S6

> Of course I do, but it's more complicated than that

773541N0
No it isn't, you stupid *tockskapp*[4].
O vreck,[5] someone's coming

Left idle, the phone went dark. There was nothing more I could do but wait and pray she'd learned *something* from me over the years and picked out a hiding spot for the phone in advance.

Meanwhile, the aloe was helping, of course, soothing the lash wounds like a girl's soft, cool hands. I'd almost prefer it wouldn't help at all, and then I'd have at least one reason to forget the girl that even Maeve—who didn't even know her— seemed determined not to let me forget.

Brave. Really? I didn't feel particularly brave at the moment, given what I was up against, nor did I think I was notably braver than any other slave who had somehow survived a life- time of the cruelest and most degrading shit imaginable. But to someone like Louisa—whose childhood, from where I stood, seemed to have been made entirely of lollipops and puppies and rainbows and unicorns—I could see why it might seem that way. It didn't mean she understood anything. It didn't even mean she *cared*. It meant I was just a project, a walking, talking charity food drive, one she could and would throw away

---

4. Stubborn person.
5. Oh, shit.

when the next shiny object came along. Because an object was what I was. Literally.

Still, she hadn't chosen *sad*, *pitiful*, or *pathetic*. She'd chosen *brave*.

And nobody had ever called me that before.

Outside, the desert sunrise was starting to brush the fronds of the distant coconut palms with purple. The housekeeper would be in any second to start breakfast.

But all of a sudden, the sound of heavy footsteps coming from the service door—definitely not the housekeeper's—sent me scrambling to my feet, shoving the phone and aloe into a forgotten bag of semi-rotten potatoes at the back of the shelf, and hastily picking up a broom.

The gardener loomed large in the doorway, shovel in hand, choking off the room with the smell of sweat and dirt and something minty, probably the homemade rotgut alcohol everyone knew he had stashed in various places around the garden. There was no telling how long he'd been standing outside the window, watching me through his yellow-rimmed, squinty eyes.

"Watcha doing in here, boy?" he demanded.

"Just cleaning."

"The hell you are. You were hiding something," he accused, beady eyes scanning the room. "Didja forget about our agreement?"

"What agreement?" I asked, though I knew. I also knew that I could deliver an entire flash drive full of hardcore snuff porn to this perv and he still wouldn't leave me alone. I still had the microcamera, though, hidden as artfully as I could without a lot of good options. "The one where you grow some teeth?"

He slammed the door and stalked toward me. "I know what you've been up to, and I know about her little crush. And so will everybody else if ya don't get me those pictures."

"Let's see," I replied, my voice even. "What did I tell you the last time we had this conversation? Oh, right. Go fuck yourself. Well, consider that still in effect."

He grabbed me by the arm and yanked me close, his grip tight, his dirty fingernails digging painfully into my skin. He brought the shovel up, pressing its metal edge sharply against my throat like a knife. "Tell me, boy, is a free girl's pussy as tight as I've always heard it is? Or aren't you her first? Maybe she's been open for business all along."

"Say that again, asshole." I twisted out of his grip, grabbing him by his dirt-encrusted shirt and slamming him up against the opposite shelf, sending jars of sun-dried tomatoes and olives smashing to the floor. I'd been dying to do it since yesterday, and now that I wasn't bleeding and chained to a post, I saw no reason not to. "I fucking dare you."

He gurgled, his neck sticky and greasy to the touch, like a pig might feel.

"You're not as tough without a whip in your hand, are you?"

"Fucking idiot kid, defending that spoiled slut," he choked out. "For what? You know she doesn't give a fuck about you, right? She'd sell you out for a pair of fancy new shoes."

"Thanks for the relationship advice, dickhead. Have you ever even seen a girl naked without having to hide behind a bush?"

He twisted his face into some ghastly bastardization of a smile. "Oh, I got a mind to do a lot more than see."

Revulsion hit me like a punch to the stomach. To think of that—to think of *her*—the perfect, glossy pink lips and huge gray eyes, full of confusion and compassion and curiosity even as I was shoving her away like an asshole—made me want to either vomit or slit his throat. Instead, I had to settle for watching him squirm as I squeezed tighter. "You do and you die. And after I kill you, I'll rip all your extremities off and throw them to the coyotes to play tug-of-war with."

"That's real funny, boy," he managed to gasp. "I figured your killing days was over, since from what I hear, you seen enough cages for a lifetime."

Fuck. Was *that* all over the house now, too? I tried to keep my voice even. "For killing *you*? They wouldn't cage me for that. They'd throw me a fucking ticker-tape parade."

In a flash, the gardener growled, reached over his head, and grabbed a jar of pickles from the pantry shelf behind him, then hurled it at me with all his strength. I ducked just in time, and the jar smashed against the opposite shelf, sending brine and shards of glass flying everywhere.

"And just what is going on in here?!" the housekeeper demanded as she threw open the door from the kitchen, flicking her careworn eyes, behind her bifocals, from him to me to the puddle of pickle juice spreading rapidly over the floor.

"Crazy kid just hauled off and attacked me!" he said, his voice rising in pitch.

"And may I ask why he had the *opportunity* to do that? You have no reason to be in here."

"But I ran out of ... salt," he said. "To, uh, kill the slugs."

The lie was painfully bad and I rolled my eyes, saying nothing, content in the knowledge that the housekeeper was the only one here who loathed this motherfucker more than I did. Ten years of ass pinching would do that to a woman.

"Quiet," she said firmly. "I don't have the patience for this nonsense on a day when the master has a dinner party planned. I want both of you out. If I see any trace of either of you in here again before noon, the master will hear about it. I'll get the maid to clean this up," she continued. "Since you've already drunk your breakfast"—this to the gardener—"I'll assume you don't need any food, so out with you, now. As for you"—she turned to me—"I'll have breakfast ready in a minute, and then you can start on cleaning the guest bathrooms, the dining room, the entrance hall, and putting the extra wings on the table settings. Oh, and all the silverware and crystal need polishing. And don't forget, we're all wearing uniforms tonight. I hung up yours downstairs. Do *not* get it dirty." She glared at the gardener again. "*You* are not to set foot in the house all evening, much to the relief of us all."

His face turned purple with rage, but he had no choice. He snatched up his shovel and slinked out of the room, muttering about how he should have slit my throat with a pickle jar shard.

Meanwhile, the gears in my head were turning as I choked down a bowl of lumpy reheated oatmeal, the housekeeper clearly keen to expend zero effort to feed us slaves on a day when she had important people to cook for. She would be watching the pantry with laser eyes for the rest of the day, but I felt confident that she wasn't going to rummage around any more than she had to. The gardener, on the other hand, would no doubt be back to sniff around for the phone the second he thought he could get away with it. And if he found it, he wouldn't bother with blackmail this time. He'd take it straight to Wainwright-Phillips, guaranteed.

That, I couldn't let happen. The earlier computer printout, I could maybe be clever enough to explain away, but not the phone with Maeve's messages. That was as good as evidence that I planned to take off. And if my master was involved with Max Langer's plot, I might find myself accused of even worse.

And Louisa couldn't help me anymore. That thought put a strange lump in my throat, and it wasn't the oatmeal.

Under normal circumstances, I could sometimes get away with using the early morning hours to go downstairs and catch a few hours' sleep. Not to mention, I wanted a glimpse of whatever ridiculous outfit I'd be stuck wearing tonight during my first face-to-face encounter with Max Langer, and to figure out how to face the guy down without killing him on sight. But exhausted as I was, it was time to turn on the charm again, whether I wanted to or not.

I found the maid at the sink, rinsing pickle brine off her hands. Sliding casually into her line of sight, I flashed her the kind of smile that never failed me. "Just who I was looking for."

HER

I wasn't exactly sure how I'd managed to go from the miracle of being nestled in his arms to being ordered to get out of his life in the course of a night, but, like the absolute ace I was, I continued to outdo myself.

Was it so crazy that I'd taken it upon myself to track down Maeve? Did I really have zero chance of ever understanding what he'd been through? Sure, the teddy bears and gumdrops of my childhood had been supplanted in his by shackles and whips, but we weren't really so far apart, right? And yeah, I hadn't actually thought of him as a person up until about a week ago, but why wouldn't he instantly trust me with his and his family's very survival?

Stupid, stupid, stupid girl. No wonder that poor slave working on campus had looked at me like she had. She wasn't scared of me. She was just astonished that anyone on the planet could be that fucking clueless.

I *wanted* to sleep. I'd safely escorted my mother up the stairs and tucked her in bed with another glass of water and some ibuprofen. But I wasn't sure I'd ever be able to peacefully sleep in my bed again, knowing he'd been in it. And if I couldn't sleep, what was the point of lying there and tormenting myself?

So it wasn't as if I were *trying* to clumsily re-inject myself into his affairs. I was well aware that I had dug half my own grave and that it was time to stop. But four in the morning found me traipsing in my glasses, camisole, pajama pants, and flip-flops through the gardens, silent except for the strange hollow call of the nightjars flitting in front of the moon, and when I passed the narrow door leading to the pantry and kitchen, voices and shattering glass greeted me. It didn't take too much deductive reasoning to figure out who they belonged to.

No, dig up, stupid. *Up*.

I kneeled and put my ear to the door.

The house had thick walls and good insulation, so I didn't hear everything. I heard the accusation of hiding something. I heard about an agreement. I heard *go fuck yourself*. And I thought I heard something about me. But before I had time to contemplate any of this, the voices got louder and more forceful —the housekeeper's, too, now—and I leaped out of the way at the abrupt turn of the knob, tripping backward over an orna-mental boulder, landing with a thud, hands scraping painfully against the lava rocks. I lay there for a few moments, frozen in fear, sweat trickling down my neck and back. The desert heat, even this early, was already strong enough to start roasting me inside my pink unicorn pajama pants.

The door was flung open, and I scrambled backward, catching my arm painfully on a barrel cactus spine, my legs barely escaping the semicircle of light emanating from the pantry as the gardener stalked out, eyes scanning the ground. He must have heard something.

It had been a while since I'd been this close to the perverted creep. When I was twelve, I'd caught him watching me undress in the poolhouse, and he'd threatened to chop me up with his chainsaw and bury me in the garden if I told Daddy. Being a stupid, weak, compliant kid, I believed him. From then on, I always undressed in my room and literally jumped in front of a moving car to avoid him on at least one occasion. But now, here, at first light, he was even worse than I remembered: the size of a bulldozer, dirt lodged in the spaces where his teeth should be, carrying a metal shovel covered with what I was pretty sure was dried blood—human, animal, or both. I tried to quiet even my heartbeat, not even daring to breathe.

At last, he snorted and turned away, heading toward the shed. He hadn't seen me.

I scrambled to my feet. I had two minutes, at best.

HIM

"I need to borrow something of yours."

The maid's green eyes widened with interest. She probably thought I was about to request her "services," especially since I hadn't been able to reach everywhere with the aloe. A few days ago, I might have asked. Maybe later, I still would. Nothing was holding me back.

Right?

"Oh? What's that?" she asked neutrally, turning around and slowly, sensually wiping her hands on a towel.

"Your brilliant skills as an actress, to keep the housekeeper busy for a few minutes while I grab something from the pantry."

She frowned, clearly disappointed, and threw down the towel. "I don't know," she said, chewing on her bottom lip. "She's in a mood today, what with company and everything. Plus, she was all pissed about this huge mess this morning. It wouldn't be wise to push her."

She was right. It wouldn't be wise at all, but neither was anything else I'd done in the last twelve hours, so why worry about it now? "Look, I promise this is nothing that will make her mood worse than it already is. And I'll owe you one, too," I promised.

"Anything?"

"Anything. Just name it."

She hesitated for a moment before nodding. Fellow slaves—especially lonely, attention-starved girls—rarely if ever forgot to call in their favors; it was one of the only forms of currency we could trade freely. Which meant I'd be fucked later, but at least I wouldn't be fucked now. And why did my life *always* seem to come down to exactly that choice?

A high-pitched shriek left her mouth, so loud I had to back away to preserve my eardrums.

"There was a *mouse!*" she squealed to the housekeeper when she burst in. "It ran right into the powder room!"

"Oh, for heaven's sake," the housekeeper replied, throwing her hands in the air. "That's just what we need: rodents running around everywhere while the master has guests."

The maid grabbed a broom. "This way. Come on." They both dashed out again, but not before she shot me one last "you owe me" look.

I didn't wait for more than a few seconds before throwing open the door to the pantry and immediately upending the bag of potatoes, scattering them across the floor. They rolled out in all directions, their pale flesh exposed to the air—but no phone or aloe bottle rolled out beside them.

Don't panic. It had to be here. But my hands were cold and clammy in the temperature-controlled room, my fingers slipping on the skins as I tried to gather them up, praying they'd be hidden under this or that one. Nothing. I scanned the shelves frantically, trying to spot any sign of them in the jumbled mess I'd made. In a panic now, I began tearing the whole thing apart, throwing all the carefully-replaced boxes and jars aside all over again. What if the gardener had discovered them first? What if they were already on their way to Master Wainwright-Phillips's brand-new desk, all laid out like a charcuterie platter?

My fear was tangible now, a dull tightness in my chest. My eyes darted from shelf to shelf to shelf, but it was too late. All I could do now was pace back and forth in terror.

In my life so far, I'd been lucky and good more often than not. But I had nothing left in my arsenal that could fix this, and now here was Maeve, the purest and most beautiful spirit I'd ever known—a girl only just learning her own name—ripped apart and destroyed because I'd failed, *again*, to save her. Like my mother. Like before. Like always.

And now here was the door opening again, as if the world hadn't fucked me over enough already just *today*.

"I thought you might have left it in here, so I went inside the pantry and dialed your number," Louisa said, staring at the cereal shelf instead of at me. "I heard it vibrate from behind the potatoes," she added softly.

Well, shit, this girl. There hadn't been very many times in my life when I wanted to sink to my knees without someone ordering me to, but this was one.

Honestly, there wasn't a single part of her I couldn't stare at for hours, and secretly—or maybe not so secretly—I had. In an endless series of stolen moments, I had cataloged and memorized—in a highly orderly and scientific way, of course—her endlessly soft spirals of hair, rose-kissed porcelain skin, pillowy lips, breasts and hips flowing like sand in some gilded medieval hourglass. But now, all haloed by the dusky swirls of light in the room, it wasn't any of those features that I saw. It was somehow, now, the soul of her; though it was crazy to think that was something I could ever believe in.

I hoped the panic from moments ago didn't show as I held out my hand, and she placed the phone and the bottle in it. A very proper, contactless exchange.

"I won't do this again," she said.

It wasn't a warning. It wasn't a threat. It was a promise. One to follow the directive I had given her. One responsible, I was pretty sure, for the shimmer of a tear in her eye behind those cute, clunky glasses, one she wasn't fast enough to hide before she turned.

Instead of in *my* hand, the phone could have been in her father's. It *should* be in her father's, after the way I'd treated her. What was any of it to her, now? I, just like the phone, should no longer be anything more to her than a throwaway thing. It was what I'd *demanded* to be. It was, I feared, all I *knew* how to be.

But this girl wasn't having it. This girl knew nothing, had been taught all the wrong things, had been spoiled beyond measure. And yet she was trying. And she got *tears* for her efforts?

Well, there went the lollipops and rainbows melting into nothing. Realistically, the most a slave could ever expect was a matter of degree: the bigger portion of food, the not-so-back-breaking duties, the less-sadistic owner. A short message every now and then from the only family you were fortunate enough to still know. You could have all of that if you were both lucky and good. And in reality, since you rarely got lucky, you had to be *really* good.

Up till now, I had been.

But this—this, now—was one of Maeve's fairy tales; her bedtime stories. It was beautiful to believe in, but I knew better. The unicorns didn't charge forward; the shackle key didn't magically appear; the hand didn't reach out through the iron bars. And yet now, after twenty years, I was seeing it all happen.

And maybe Maeve was right. Maybe it really was as simple as that.

"Louisa, wait."

9

HER

"I didn't look at anything on it," I blurted without turning around. "When I gave it to you, I gave it to *you*."

"That's not—I just want to talk to you, yeah?" The statement was haltingly phrased, almost tentative, like he actually thought there was a chance I'd say no.

I had resolved not to look at him, even though looking at him was literally the only thing I'd wanted to do for weeks. But why look at someone who didn't want to see me and didn't want to be seen?

But he was here. He wasn't leaving, wasn't hiding. Wasn't accusing. Wasn't demanding, *why are you still in my business when I literally just told you to stay the hell away from me?*

He was just standing there, his long, sculpted arm with its scarred fingers still curled loosely around the phone and aloe bottle. But he wasn't looking at them. He was seeing me, through the eyes of a boy who had long ago learned the slim odds of any given roll of the dice turning out in his favor, but who kept playing because it was all he'd ever known how to do.

And now he'd just bet his life, lost it, and seen it placed back in his hand.

He opened his mouth but didn't get a chance to speak.

"Loulou? Is that you?"

Daddy, of all people, was in the kitchen, just on the other side of the door, raising his voice over the fizzing of the espresso machine. Why did there have to be so goddamn many people in this house? "What do we—" I started.

"Shhh. I'm not supposed to be in here," he admitted. "Meet me after your class. Downstairs."

"The slave quarters?" I hissed.

"Why not? No one's going to look for *you* down there."

"True."

A second later, he had disappeared outside through the other door, leaving me standing alone in the cool, silent pantry and—not for the first time with him—unconvinced I hadn't dreamed it all.

Well, I didn't exactly relish a chat with my father given the state I was in, but I couldn't stay *here*. I opened the door to the kitchen, only to practically smack into Daddy, clutching an espresso cup.

"You're up early," he said, his voice brighter than I'd heard it in a long time. Why?

"Well, I have an early class today." Not one that required me to be up at dawn, but it wasn't like Daddy had nothing better to do than memorize my school schedule. Although these days, who knew?

"How's the tutoring going?" he asked, of all questions. "Has it helped?"

Fucking hell, had my parents hatched some fiendish conspiracy to siphon my every thought and feeling about the boy right out into the open? Could the half-demented smile I'd pasted on my face possibly convince him that opening that chemistry book hadn't started an earthquake that might as well be knocking pictures off the walls as we spoke? "Um, good," I said through gritted teeth. "Really good."

"I know using a slave as a tutor is a bit unusual, but apparently, his former owner made it into a lucrative little side business for himself," he said, apparently oblivious to the way my eye was twitching as if about to burst. "But it's all about thinking outside the box and leveraging your strengths, right?"

Like punishing the boy for tutoring me and then taking credit for the idea? Yeah, that was a real power move right there. "I really have to run to my psychology class," I squeaked, even though I knew the only psychology I was going to be capable of today was the psychology of how I could sit in a lecture hall for an hour, ruminating over everything he might possibly say when we met, without collapsing into a boneless heap on the floor.

"Well, just be sure to be home in time to get ready for dinner because I have big news to announce," he blathered on. "You may as well know that Max Langer and I are formally announcing tonight that I'm going to become a partner in his new venture."

So that was it. That was how he planned to save us all. By hitching what remained of his splintered, broken-down wagon to, of all people, Corey's boss. I took a deep breath in an attempt to sound slightly less hysterical than I felt. "Daddy, don't you know that his old partner dealt in slaves? Is that really the reputation you want in this era of corporate social responsibility?"

"Well, I can see your scholarship money is being well-spent at that college," he said lightly. "I love that you have strong convictions, sweetie. I did, too, at your age. But you have nothing to worry about. In fact, Max is planning on disrupting the whole industry of slavery. He says that era may be coming to an end, and who knows? He's a genius. Maybe he's right."

"So ... what, we're going to free all of ours?" I couldn't help it.

Daddy chuckled as if I were just too precious for words. "Six months from now, when this pays off, it'll be the start of a better life for all of us. You can live in the dorms next year. We can start going on vacations again. You can finally have that new Chanel bag and a car."

As if any of that stuff mattered. "I just want us to be happy. Like before."

"This *does* make me happy, sweetheart," he said. "Providing for you and Mom, that is. I know you've had to endure a lot of hardship recently, and you deserve it."

Endurance? *Hardship?* The fuck did he know about those? He was speaking an archaic language, meant to communicate with a version of *me* from a previous lifetime, a Louisa obsessed with pink-and-green dorm decor, who would go to homecoming with a guy like Corey and come home crying because another girl wore the same one-thousand-dollar dress.

"Besides, I would never do *anything* that my little Loulou objects to. I promise." He kissed the top of my head.

"You said it would pay off," I said. "But what if it doesn't?" He seemed not to have heard, so I asked again. "Daddy? What if it doesn't pay off?"

He spoke carefully. "That's not anything you need to worry about. It's not going to happen. The only thing you need to concern yourself with right now is school. I mean it."

"Daddy, I'm eighteen. I'm an adult now. I know I don't always act like it, but I can handle this. I need to know what we're up against."

He set the cup down on the counter as if it had suddenly grown heavy. "Then we sell off everything, starting with the house. And the slaves."

It wasn't really the basement.

It was an entirely separate wing of the house, a bunker, really, a windowless slab of concrete built in the desert where lower floors were expensive and totally unnecessary, except to allow maximum separation from the bright and beautiful parts of the home. Maximum ignorance, on my part, of everyone who was forced to inhabit it. And maximum chances, in the time it took to traverse from the main house to the other wing, to allow me to turn back from making a horrible mistake. One so all-consumingly awful that just thinking about it during my lecture, after chewing the erasers off not one but two mechanical pencils, I mounted another attack on the cap of a ballpoint pen. When you got right down to it, there were at least a million reasons *not* to make the trip down those stairs, and only *one* reason to go.

And Option A still didn't have a chance.

The worst part was, once I got home, I had no time left to freak out about it. Ten minutes at most. If I waited any longer, he'd be ordered upstairs to do some thankless task, and I'd miss my chance, maybe forever. All I could do was hope my legs held out as I forced them to carry me out the access door, down the path of lava rocks, behind an artfully placed clutch of palo verdes, to another, smaller door that opened to reveal the top of a narrow staircase, where I paused. I already felt utterly disrobed under the lurid yellow fluorescent light and its passive-aggressive buzzing that was nevertheless not loud enough to drown out the hammering of my heart and the churning of my insides as I descended, trying to keep my footsteps light.

At the bottom was an empty corridor. And at the end, more cinder block, more fluorescence, and another door—*the* door, probably. I glanced at the walls, suddenly fearing danger. Security cameras? Microphones? Or maybe a two-way mirror, or a curtain allowing my second-grade teacher to jump out and announce she was hereby revoking that "Excellent conduct" score I'd earned on my report card all those years ago? I knew it was ridiculous, but—

"Lost?"

I jumped. He stood right there in the doorway at the end of the hall, arms crossed. He looked better rested and was wearing a shirt I hadn't seen before, a soft aqua blue one that somehow fit him perfectly; it hugged his torso and even under the harsh lights, seemed to turn his eyes and hair to liquid gold, a glittering treasure submerged in a coral reef.

A few mangled erasers were a small price to pay.

I couldn't see much of what was in the room behind him. More cinderblock: what a surprise. Also: a few narrow metal bunks, the threadbare sofa that used to be in our media room and that I thought my parents had thrown out years ago, and light struggling to spill through a single high window in the corner.

So this was it. His everyday reality. For some reason, I felt grateful that he was letting me into it, even though technically, I could have come down here years ago, at any time. Yeah, it was supposed to be off-limits, but it was *my* house, for God's sake.

"I'm sorry," I said.

"About what?"

"About this." I gestured lamely to the dismal space. "Believe it or not, I had no idea."

He seemed confused. "Are you kidding me? I mean, there's a window. And a *sofa*. Trust me, the place is a palace."

"I really don't want to know what you're comparing it to."

"No, you don't," he said, even though he must have known that actually I did. "Come," he said, and for one absurd second, I actually thought he might *take my hand*.

He didn't, though, just beckoned me around another corner, where we found ourselves in an alcove made of yet more cinderblocks, plus the bonus of a dingy area rug, a dented metal stool lying on its side, and a broken bookshelf stuffed with old cookbooks and dated encyclopedias. Down the hall, another door was ajar, and I could just see more bunks, one with a handmade quilt—the women's quarters, I could only assume.

"Sorry I can't offer you a drink," he said, raking his hand through his thick golden strands as he followed my gaze. "Or a chair." He turned around and offered me a sheepish half-smile. As if I would ever criticize *this* view.

I glanced behind me. "Should we be—"

"It's okay," he assured me. "They're all busy. You should see the housekeeper's to-do list for today. Reading *Advanced Quantum Mechanics* was less scary. Nobody will be down here for hours. Oh, and there's no security camera. Not in this spot." He reached into his pocket and pulled out a thin wire. "And not as of this week. Anyway." With that one word, his easy confidence melted away, replaced by that hesitance when he'd called back to me in the pantry. "I just wanted you to know that my sis —Maeve's—messages were on that phone."

So he'd spoken to her. I knew, now. I knew why he'd given me the indescribable look he had when I'd walked in, like he was seeing something in me I'd never even seen in myself. That look he was almost giving me again, now.

"I don't know how you did it, or what you had to do."

I closed my eyes, trying not to think about what I'd had to do, or what I'd heard between him and the gardener, or whether any of it should, or did, involve me. It all could wait.

"But you were amazing."

I popped my eyes open. "Wait. *I* was amazing?"

"Are," he clarified. "Are amazing."

For the first time in twelve hours, I genuinely smiled. "Is … is this a thank you?"

"A really, really incredibly shit one, but yes, it is," he said, rushing ahead. "Also, I, um—I'm sorry."

"*You* don't need to apologize!"

"Yeah, I do." He kept running his hand through his hair. It was a nervous habit of his I'd noticed right from the start, one he would probably never admit to having. But I'd never seen him do it *this* many times in a row. "And I'm completely fucking it up, too. I guess because I—we—don't do this very often. Not for real."

"What do you mean?"

"*So sorry, sir, thank you, sir, please don't beat the shit out of me, sir.* It sort of loses all meaning after a while."

"What? You mean that stuff isn't sincere?" I asked, pretending to be shocked.

He shook his head. "Sadly, no. I hate to be the one to break it to you. Anyway, let me try to explain something. About what I said last night." He took another deep breath. "Nobody does anything for me. Ever. If I want something done for me, I do it, or it doesn't get done. That's the way it's been for a very long time. And I'm not sure I would know what to do if that ever changed."

After a pause, I said softly, "It has changed."

"I know," he admitted, slumping back against the wall. "Fuck. I know."

For some reason, my smile only grew.

"It's just," he continued, "I never thought the person who would do it would be someone who can get me thrown down a mine shaft just for *thinking* about ..." He trailed off all politely as if there could be any possible chance I didn't want to know exactly what it was.

"About what?" I didn't think my heart could pound any faster than it had at the top of the stairs. I'd been wrong.

"Things a good slave should never even think about."

"Sure, but I don't know why that would ever concern *you*."

That made him laugh. He rested one shoulder against the cinderblock wall, like he wanted a better view of me, though he kept his eyes slightly averted. As he spoke, he trailed a finger slowly along the grout between the cinderblocks, and for some reason, I found it fascinating to watch. "And why not?"

"Well," I said, "because if you were a good slave, we wouldn't be *here*. And yet here we are."

"Here we are."

He met my eyes again suddenly and spectacularly, the weight of it nearly knocking me off-balance. Something had shifted. The energy around us hummed like a field of charged particles. He stood up straight, raised his hand for a second, dropped it, raised it again, killed me with how close he was to doing something, while I killed *myself* over how I shouldn't be allowing him to do it. Not just for my own sake, but for his. Maybe even *more* for his. My entire moral compass was breaking down in real time, realizing that I now cared so much that the only right thing to do was to *stop caring*.

"We—we *shouldn't* be here," I said. *No. Don't listen to me. You know I'm an idiot. I'm failing chemistry, for fuck's sake.* "What if someone—what if you—and what about Maeve—and the mines, and the—"

"Fuck, Louisa, what did I just say?" he cut off my desperate babbling. "Why would I have gone through with that whole fucking embarrassing speech just now if I didn't want to be here? Can you just trust me enough to know what I want? Because I know what *you* want."

"What do I want?" I asked in a small voice.

"You want me to touch you." His gaze lowered under those long lashes, like he was seeing my body for the first time, drinking it in, *inhaling* it, taking a slow voyage across every visible inch of my skin and using his imagination to fill in the rest. "Not by accident. Not for comfort. But just because you want it."

That *look*, so serious, the kind of seriousness he'd only worn up till now when trying to puzzle out a particularly thorny chemistry problem. In some ways, this wasn't much different. In other ways, well, it was.

"You're doing it already."

It was true. One of his knuckles had brushed mine. Like an accident. I knew it wasn't.

"Am I?"

He kept going, letting our fingers intertwine for a brief second, come apart, then intertwine again. His thumb traced along the top of mine, gentler than anything so roughened by hard labor had any right to be. His other hand traced a delicate pattern on the exposed skin between the bottom of my crop top and the waist of my corduroy miniskirt with the buttons down the front.

I must be flushed red from my head to my decolletage right down to my toes, and I hoped to God he was enjoying it. As for my insides, they had melted into a puddle of thick, viscous fluid, and I hoped he was enjoying *that*, too, because there was no way he couldn't have sensed it somehow.

"Yes. You're touching me."

"Oh. So sorry, miss."

One little deft flick of his wrist and I was somehow propelled forward against his chest, with one of his hands migrating to the small of my back.

"So I was right." He could breathe the words into my ear now. "You, of all people, should know I'm always right."

"About chemistry, maybe," I breathed back.

"About so much more than that."

A second later, somehow, a roughened thumb was tracing the line of my jaw, tilting it closer to his mouth.

Well brought up, schooled in propriety and decorum, I should have run away and screamed and yelled and—oh, now I was ruined, ruined. Eighteen years' worth of straight As and gold stars and proper deportment just to let a slave kiss me—and kiss me like *that*.

Not only chemistry anymore. Physics, too. Torque. Velocity. Gravity. Things powerful and explosive and dangerous, unavoidable and immutable, capable of blowing off all the chains and locks and bars in the world.

His mouth was moving farther along my jawline now, finally arriving at my neck with a playful and exploratory little nip, prompting me to flip up my chin, my mouth forming a wondrous O directed up toward the crumbling ceiling plaster.

"Touch me," I whispered breathlessly. "Now."

"Where?"

"Anywhere. Everywhere. I just want your hands on me."

He obeyed immediately, his rather large, rather graceful hand sliding underneath my tank top. Instantly, the juxtaposition of the hard metal chain on his wrist against my softest and most vulnerable parts sent a sublime shiver shooting through my body as if it—my body, that is—just wanted to race ahead to get to the good part and didn't care what else had to happen to get there.

I did, though.

The kisses that had started out gentle gradually became more assertive: warm, wet, famished nibbles aimed at the exposed skin around my ear, shoulders, and neck. His fingers trailed up from my navel and across the sides of my purple lace bra, pulling the fabric aside; I sharply inhaled when my nipples poked out and greeted the cold basement air. While he—ever the scientist—puzzled out the straps and hooks with one hand, he stroked the inside of my thighs with the other, caressing the soft tissue of my bare leg all the way down to the back of my knee, cupping and lifting it lightly up close to his side.

That's when I felt his excitement for the first time, unable to help letting out a short, sharp gasp when I felt it, straining against the insides of his shorts and digging, bold and brazen, against the bare skin of my leg. He barely seemed to notice, as keen as he was on exploring—and claiming—the new world of *me*. Not quite sure what to do with it yet—if anything—my hands ventured behind him instead, landing tentatively on his broad back, eagerly and breathlessly working their way around that wondrous strip of soft skin and baby-fine hair just above his shorts and beneath his shirt, my fingers breathless with anticipation as they kept ranging farther. But they stopped immediately when I collided with the pain.

How the hell could I ever forget that he'd been *brutalized*? He still wore the lifelong marks of the old wounds and the distressingly new. Fuck, the file. The gouged, puckered disaster that was his back, starker than even the cinderblock and metal of all the places they'd caged him.

*What am I doing? He can't—and I shouldn't—and—*I snatched myself away. What if I'd *hurt* him?

"It's okay," he whispered reassuringly. "I'm okay. You can touch me, too, if you want."

I managed a smile, though every part of me still hesitated. "Are you sure?"

He raised an eyebrow, then went in for a playful kiss. "Are you kidding?" He kissed me again. I'd frozen up, and he knew it would melt me. "You know I know what pain feels like, Lou. And this isn't even *close*."

Buoyed, I returned his kisses with relief, even brushing some golden strands out of his face to reach it better, while he went right back to business, unfolding his fingers again on the inside of my thigh, the tips brushing just under the seams of my panties—also lacy and purple, though, oh so creatively, a different shade from my bra—and over the mound, every centimeter he explored reducing a greater percentage of my insides to warm goo.

The intercom buzzed nastily from around the corner, dropping us out of the heavens. Was there *anywhere* we could go to be alone?

He looked away, his eyes startled, but not panicked. Not yet. "We—"

"Keep going," I said, a purr verging on a growl. "Just a little more. Please. Whatever you do, don't stop."

"I won't," he breathed into my ear. "I promise. But you have to help me, yeah?"

"Okay, I—"

He quieted my mouth with a kiss. He forgot about the hooks, just sent one hand boldly straight up under my bra to firmly enclose my breast and claim my nerve endings with his calloused fingers. His other hand I clasped gently and guided along—to save time, to make it easier for him, but God, he *was* almost there already, magic boy—coaxing it to curl into the delicate space where my clit hid, shy and blushing in its solitude. A team effort. We were both rewarded with a long tendril of euphoria unfolding throughout my body, my knees dipping in response, and I whimpered as loudly as I dared to encourage him to push even harder against the outside of my mound, even as his knuckles still just barely brushed against the outer edges of my soaking folds. My back stretched and went rigid as he drove that powerful hand firmer, confoundingly delivering more and more of that incredible friction to my clit, its divine pulsations rhythmic and close, now. I somehow signaled to him, *harder*, and I kept my eyes squeezed shut, my manicured nails clawing into those massive shoulders and tugging at all that shining hair, already slightly damp with exertion, pulling his head close to rest briefly on my shoulder.

There was infinitely so much more to want—yes, *of course* I wanted to touch him. To reach for whatever awaited me beneath those strained shorts, for one thing. To undress him completely, to have him undress *me*, to touch and tease and watch every gorgeous inch of him swell and brighten and come alive, to invite him to do the same for *me*, to moan as loud as I dared, to *scream*, to lay all afternoon in a field of wildflowers— but there was no time, no space, and yes, that was the fucking housekeeper shouting from the top of the stairs, her intercom buzzing having gone ignored—and this was all we would get, for now or maybe ever, and I muffled my outburst, following his lead, back braced up against the wall, arching, catlike, then the sudden release, my body becoming a gauzy ribbon floating blissfully to the floor. He caught me just in time.

My eyes fluttered open to find him gazing right back, shoulders heaving. He shook some of the damp golden hair off his face to reveal a little bit of wonder in his eyes, if I wasn't mistaken.

"What just happened?"

He rested his head on the wall, catching his breath, but glanced back with the trace of a smile. "Among other things," he replied, "something you can never, ever tell your dad."

With no answer, the housekeeper had given up, and he'd mashed the intercom, coming up with an elaborate excuse involving yard waste and wheelbarrows and the end of monsoon season that made absolutely no sense to me except that it somehow bought him five minutes longer by my side— five minutes we had to spend talking instead of fucking, unfortunately, if only because we had to figure out just what the hell we were going to do with ... *this*. Whatever *this* was.

"Are you okay?" Fuck, I couldn't leave him to go do *chores* like this.

He sighed. "Well, I've been through worse torture. *I'm kidding*," he added before I could gasp in horror. "Seriously. I'm fine. Come." He wrapped his arms lightly around my waist and drew me closer so we were face-to-face again. He did seem relaxed, genuinely satisfied just to have satisfied *me*, and the wonder and curiosity in his eyes were enough to indicate that he believed there'd be a next time.

Next time. Fucking hell. I was already never, ever getting over *this*.

"What's going to happen now?" I wasn't sure whether I was talking about the next second, the next day, or the rest of our lives.

But he began, quite logically, at the beginning. "Well, you're going to go upstairs and get some sleep because you need it. And then, you're going to review all of Chapter Nine, making sure to focus on aldol condensation and esterification."

"*Seriously*?!"

He looked genuinely confused. "What? I'm still your tutor. You thought I forgot about your exam?"

I rolled my eyes. "It always has to be about science with you, doesn't it?"

"Always," he said with a laugh. "Anyway, after *that*, you're going to get ready for tonight," he said, reaching up to tenderly place one of my long curls behind my ear, sliding his fingers down its silken length, lingering as if he didn't want to let it go. "When I'll see you again."

I closed my eyes. Yes, he'd see me again. And he would have to pretend not to. And that was what he'd have to do *every* time he saw me in public, from this point forward, if he didn't want to get us both killed.

What the fuck kind of ending was *this* to our story?

The answer was, it wasn't one.

"But what about you?"

Wrong question. The subtle change in his expression told me instantly how little he wanted to contemplate what the day had in store for him.

"Quantum mechanics?" I teased, trying to coax a smile.

"Molecular orbital theory. Diatomic *and* polyatomic," he said. "Followed by floor scrubbing and silver polishing. And now I'm behind, for obvious reasons," he remarked. "*Good* reasons," he added, his thumb stroking the bare skin between my top and skirt reassuringly.

Fuck. Why was he always comforting *me* over *his* life being a nightmare? I dug deep for anything that might cure that look of sad resignation in his eyes. Other than an orgasm, but that would have to wait.

"So about tonight," I said. "Anything in particular I should wear?"

"Wait." He sounded puzzled, though intrigued. "Do I actually get a say in this?"

"Well, you and I aren't going to get to do much talking during dinner," I said sadly. "So yes, you do. Within reason," I added. I suspected it wasn't every day he got asked about his tastes in women's clothing, and I didn't want him to get *too* carried away. "So?"

"Anything that makes you feel good," he said.

"I love that you're trying to be gentlemanly, but come on."

"Hey, I gave it a try," he said, then added eagerly, "Something short that shows off your back?"

"That's more like it." However, mention of the party jogged an unpleasant recollection. "Just to warn you, Corey's coming. And his boss."

"Max Langer," he said immediately. "I know."

I was surprised he knew who Corey's boss—the man whose success all of our futures apparently now hinged on—even was. Then again, he missed nothing. Hell, he probably knew more about Max Langer than *I* did.

But I did wonder why.

With a swallow, I remembered how my last conversation with my father had ended. But I couldn't bear to remind the boy in whose arms I now felt so safe that he was property in danger of being sold, any more than I could bear to remind myself.

"So how is your boyfriend going to dazzle us with his brilliance this time?" he asked. "An erupting papier-mâché volcano?"

I giggled. His barely disguised loathing of Corey, after what had just happened a minute ago, was completely absurd, as much as it secretly delighted me.

"You're adorable when you're jealous. Did I ever tell you that?"

He rested one elbow on the wall, rakishly leaning on it, his face angled down toward mine. "You never told me I was adorable, and that's the only part I'll accept. I prefer 'devastatingly handsome,' though."

The intercom buzzed angrily to life again.

"Shit." He broke away, hand in his hair, his eyes shooting toward the door. "Someone could be down here soon. You have to go."

"But you said—"

"I lied."

Could I blame him, really?

"Relax," he assured me, turning toward me again. "It's okay. Nobody saw anything."

"What if someone sees me on the stairs?"

"Make up a story. You just learned from the best," he said, nodding toward the intercom.

I paused to brainstorm. "I'll tell them I came down looking for the maid."

He shook his head. "Slow learner. No. Tell them you came down to find me."

"What? Why?"

"Because they'll figure if you really came down to find me, you'd say you were looking for the maid. Come." He kissed me sweetly, casually, but—just for a second—hesitant to let me go. "You have a lot to learn about lying, young lady."

"Know where I can find a good tutor?" I whispered slyly in his ear before sprinting up the narrow staircase in a daze. The cinderblock, the stark yellow bulbs, and the creaky wood no longer seemed quite as menacing. In fact, they were almost laughable, a weak attempt at muting the wonder I'd found.

I knew that wonder wouldn't last. I knew I had to get upstairs and out of that basement fast. I knew we were in danger, and when we came together again at the party, we'd be in even *more* danger. I knew what we'd just done wasn't going to lead to snuggling in front of the TV, elegant dinner dates, or autumn strolls in the park hand in hand. The exact opposite, in fact. For a second, though, I'd forgotten.

I shouldn't have.

Before I could dart outside and dive behind a barrel cactus for cover, the door flung open with a thwack against the wall, and I was enveloped in the hulking shadow of the gardener, looming over me like a poison gas cloud.

"Hey there, princess," he sneered, eyes gleaming with a

rheumy film that made my stomach turn. "Lovely afternoon for a trip to the ... basement."

My entire body turned ice-cold. He leaned against the doorframe, grinning like a demented clown, revealing rows of empty tooth sockets as I felt myself almost literally shrink under his stare. Then I saw what was in his grubby hands: instead of a spade or shovel, it was a battered old tablet held together with masking tape, the screen glowing with that sickly light I'd only seen in one type of video—not that I made a habit of watching *those*. As he watched it silently, his lips curled up again, but it was nothing resembling a smile.

It couldn't be. The slave boy—*my* boy, as maybe I could call him now, for lack of anything better—had *disabled* the camera.

Well, the one he knew about. And the one my father knew about, evidently.

"Ya know, I was real pissed off when the girls boarded up the basement window," the gardener remarked. "Ruined the only real fun I ever had. And every time I tried to get into someplace better ..." He cackled before trailing off disturbingly. "Anywho, one of the old garden slaves used to take a peek with me. He was a real clever guy. Knew how to read, too. Before your daddy sold him, he set me up with this thing real good." He waved the tablet. "Now I get to watch movies every night, just for me. Don't even gotta do nothing but keep it charged. This time, though"—he paused to let loose a wheezy laugh—"it was a blockbuster."

I could have vomited right there on the steps. "G-give me that." I tried to grab it, but he snatched it away like a schoolyard bully. "Or I'll tell Daddy." I tried to force some authority into my voice, even though this sick fuck found me about as intimidating as a piece of construction paper covered in glitter and glue.

Batting me away handily, he tapped the screen with a dirty

finger. His contorted lips twisted further, and bile rose in my thick throat, heart hammering so loud I was sure he could hear it. I watched his jaundiced eyes flit across the screen as if he were enjoying every second of what he was watching. Enjoying it as much as *I* had enjoyed it. "Let it go," I hissed, desperate not to cry or scream for the boy I'd just left in the basement, like having him here would do anything but fuck us further. "Or, I told you, I'll tell—"

"Sorry, Miss Loulou." He caught my wrist, and I barely stifled a shriek as he pulled me closer, like we were about to snuggle and watch a rom-com. In all the years he'd terrorized me, he'd never actually touched me—after all, he valued his life. And that he suddenly no longer seemed to care about *that* was the most terrifying thing of all.

He tapped the tablet again, then flipped it around. There was the basement, and there was me, caught in a moment I wished I'd never been stupid enough, even for a second, to believe wouldn't be my downfall.

"Safe to say the only one telling Daddy anything from now on," he said, "is gonna be me. Unless," he continued as I choked on his toxic breath, "you tell your boy he's gotta keep his word and share."

10

HIM

I'd waited two years and traveled 5,000 miles for the night I'd finally encounter Max Langer face-to-face, and now that it had arrived, all I could think about was what dress a girl would be wearing when she appeared at the top of the stairs.

Yeah, there might be a problem.

I had *not* planned this. Really. Sure, I'd gutted the down-stairs security camera, but I'd done that weeks ago simply as a best-practices thing, long before I ever imagined I'd be fingering my master's daughter to orgasm in a stark, fluorescent-lit hallway with an old woman's voice screeching at us over an intercom. Nor had I had any idea that Louisa—through no fault of her own—would leave me unable to go upstairs until I'd finished myself off, back against the wall, stroking my dick to the memory of the way her lips had formed that perfect shape when I found the spot I'd been searching for, and every single *other* shape I imagined them making, every other shape I imagined between them. Yeah, I'd told her I was fine, and I was. Now.

As shocking as it was to me, I was *glad* we'd stopped there. Not just because there was no time or that she'd hesitated at touching my healing wounds, or that the atmosphere sucked— and the fact that I even cared about *that* was weird enough— but because I didn't know how far she wanted to go, or could go, or had gone. Slave girls let *me* call the shots. I couldn't play Louisa that way. In fact, I couldn't remember a time when I'd been so genuinely concerned about someone *else's* pleasure. Of course, as a slave, that was all I was *supposed* to care about. But as *me*? Well.

Still, I tried not to look too smug when I finally went upstairs to face an assault by one of the housekeeper's mixer blades and two massive cabinets full of unsorted silverware that I spent the rest of the afternoon on my knees polishing, only interrupted when she broke down and slipped me one of her vanilla meringues. I smiled up at her, amused by what she'd think if she knew what I'd *really* been up to earlier.

But the *real* problem was that Louisa, for all she'd done to help me find Maeve, still had no idea that the man coming to dinner—the man who was supposedly about to save her family from ruin—had my sister. And for now, it had to stay that way. After all, how could I possibly explain that to her as she was dashing up the stairs wearing that impish, rosy, well-kissed grin, so self-conscious that she didn't realize *I* was looking at her like some floppy-eared puppy?

Oh, and then there was the gardener. Earlier, I had scanned the entire terrace, including the outdoor dining and pool areas, just to make sure the gross toothless bastard a. wasn't skulking around and b. hadn't left any incriminating evidence, like the printed map to Langer's warehouse he'd swiped. I'd found nothing and no sign of him, but it didn't make me feel any better because I needed to warn Louisa, and I couldn't without explaining everything. And *everything* would include what else

I'd been doing in her room during our tutoring sessions—other than mentally undressing her, which was probably no longer much of a secret.

Yes, Maeve was right. Louisa had risked a lot to get me that phone. She *cared*, and that was terrifying enough. She *shouldn't* have done it, and I shouldn't have accepted it, but it happened, and there was no going back. But if the time came to choose between me and her family—especially after she learned I had not, to put it lightly, been entirely truthful—I knew the choice, for her, would still be an easy one.

So yeah, there was a lot I couldn't tell her, and worst of all, it was all stuff she deserved to know. But after a lifetime spent aware that one carelessly dropped fact could earn you a flogging, a caning, or some other random method of unspeakable torture, lying wasn't an easy habit to break. So maybe she'd cut me some slack?

Yeah, right.

With all her gold stars and high expectations, even as she grew and changed before my eyes, this desert princess would—despite knowing everything I'd been through—expect *me* to be better, too. After all, she was used to the best.

And that's why my first priority—besides brainstorming places to take her next time besides a dusty alcove full of broken furniture—should have been finding a solution to this problem. Unfortunately, I didn't get to choose my priorities. So instead, I dutifully took up my post by the door in an all-black uniform I'd been given to wear. I'd been given a few dress shirts to wear in my time and generally found them too tight in the shoulders, but to my surprise, this one fit me as perfectly as if the house-keeper had worked some kind of magic on it.

The maid stood next to me in a black skirted outfit, holding a tray of champagne flutes, which she was efficiently offering to the arriving guests before directing them to the sprawling terrace, where more cocktails would be served before dinner. *My* only job during this part of the evening was to stand there like a marble pillar and take coats, bags, and anything else people wanted to dump on me, and to ensure the guests knew immediately that despite what they'd heard, Keith Wainwright-Phillips wasn't so broke that he couldn't afford a brand-new, good-looking slave.

In fact, I felt one guest's obliging eyes on me before I even saw her: the thirtysomething redhead in the corner, champagne flute twirling in her hand, was already checking me out like I was on the menu. I knew the type—rich, bored, undersexed, and always leering at slave boys like we were streaming entertainment. Still, up until recently, I would have played along, but tonight? The way she looked at me—hungry, expectant—just made my skin crawl.

Whatever. It was what it was. Better to be a piece of meat here than chained and half-naked at a public auction.

Actually, given that it was October in the desert, none of the guests—which so far seemed to be mostly Wainwright-Phillips's friends, business associates, and their spouses, but no Langer—wore a whole lot of extra layers, which meant that so far, I hadn't done much of anything. Which gave me a lot of extra time to covertly scan the top of the stairs. That would have been fine if it weren't for the *next* guest noticing it immediately.

"What are you looking at, slave?" The Big Douche on Campus, who'd just arrived with his parents, wore a light leather jacket reeking of menthol cigarettes, which he made a point of aggressively chucking at me like he'd somehow known ahead of time I'd get assigned to do this.

There was no torture quite like coming up with a million of the wittiest, most scathing retorts you've ever heard and then not being allowed to use them, but it was one I was all too familiar with. But with all the guests around—and Langer on his way—there was too much at stake to waste them, even on someone as loathsome as Corey Killeen. All I could do was bite down hard on my lip and direct my eyes back to the floor where every person there—except maybe one—thought they belonged.

"Nothing, sir."

"Good. Fucking keep it that way."

Tonight was going to be rough.

773541N0

Abee jo,[1] *Brudderhäerz,*[2] are you there?

773496S6

I'm here, Maeve

Here meaning the wine cellar, desperately trying to tap out a message before the housekeeper burst in and demanded to know why I wasn't back yet with that extra bottle of Marsala I'd lied and told her we were out of. Personally, *I* just wanted to know why I was such an idiot. This goddamn phone would have gotten me killed twice already if it weren't for the grace of the girl in the backless dress, and yet here I was *still* carrying it around instead of stashing it in the empty birdhouse next to the

---

1. Hi.
2. Literally, "brother heart," an endearment.

garden shed that would have made a damn good hiding place had I bothered to actually use it.

Too late.

773496S6

What is it? Did you find something?

773541N0

You were right, about the research
They're doing experiments
On our microchips

773496S6

What do you mean?

Who?

What kind of experiments?

773541N0

I don't know, but Resi said that's why they needed me
Because my chip is still transmitting, but no one is
looking for me
Same with the other girls

That would make sense, actually. You couldn't experiment on a chip that had been disabled, but a runaway slave with a working chip would be tracked immediately. That must have been why they went after Maeve, after her owners abandoned her.

773541N0

Resi was helping with the research but they went too far, she said

Now she wants out

But we have to be smart about what we're doing, or they'll catch on

773496S6

Who'll catch on? Max Langer?

But Maeve didn't answer right away, almost like she knew something but for whatever reason was afraid to tell me.

Fuck. I never should have gotten her involved in this, let alone anyone else. I kept my circle small for a damn good reason. Maeve, on the other hand, was always doing stupid shit like opening up and trusting people. When would she learn?

773496S6

Maeve? I want you to stop whatever you're doing

And stop talking to anyone

773541N0

But you told me to

773496S6

I don't care, it's too dangerous

Leave it to me from now on

I'm coming for you, I promise

I'm going to get you out of there

773541N0
But Resi's going to free us
She just needs more time

Our next two messages got sent nearly simultaneously.

773496S6

Free you?

How long is that going to take?

And what if someone catches on?

773541N0
Nondikass
Someone's coming, I have to go

But she didn't go. Instead, more dots appeared, then disappeared, like she was trying to tap out an answer to my questions as fast as she could before she got caught. *Someone's coming, Maeve. Hide the phone, for fuck's sake.* Had someone...? Was she...? I could only stand there in the dark, frozen to the spot, heart racing, watching those goddamn dots, waiting for them to stop, waiting for a message, anything. But they just kept pulsing. My pulse hammered in my throat. *Say something, Maeve. Please.*

Suddenly, the dots disappeared. Then, one final message appeared:

773541N0
He's here

HER

Upstairs, I opened my textbook.

Sure, it seemed ridiculous to return to alkenes and alkynes now, but he'd never let me hear the end of it if he found out I hadn't studied. But I might as well have been back to square one. The formulas on the page just swam. All I could see, all I could hear, all I could *feel*, was the gardener's sneer, that sickly light, that awful tablet clutched in his grubby hands.

He'd given me until midnight. Even offered me a deal, of sorts. A nauseating, horrific, impossible, unthinkable deal. One I could never make in a million years, which I'd told him before sprinting upstairs and straight into a long, scalding-hot shower that I hated to have to take because it washed all the good stuff off with the bad.

But as bad as the deal was, the alternative was worse. For me, it meant ruin. For the slave boy? Death.

And I knew that if I didn't go to the gardener tonight to give him my decision, he would come for me. And as repulsive as that was, it was also my only saving grace. That he was so blinded by four years' worth of lechery that he was going to try to hold out instead of going straight to Daddy and losing his only bargaining chip.

It gave me time to think of a plan to destroy him.

Because if I couldn't, he *would* expose us. It was only a matter of time. But how should I do it? Should I go to Daddy and try to—

No, no, no. Every single choice was wrong. Catastrophically wrong. Maybe it was too late to do *anything*. And plus, what if he *didn't* hold out? Maybe he'd been to Daddy *already*. But no. The gardener got banished to the far reaches of the property at parties, so maybe he wouldn't be able to reach Daddy. Maybe he wouldn't be able to reach *me*. But I couldn't count on that.

And what about my boy? I had to tell him, and I had a *way* to tell him, now, I thought, staring at my phone. Didn't I?

Or maybe, I should first try to figure out what the gardener meant by *keep his word*. Was it possible that—

No. It was impossible. When it came down to believing a disgusting old pervert versus the magic boy who got me loving chemistry and who had kissed my forehead as gently as a prayer, it wasn't really much of a competition.

Right?

So heart pounding in my ears, I swiped open the messaging app and selected "Albert Einstein" from my contacts. Took a deep breath and started typing.

> The gardener saw

Deleted.

> Someone knows

Deleted.

> We need to talk

Deleted.

> I need to talk to you

Deleted.

> Find me at the party. It's important

Deleted. I turned my phone over and pushed it away. I needed to think more about what to say, but I also knew there was a good chance he'd hidden his phone and wouldn't see it, in time or at all, and we were both fucked either way.

And now, shit. According to the clock, it was time to pick out something to wear.

But strangely, it made me feel better. Hey, I grew up in Scottsdale, okay?

It felt like a form of meditation as I started cataloging all 700 or so clothing pieces in my closet, focusing on how well they checked off my boy's two hopeful requests—short and showing my back. But even then, I couldn't shake the dread curling in my stomach. I had to tell him. But what would he do if and when I did? What *could* he do, other than run away screaming from the girl who seemed destined to get him thrown in a mine no matter how smart and careful he was?

I had no answers, of course. But at least I'd find out in a minute how I did with the dress. Oops, less than a minute because I was at the top of the marble staircase now, and he was at the bottom. My heart was thudding almost audibly, not just from the excitement of seeing him, but from sheer terror. How was I supposed to act normal? What even *was* normal, now?

Surprisingly—and by "surprisingly," I mean "not surprisingly at all"—he was indeed devastatingly handsome in the black uniform, a step up from the cast-off and borrowed T-shirts and shorts he normally wore, not that he had any choice in it. He'd also done something to his hair—I wasn't sure what —and the thick, sun-bleached strands, often flipped chaotically over to one side to hang in his face, looked more ... polished, somehow. I'd have to be careful not to stare at him. Okay, fine, I'd already failed at that. I'd have to be sure not to stare at him for more than fifty percent of the night. I didn't like my chances much there, either.

For his part, he didn't seem to be looking directly at me, but

I knew that didn't mean anything. Under that forelock of hair, beneath those long lashes, behind that submissive bow of his head, he was drinking me up from top to bottom.

He was that good.

The question was, though, could he read in my face that something was wrong? Probably. And if he could, how could I tell him the truth? Conversely, how could I *not*? Head swimming, I continued down the stairs, each tap of my black open-toed heels on the parquet bringing me closer to him, closer to the moment where I'd have to decide if I could keep up the act or crumble.

And as much as I wanted to make eye contact—to somehow coax out that bright, curious gaze and beautiful smile, just for a second, just for me—I knew that even trying risked getting him in trouble, and I would never ask it of him.

Instead, I was supposed to just walk by him as if he were a living coat rack, as if he weren't even there, as if all the bones in my body, and plenty of other parts, too, weren't so acutely aware of him that they could all jump out of my skin at any time.

The maid was standing there, holding a tray of champagne flutes, and as much as I hated interacting with her—and as much as I knew alcohol wouldn't help anything—I was dying to grab one of the glasses and down it while slinking out to the terrace and awaiting my fate. Realistically, though, the easiest option would be to ignore both of them, much as it made my heart ache. And either way, I couldn't stand on the stairs any longer. So I had to start moving my legs, little of which were concealed by the sleeveless black butt-grazing cocktail dress I'd chosen.

And wouldn't he choose that moment to raise his head under the guise of shaking some hair from his eyes. But what happened next was a total surprise.

The coats still draped over his arm, he grabbed one of the flutes from the maid's tray, and I could only watch in slow motion as yes, that stupid fucking idiot was on his way toward me, so what choice did I have but to cut the distance and walk toward *him*? And reach out to let him place the glass gently in my trembling hand as if we were the only two people in the room. And if his finger happened to brush mine, well. A hazard of the job.

"Thank you," I said, hoping I could somehow imbue the two words I *could* say with everything I *wanted* to say.

"You're welcome, miss," he replied, his golden eyes averted respectfully, while the part of me screaming *please look at me* and the part of me screaming *don't risk it* punched each other out in a full-on battle royale.

Had he seen the message? It didn't matter. Now or never. I had to tell him. It would shatter us both to pieces, but I had to. I cleared my throat. "I—"

"Just look at this, Loulou."

But it was the glass that almost shattered—in my hand—as Daddy appeared to obliviously kill the moment. To my surprise, though, he was smiling, and for the first time since I'd left the basement, I actually breathed.

Daddy doesn't know. The gardener didn't tell him—well, show him.

Yet.

That meant there was still a little time. Time to figure *something* out. Luckily, I now knew someone very well—well, better than I had that morning, anyway—who was good at figuring things out. If only he knew that there was anything *to* figure out.

"What did I tell you? Does he clean up or what?" Daddy jerked the slave boy toward him by the arm with enthusiasm and turned his chin, admiring him as if he were an expensive oil painting he'd just hung over the mantelpiece. Meanwhile, the maid's customary pout didn't change, but I could swear that smug little minx was silently sniggering at us.

Sometimes I wondered about Daddy.

Then again, maybe he was just in a good mood. A deal with Max Langer was apparently a big deal, enough to get him to shave and put on one of his expensive tailored suits for the first time in a year, befitting the multimillionaire CEO he at one point had been and hoped to be again. And as much as I resented him for tearing us away from *that* moment, I couldn't pretend it wasn't refreshing to see him like this.

I was considerably less enthusiastic about Langer. Corey had said he didn't deal in slaves, but Corey couldn't exactly be trusted to be objective about the boss who was offering him a six-figure salary fresh out of school. But maybe that didn't matter. If they were working on a deal that was supposed to save my family's fortune, I *had* to be happy about it. Right?

Because it wasn't only my own fate in the balance. It was my boy's, too.

But then what? What kind of future did we have even then? Call me naive, but I knew damn well how the world worked, and that even if Langer somehow transformed my over-the-hill father into a tech billionaire, my boy was still legally as much Daddy's property as the coffee table or the TV. Daddy could still sell him anytime, and *I'd* have to shut up and watch him go. And even in the unlikely event we could come up with a plan to foil the gardener—being able to talk to each other might help—it was probably only a matter of time before Corey, or the maid, or some other foe we didn't even know about yet, picked up on the flux of pure sex hormones I was certain we were both giving off pretty much around the clock and decide to ruin both of our lives out of jealousy, vengeance, spite, or all three.

Well, *that* sure killed the party mood.

I stood in an unblinking daze as the last few guests filed in and Corey, in a cloud of menthol—when the hell had he taken up smoking?—returned to glom onto me, directing me imperiously toward the back of the house.

Helplessly, I followed him. As much as it killed me, I hated even more what it would do to my boy, despite his earlier unconvincing denials of jealousy.

But, oh. The maid had returned to the kitchen, and everyone else had dispersed from the foyer. The jackass walking next to me was caught up in his usual self-absorbed bullshit. There was only one person left by the door, but he'd be gone soon, too. And I *wasn't* powerless, at least not in every way.

My long, thick curls still hung down over the back of my dress, and as I walked away, I flipped the curtain of hair up over my shoulder to give him an exclusive glimpse of my nude back, framed in two delicate panels of black lace.

I couldn't turn back to see his expression, of course. But I could feel it. And that was almost as good.

And then, while I was sure I had his attention—though still without turning back—I held up my phone and tapped the screen.

Which meant I'd better send a goddamn message.

HIM

Yeah, grabbing the flute had been a stupid thing to do, and no, it hadn't been planned. But then again, was *any* of this planned? She'd just looked so hot and so brave and so scared all at once, standing there on the stairs, trembling in the dress she'd chosen just for me. And since I couldn't envelop her in my arms, couldn't caress that luscious, peachy back, or tell her what I really thought—that I could live a million years and never get over the fact that a girl like her would give a damn about my fantasies, let alone fulfill them—a glass of champagne and the brush of a finger would have to be enough.

Enough to airbrush out the slimeball walking next to her when she flipped her hair. Enough to armor us for whatever the night held.

And enough to cushion the shock when I finally put the coats in the closet and arrived at the terrace, only to find that Max Langer—billionaire, tech wizard, homicidal maniac?—apparently was too important to bother with front doors.

He had, the entire time, been standing there, amid the complicated terra cotta stonework, prickly pears, and lava rocks. And there was no other way into the property except through the large circular driveway, which meant he must have driven in, gotten out of his car, and gone around the side of the house. That was unsettling enough on its own. And all of this was even *before* I got a good look at the guy I'd only glimpsed while furtively scrolling through search results in a German science lab 5,000 miles away.

The icy blue lights of the swimming pool behind him, combined with his blue eyes and sharp cerulean blue suit, made him look like a glacier. He was good-looking in the way of a slab of granite not yet quite sculpted, with a lean, muscular frame, pale skin, full lips, and thick waves of dark hair that seemed to almost defy gravity. And when he spoke, he had the trace of an accent that sounded more than a bit familiar.

"If you look at anyone successful these days," he was telling Wainwright-Phillips and some of his colleagues, who were gathered around him like worshippers at an altar, "odds are they didn't get there on brains or talent; they got there by shouting louder than the other guy. By selling, and the product is themselves. It's why I prefer scientists and engineers. Of course working with *them* is like going out with a girl looking for true love. No matter how hot they are, you'll inevitably let them down, and then not only do they walk out on you, they take your entire computer system down with them when they go."

Louisa wasn't in that group, much to my relief. She was a few feet farther away in her tiny little black dress and killer heels, near another arrangement of wicker lounge chairs, chatting easily with a man and woman closer to her age.

I was familiar enough with her adorkable side by now that I'd almost forgotten she was a girl of society, schooled in the social graces, just as *I'd* been schooled, fairly unsuccessfully, in subservience and submission. That was my girl.

Mine. And how was that for irony?

But I also knew, by the way her eyes darted warily around the room as she giggled and cooed and spoke of everything light and pleasant and tried to ignore me, that something was wrong.

Really wrong.

Like an idiot, I patted my pocket. Slaves didn't carry phones or wallets or car keys or money, so it would look weird. I'd put the phone on silent, of course, but I shouldn't have brought it at all. And despite her gesture, I hadn't felt a vibration. Still, I had to—

"Well, don't just stand there."

I turned around with a start, but it was just the house-keeper, passing by on her way to the kitchen with her customary thump on my arm and no indication that she'd noticed anything except that I was slacking off. I noticed the maid was already trotting around with trays of stuffed poblano peppers and chili-lime shrimp cups.

"Make yourself useful."

With a frustrated sigh and without risking another glance back at Louisa, I turned back to the only thing I was *supposed* to be worrying about, right now or at all: serving. If only food, and its assembly and distribution, had ever made even a fraction as much sense to me as chemistry or calculus. The housekeeper was well aware of that, but she'd also made it clear earlier that I'd be expected to do something more useful during the party than clear the table, so I'd made the mistake of telling her I knew something about drinks. I thought that would mean I'd be put in charge of the wine cellar—which I could probably handle, thanks to my years with the professor—but the ancient valet was doing that, and the housekeeper had neglected to mention that the guests, and Langer in particular, liked tequila. So to my dismay, I soon found myself at the outdoor bar with bottles of silvers and golds and reposados and exquisite little arrays of herbs, twists, and bitters, desperately trying to make any of it make sense to my European soul.

A minute later, *some* sort of drink was in Langer's hand, complete with a carefully placed sprig of rosemary at the top that I thought might fool someone into thinking I knew what I was doing. I turned to go back to the bar area, hoping to catch a break *somehow* and either talk to Louisa or get my phone, even if it meant pulling some kind of con that would let me, and then her, leave for a minute or two. And through it all, I kept watching the tech mogul out of the corner of my eye.

Langer took a sip of the drink, made a face, and put it down on the edge of the firepit behind him. "Hey. Kid."

Instinctively, I braced myself, waiting to be scolded.

"What's your name?" Langer asked.

Wainwright-Phillips overheard and gave me an odd look. "Come on, Max, you know they don't have names."

To probably everyone's surprise, Langer laughed throatily, like this was some funny notion to him, like he and Wain-wright-Phillips hadn't been living in the same world for the past forty years. "And why shouldn't they?" he said. "I mean, what are we trying to do here? Disrupt slavery, yeah? You were in the corporate world too long, that's your problem. You don't question things anymore. Disruption, like almost everything, comes down to science. It starts with a hypothesis. A question. Why is this the way it is, and can our product make it better?"

Make *what* better? The process of dismembering and killing slave girls? Clearly a million-dollar piece of IP, right there.

My master, though he'd gone quiet, seemed to be pondering this seriously. "Well, I—"

"And I'll tell you right now, Keith," Langer continued, "if you don't ask it, your competitors will, and they'll have cornered the market before you even know the market exists."

I stood rooted to the spot, looking from one man to the other, not sure if I was yet permitted to walk away. And not having expected to suddenly become the center of attention. It's not that I was opposed to it—even if it was only for serving Langer a piece of shit beverage—but this also had the potential to go south very quickly and rob me of *any* chance to figure out what was going on with Louisa.

"Well—" Wainwright-Phillips paused, clearly racking his brain. "We're using him as a tutor for Louisa. How's that for thinking outside the box?"

Langer's senses seemed to sharpen. "Is that right? Which subject?"

He seemed to be asking Wainwright-Phillips, but he was looking straight at me. Once again, I didn't dare respond. Of the millions of things a slave should never, ever do, making your master look bad in front of his guests was pretty damn close to the top, and getting smacked across the face right in front of Max Langer wasn't even close to what I'd had in mind for our first encounter.

"Well, she's pre-med, and—" Wainwright-Phillips began.

"Hey, is he deaf or mute?" Langer interrupted. "You're not, are you, kid?"

"No, sir."

"Then let him answer."

I was stunned at how fast my master shut his mouth. Well, then. *Let's go.* "Organic chemistry, sir."

Langer grimaced. "They're still making pre-meds learn that?"

"Unfortunately, sir," I replied. "And slaves, too."

Langer laughed, a sound that, while not unpleasant, definitely insisted on making its presence known all over the room.

I could already see that if Langer had hurt Maeve or anyone else, how easily he might have done it, or ensured that it was done. He was everything Wainwright-Phillips perhaps had once been and wanted to be again: young, rich, smart, handsome, charming, and ideally positioned to get away with *anything*, including the worst things you could possibly imagine. "How old are you, and where are you from? I detect an accent."

"Nearly twenty, sir." Under my hair, I glanced up. Where was Louisa? I needed to know where she was *now*, for her sake and mine. "And Luxembourg."

"Beautiful country. I partly grew up with my mother in Germany, but I used to go to Luxembourg on business. Last time, I shipped back an entire case of that Cassero liqueur they make. I'll bring over a bottle sometime for you."

He made it clear that the "you" meant me and no one else. Like he could just stop by the house one day and start boozing it up with me like two old buddies. Was this man completely and utterly delusional? Yeah, like a fox.

"I expect that's more up your alley than tequila—which, pro tip, next time, use the silver," he continued. "The name's Max, by the way. My dad made me call him 'sir,' and that's the last thing I want to be known by, considering I hated everything about the bastard, except for the million or so worth of startup capital he left me when he died. Also, just so you know, it freaks

me out to have you looking at the floor when you talk to me.
Makes me think my cosmetic surgeon isn't worth what I paid
him for that eye lift. Anyway, good to know you."

Look, it wasn't as if free people *always* treated slaves with
contempt and scorn. At various times, I had been fawned over
and indulged by lonely women; sympathized with by the occasional closet abolitionist; and all too often, just ignored. But I'd
never encountered anyone who quite simply refused to
acknowledge that I wasn't free.

Max Langer acted as if the rules didn't apply to him. That
made him dangerous.

I raised my eyes. Whatever the rest of them thought, I'd
have to be an idiot to pass up this free opportunity to look this
motherfucker full in the face.

Langer held out his hand.

I stared at it.

For me, it was a rare offer, but I knew that in the world of
free men, having a firm grip said a hell of a lot about you. What
kind of man you were. Whether you could be trusted. Whether
you could be reckoned with.

Control the center, control the game, boy.

If he wanted disruption, I'd give him disruption.

So with my master standing right there, I shook the hand of
the man I'd been hunting for a year and looked him straight in
his frigid blue eyes. I hoped my message was clear.

*I'm not buying what you're selling, asshole. And if you touch my
sister, it'll be more than your limbs the coyotes will be chewing on.*

Wainwright-Phillips, to his credit, seemed to notice none of
this. He just nodded cluelessly at the eccentric behavior of those
richer than him and wandered off to greet some more guests.
But Max Langer remained, his smooth, firm hand still gripping
mine. And as he leaned in close, the phone in my back pocket
took that exact moment to start buzzing audibly.

Fuck.

I went rigid, and I know Langer felt it. *Of course* I'd been too stressed out and distracted to get the volume settings right. In horror, I looked up at Langer again—right in the one place a slave was never supposed to look.

But he didn't even blink. He just quirked an eyebrow and leaned in closer. "You might want to answer that, kid," he whispered, his breath cold in my ear, "and let her know she shouldn't dig too deep—or she might get exposed."

❤

The phone stopped buzzing, thank fuck, but it still took about fifteen more minutes and the housekeeper handing me a garbage bag—full of about fifty empty liquor bottles and a broken lamp thanks to Louisa's mom—to give me my chance to finally look at it. And as soon as I had the bag, I hurled it into the garbage bin and ducked behind the bin, out of the way of the security camera I knew was situated on the eaves, frantic to see what Maeve had written.

But the first message wasn't from Maeve.

MARIE CURIE

It's the gardener, he has evidence

About us

Motherfucker.

She was goddamn right we had to figure out something to do: kill him. What else *was* there to do?

Okay. I took a deep breath. When I'd left the terrace mere minutes ago, Louisa had been by the pool, talking to some of her parents' friends seemingly without a care. She was safe, for now.

But if he had evidence, that didn't matter. He could throw it all in the middle of the goddamn dinner table if he wanted. Hell, he could nestle it lovingly in a bed of romaine lettuce right on Louisa's dad's plate. Or he could—

MARIE CURIE

But I'll take care of it

I dropped the phone on the lava rocks with a crunch. Not for the first time that night, horror crashed over me like a rogue wave.

She was wrong. The gardener didn't want to expose us. He didn't give a fuck. If he did, he would have done it already. But I knew exactly what he did want.

Oh, I got a mind to do a lot more than see.

And after he did *that*, he'd expose us anyway, just for shits and giggles.

Why, why, why had I ever let Louisa out of my sight?

I knew she cared. Too much. She'd proved it by risking her own neck for me, and to keep me out of the mines, I knew she'd do it again.

But I couldn't let her. Because the price he'd ask wouldn't be her neck. It would be a price too high for her to pay. For *anyone* to pay.

I knew because my mother had paid it.

And of all the fucking awful memories shoved into the far recesses of my brain, it was *that* I was reliving as I stood there, watching the phone as it buzzed angrily in the rocks. Another message was coming in.

This one *was* from Maeve. But the timestamp was hours

ago, as if some tech glitch had prevented it from reaching me until now.

773541N0
You asked how long it would take Resi's people to
free us

Forget about Resi. Forget about her people. She'd said *he's here*, and it was *he* I wanted to know about. I didn't expect Maeve to reply right away, but I sent her a message anyway.

773496S6
I don't care

I'm coming for you

But to my shock, she did reply.

773541N0
No, you don't get it
We can't stop now

773496S6
Why not?! Yes, you can

You have to

You literally told me today that Max Langer
knows what you're doing

773541N0
We can't
Because we have to stop Max
And because we're not just freeing me and the other
girls anymore

"Boy, is that you in there?"

The housekeeper, pounding ever closer. "Stop dawdling, for heaven's sake! Mr. Langer's asking for another cocktail. I'm busy plating these entrees, and if it's not poured in the next thirty seconds, it's my head!"

It was only eight-thirty, but she sounded about ready to collapse, and I didn't blame her. Yes, she was a serious thorn in my side tonight, but she was also carrying this entire goddamn party on her creaky, overburdened middle-aged shoulders, and I sure wasn't pulling *my* weight to help. But that didn't mean I wanted her to find out why.

As fast as I could, I murmured a voice message in Luxembourgish: "Not just freeing you? What are you talking about? Who are you freeing?!"

"Who on earth are you talking to in here?" the housekeeper demanded as she flung open the door.

"Myself," I blurted out. "Sometimes a guy just misses hearing his native tongue, you know?"

Her eyes narrowed, but I knew she was too softhearted to condemn a poor homesick boy. Mostly, I was hoping she didn't notice how my head was swimming. Because Maeve had replied immediately, and before I slipped the phone back in my pocket, I had just enough time to read her answer to *who are you freeing?*

773541N0
Every slave on Earth

11

"Loulou, I need you to check on your mother, please," my father whispered from a few places down.

Fuck. Mom's cocktail hour had started around eleven this morning, so it wasn't surprising that halfway through dinner, she'd gone missing from the table. That meant as usual, Daddy wanted me to go look for her and make sure she hadn't passed out on the floor of the powder room in a disgusting puddle, especially not during a party with our entire family fortune on the line.

It likely also meant going into the garden, which was why I wasn't, yet. Not until I'd spoken to my boy. Not until we'd figured out a plan.

But how? Time was running out. If I didn't find the gardener, *he* would find *us*. And the video would find Daddy. And then it would be too late. And worse, I didn't know if my boy had even seen my message yet. I didn't know if he *would*.

Twilight swallowed the sunset's final glow. Candles flickered in tall glass holders, the firepit crackled, and the pool shimmered, reflecting the firelight and the darkening azure sky. Roasted tamales, peach salad, and chile-crusted branzino with squash puree all made their appearances, the housekeeper no doubt seizing the chance to remind everyone that her master had once had enough money to send her to a high-end culinary academy.

The terrace helpfully had its own bar and kitchen, which meant the slaves didn't have to go back and forth to the house every time someone wanted something. It also meant I was acutely aware of his whereabouts every single second of the evening but still couldn't risk saying any more to him but a *thank you*, even when he'd served me another champagne cocktail as I stood amid a group of my father's friends' kids, or when I'd watched that bold handshake with a man rich and powerful enough to be an effective supervillain was one of the most reckless—and dare I say, sexiest—things I'd ever seen. But it wouldn't matter how sexy it was when my father opened his phone to see a softcore porn video starring his daughter and his slave.

One thing was clear: this couldn't go on. Now that dinner was in full swing, my boy was as rapidly in and out of the kitchen as the other slaves, and I couldn't exactly go chasing after him, pulling him away from his duties and *myself* away from the table. Come to think of it, had he—or the other slaves, for that matter—had a moment's rest all evening, or anything to eat? And why the fuck had that *never* crossed my mind at a party before?

So yes, *that* was all agonizing, but *surely* it couldn't be more so than having to store all the lovely Santa Fe art you'd just bought while waiting for your 1.2 million-dollar home remodeling job to finish, which was the one currently bedeviling the woman sitting next to me, totally oblivious that my focus was

completely and entirely elsewhere. I made polite noises and
pushed back my chair. But before I could leave, I stopped.

"I mean, who would have thought that the most expensive part of a rocket would be the part you throw away?"
asked Langer, who had hardly touched his branzino, the
plates for which the slaves—except for one—were now
quietly clearing away from the dining table. The glow of the
soft tabletop candles and overhead lanterns obscured
Langer's icy blue eyes as he held forth. "When I decided to
invest in Orbital Dynamics, they told me they thought they
could make spaceflight affordable by reusing those parts.
Problem is, they sent up five of them and only two of them
came back, and the ones that came back had their fuselage
gutted like a herring by space debris. Now they tell us it's
going to take months to repair, which you have to admit kind
of undermines the whole concept. And the other partners are
talking about cutting their losses, after twenty years and
billions invested."

"So what you're saying is that it's not economically feasible
to send up these rockets?" asked one of Daddy's colleagues in
dismay.

"Not if you want them to come back," said Langer, leaning
back in his chair.

"It's pretty obvious," said Corey a few places down,
prompting some heads to turn. Much to my relief, *he* was
expending most of his effort that evening sucking his boss's
dick and had temporarily left off worrying about his own. "If we
can look at the data from the rockets that came back intact, we
can see where the holes were made. If the fuselage is destroyed,
logically that's the part whose structural integrity should be
reinforced."

It sure *sounded* smart. All across the table, more heads spun
to look at him. And at the very end, one of the slaves—guess

which one—had paused with three plates balanced in his hand and was clearly listening, too.

"What do you think, kid?" asked Langer, noticing immediately.

"What would he know about it?" snapped Corey. "We're talking about rocket science, not how to load the dishwasher."

His boss ignored him and nodded at my boy.

I sat down.

Every other slave I had ever met, at this point, would have given him the *Oh, it's not my place to say, sir* routine.

But if it wasn't clear already, we were not dealing with every other slave.

"With all due respect, sir—I mean, Max—your intern here has a fantastic idea," he said. "For losing both all the rockets you have left *and* your remaining stockholders."

Corey's face turned an unattractive shade of eggplant. My father practically choked on his wine. "Excuse me?"

Langer held up his hand, shutting my dad up yet again without a word. Holy shit, did money ever talk.

My heart pounded as I reached for my glass of ice water and downed it in a gulp, not daring to look. But it didn't matter. I could have stared right at him if I wanted to. Everyone else at the table was staring at him, too. They were mesmerized. Even the slaves had stopped, whatever they were carrying juggled precariously in their hands.

Even the gardener's threats now seemed minor compared to what was happening. Desperately, I tried to catch his eye, but the glare from the lanterns and candles made it impossible. I had to tell him to stop, to be careful, to have *some* instinct for self-preservation. Jesus, we were already fucked enough tonight. But still balancing the plates, his gaze remained fixed on Langer, the only one there who'd permitted him to speak to him normally. But that wasn't the *only* place he was looking.

"Go on."

No, no, no—

But wait. Did he have a plan? He usually did. And maybe this was part of it. Maybe—

I stared at the bones of my cold, half-eaten branzino, and listened closer, heart pounding, trying to figure it out.

"Well, first, let's assume the lost rockets actually did get hit and didn't just run out of fuel and fall out of the sky because some boy genius on your payroll forgot to carry the one," he said with another veiled glance at Corey, the look on whose face would have been hilarious if it weren't so homicidal. "Forget about the fuselage. You know it can take it. You look where the holes *aren't*. Think about the rockets that didn't come back."

Beside Corey, his parents—how ironic to have such a dyspeptic-looking mother when his father owned an empire of high-end restaurants—began to murmur angrily. His father pushed back his chair.

"Nine times out of ten," my boy continued, "that's going to be where they broke up. Reinforce those areas next time, and they might survive long enough to meet your revenue goals next quarter."

"Okay, that's enough," Corey said. He was a ticking bomb and clearly, the only thing preventing him from detonating was that his would-be-billionaire boss was sitting next to him, rapt. "We get the idea."

My boy didn't even have to wait for Langer this time to signal to him to carry on. "But here's the thing," my boy continued. "Even if by a one-in-a-million chance you get lucky enough to reinforce every single critical portion of your remaining rockets, you still have to face the fact that space is a vast, scary, unpredictable place and you're trying to blast your way through it on the calculations of scientists just out of school, who are probably regurgitating everything they know out of textbooks written decades ago to feed some C-list professor's drug habit."

I couldn't help but giggle at this, horrified as I was.

"See, at some point, whether it's a solar flare, radiation, or killer green space blobs from Mars, you'll find out eventually that the numbers and formulas can only take you so far. They say, follow the science, but eventually, it's not about science anymore. It's a gambit. And it's your move," he finished. "Max."

The table was silent as everyone took a second to pick their jaws up off the floor. His poker face was excellent, though, except for the hand through the hair: his tell. Nobody besides me could have possibly known it, of course. But I couldn't imagine how nervous he must have been; how fast his heart was pounding; the knowledge of what could happen if this plan —whatever it was—went wrong had to be unbearable. But what could I do to help?

"He's right," I said. *No, you idiot, not that,* the smart part of my brain scolded me. The stupid part just went right on talking. "I mean, I study pre-med, not physics or engineering, but speaking from that point of view, if you go into a medical tent during wartime and look at the soldiers recovering, you're going to see a lot of gunshot wounds to the limbs and hardly any to the chest or head. But that doesn't mean you should wear Kevlar on your legs. It's the same principle."

At last, he turned, meeting my eyes dead-on. And there on his face was that beautiful, life-affirming smile I'd been trying to coax out all night. Turned out, making a fool out of his asshole rival and impressing a billionaire hadn't done it for him.

I had.

I smiled back before looking down at my plate again, face aflame.

"Well said, Loulou." Daddy nodded at last.

"All right, then," Langer said slowly. "So then what do we do to fix the holes?"

"I don't know," my boy replied, quickly tearing his eyes away from me. "Slap some duct tape on them? I mean, I'm not a rocket scientist."

That got Langer laughing, and seconds later, my father and most of his friends and colleagues joined in. He used the opportunity to slip back inside the house with the plates. It was all I could do not to run after him and either hug him, kick him in the nuts, or both. It was a miracle that he'd made it away from the table with any skin left on him, talking to free men like that.

I sure couldn't laugh. But at least I could finally breathe.

Corey, however, was barely doing that. He was seething, his knuckles so white on his glass it was astonishing it wasn't already in smithereens.

Langer, for his part, turned to Daddy again. "And all you've got this kid doing is serving drinks? Come on, man. You're breaking my heart. I've told you this over and over. How do you expect buy-in from investors, buy-in from your team, if you can't buy in yourself?"

Meanwhile, my father's eyes were as wide as if a dinosaur had walked through the backyard or a flying saucer had just landed on the roof. He cleared his throat.

"Well, Loulou," he said, "for starters, maybe the boy should be tutoring you in more than just chemistry." He lowered his voice, and for a second, my heart twisted in my chest. Had he noticed how I'd looked at the boy? Or had the gardener gotten to him and—

But no. He was only repeating his request from earlier. "Your mother, please." He looked genuinely worried.

Now I *did* have the urge to start laughing hysterically as I pushed back from the table, but not because anything was funny.

Okay. It was fine. Mom would be upstairs. The gardener wouldn't be up there. He wasn't *allowed* up there. I'd find her, tuck her into bed, and get the hell back to the party as soon as I could. By that time, Rocket Boy would have seen my message, and then we'd come up with a plan to deal with this. He was the smart one. Fuck, he'd just solved a major engineering problem for a Fortune 500 company in five goddamn minutes. He'd know what to do about this.

Ducking behind a mesquite, I pulled out my phone and, heart pounding, tapped out another message to Albert Einstein. Pressed send.

No. What was I doing? For fuck's sake, he didn't have enough on his plate already? He'd barely escaped being chained to a post and flayed alive, and I wasn't even sure he *had* escaped it. Daddy's wine might be calling the shots right now, but it wouldn't be tomorrow. And what about Maeve?

I deleted the message.

I couldn't do it.

He had enough battles to fight. He'd spent his entire *life* fighting.

It was my turn.

I swallowed. My heart was pounding in my ears, but my mind was made up, and I started down the Mom Trail, trying to breathe normally and mostly failing. I had just until I found her to come up with a plan to save us.

Or just save *him.*

I hesitated, glancing at my phone one last time. Was I really going to handle this on my own? Not to mention, I still had no clue what the gardener had meant by *keeping his word.*

But that wasn't enough to stop me.

Tracking Mom was like tracking a wounded animal sometimes. A dropped napkin by the sliding doors led to an abandoned glass of chardonnay on an end table, giving way to a pair of strappy cork wedges lying on their sides by the open pantry door, next to a half-eaten packet of saltine crackers. I went inside, then pushed open the exterior door.

"Mom?" I called, rounding the corner, following a scuffling noise on the lava rocks. "Is that you?"

Nothing.

After darting through the garden, in through the sliding doors, and upstairs, I finally discovered Mom leaning woozily on her bathroom vanity, trying to powder her face but mostly powdering the basin instead. She protested when I arrived, insisting the party was still going and she had to get back to it. After pouring her a glass of water, guiding her to the bed, and settling the covers around her, I started down the stairs. So far so good. I took another deep-as-I-could breath and started back down.

That was until I smacked into a tall form standing silently in the doorway of my father's study, skin translucent and alien in the light of the moon.

"Looks like I wasn't the only one making deals tonight."

HIM

What?

Something must have been lost in Maeve's translation. The SLA had *tried* freeing all slaves, thirty years ago, and failed epically. All those poor bastards—save for Louisa's professor, apparently—were in the mines, or dead, or most likely both. No one had tried since.

Mistranslation or not, this Resi woman knew *something*. Something about what Max Langer—and maybe my master— were plotting with the microchips. Something she was trying to stop. Something that Max Langer *knew* she was trying to stop.

And now she was in his crosshairs. And also thanks to me, so was my sister.

And so was I.

But I didn't serve causes. I served science and logic because those were the only ways to win. *Think several moves ahead, boy, not just the one in front of you.* This was about Maeve and only Maeve.

Back on the terrace, the announcement was official. The deal between Wainwright-Phillips and Langer had been cemented. The toasts had been made. It was time for more expensive liquor and cigars around the outdoor firepit. The men were congratulating themselves on being captains of industry; the slaves were inside washing dishes, except for me.

Me? I had saved billions of dollars in rocket fuselage, humiliated the biggest douchebag I knew, criticized and even outright insulted several rich, powerful free men, and lived to tell the tale. More importantly, my plan had worked. I may have no skin left on my back tomorrow, but I'd kept Louisa safe at the table for five minutes, five minutes where the gardener couldn't touch her, and she couldn't touch him.

But now as I exited the kitchen expecting to see her face, my eyes flitted to every corner of the terrace, and a cold knot of panic twisted in my gut. She wasn't in any of them. Where the hell was she? My breath hitched, heart thudding as if I'd been sucker punched. In the five seconds I'd taken to check her message, she must have slipped out.

So fuck the housekeeper. Fuck this party. Fuck cleaning up and fuck being a good, obedient little slave.

Only one thing mattered: finding her before *he* did. Or before she found *him*.

I shot down the dimly lit garden path, darting between the mesquites and palo verdes and the distant hooting of a desert owl, nearly drowned out by my heart drumming desperately in my ears. I knew exactly where I was headed.

But before I could even reach the garden shed, the door creaked open, and I nearly dropped the phone. The gardener's bulky shadow fell over me, his body blocking off the doorway, his presence thick with a kind of sludgy, satisfied calm that made me want to retch. "Whatcha doin', boy?" he drawled, leaning casually against the frame, bracing himself on a spade. "Looking for candy?"

"Where the fuck is she?" I growled as I slammed him into a wall full of garden tools, sending spades and shovels clattering to the ground, veins pumping with bloodlust for this mother-fucker. "And where's the evidence? You've got two seconds to tell me before I gut you with your own pitchfork."

He just chuckled and shrugged, even as I tightened my grip on his filth-coated windpipe. "Don't got it no more."

"What?"

"Gave it all up," he rasped. "To Mr. Langer, that is. To get myself a much better deal."

I froze.

The cold whisper. The icy blue eyes. The lean-in. *She might find herself exposed.*

I'd had it all wrong.

The gardener was still wheezing like a demented hyena in my grip. "Looks like you got your lines crossed, boy."

I tossed him aside like a garbage bag, gaping down in horror at my phone, then back up at the sleazy idiot's grin oozing across his face as I took off running *back* toward the house at full speed. "Don't get too comfortable in there, asshole," I shouted before I left. "I'm coming back."

But amazingly, he was only my tertiary concern now. Because Langer *was* onto me, and he *had* made a threat, and he *did* know everything.

But not about Maeve.

About Louisa and me.

HER

Max Langer's icy blue eyes raked me up and down like shiny blades as he opened the patio door and ushered me outside. He wore a faint smirk on his pale lips, which still looked cool and almost otherworldly in the blue moonlight.

I swallowed hard and crossed my arms in front of my chest as if I had anything to hide in my high-necked dress, and forced myself to stay calm. "What are you talking about?"

Langer raised an eyebrow, clearly amused by my attempt at composure. "Just that you and dear Rocket Boy won't be seeing your dentally challenged friend again for a long time, and by that, I mean ever. So you can enjoy each other's company unmolested, if you'll forgive the expression."

My knees practically buckled.

He knew. Max Langer knew. How? Why? I—

"What did you do, kill him?" I gasped.

"Oh no," he replied, waving dismissively. "I mean, I'm not opposed to killing people, but the messy stuff isn't usually my first resort."

"Did you buy him, then?"

"Oh. I forgot you weren't there when the whole 'disrupting slavery' thing came up. Nah, not interested. No, really, we just had a nice little chat in the garden over a glass of some of his artisan, small-batch, triple-distilled spirits, where I convinced him that there might be a better use for his talents than blackmail. He'll be gone by tonight."

"What are you two up to back here?"

I inhaled and whirled around, only to see my father emerge from the other side of the house holding a glass and a smoldering cigar. I took a step back dizzily, my heart screaming in my chest hard enough to topple me. I was trapped. *We* were trapped.

Meanwhile, Langer just grinned casually. "So I found out something about your daughter tonight, Keith." He threw an arm around my shoulder, though I was shaking so hard it was probably making *him* vibrate. "Something I found very interesting. And no doubt something *you'd* find even more interesting."

Here it was. Over as soon as it started. That boy who had held me like I was the only good thing he'd ever found in this world was about to find out that with one touch, I'd *destroyed* that world. That I'd destroyed *him*. That he'd be cursing my name for the rest of his short, brutal life toiling at the bottom of a mine shaft in chains and—

"She has a very shrewd business mind. In fact, I think medicine might not be her true calling." Langer turned to me, shamelessly looking my body up and down again while distracting my father by talking about my brain. "Never too late to switch to the school of management, you know." He winked.

Daddy chuckled and puffed his cigar.

What?

"Well, Max—" Daddy began before looking up in surprise at a noise from deeper in the gardens. And just when I thought this little confab couldn't get any weirder, a fourth member sprinted up the manicured garden path, launching it from weird clean into Bizarro World.

My boy had finally found me.

While Langer looked alien in the moonlight, *he* looked like some translucent, ethereal creature of the mist, except for the wild look of sheer terror in his eyes and the way his broad shoulders heaved as he tried to catch his breath, reminding me that he'd been bearing the weight of the world on them all night—and long before that, too.

And that was all *before* he saw his master standing there.

"Sir." He took an instant step back from the rest of us and bowed his head as he visibly probed his brain for an appropriately slavish explanation for why he was here. "I was just—uh —tidying up the garden paths before the guests noticed." For a split second each, his eyes darted to me, then to Daddy, then to Langer, then down again, his gears turning as the poor guy tried to figure out just what the hell was going on and whether it would in any way involve him being put in chains and dragged off to die in a mine.

Daddy opened his mouth, an unmistakable remember-your-place-boy look on his face, but before he could say anything, Langer smoothly interjected. "A rocket scientist *and* a landscape engineer? Keith, you've hit the jackpot with your daughter *and* your slave. You're a lucky, lucky man," he said with an awed shake of his head. "The three of us were just going to meet back here to talk about the best ways to improve the irrigation system on that Central American banana farm I inherited. I mean, with little Loulou's studies in biology and your boy's familiarity with physical sciences *and* groundskeeping, I thought they were just the minds for the job." He glanced at my father with a disarming smile.

"But—" my father stammered, befuddled, smoke wisping around his head.

For fuck's sake, Daddy, just stop saying things. Please. I'm begging you.

Langer stepped in again, though. "Why don't you go grab another glass of that Anejo I suggested?" Langer nodded at Daddy's glass, releasing me and almost bodily redirecting my father back toward the terrace. "In fact, tell the maid I'll take another, too. We'll just finish up back here."

And Daddy left. Miracle of fucking miracles. What was *happening*?

Only Langer could answer, so it was no surprise that both me and my boy were now staring straight at him, waiting for him to do just that.

"What?" he asked innocently. "Oh. You're probably wondering what happened to that charming little device Big Toothless Joe was using to blackmail you." He reached into the silken inner pocket of his crisp, perfect cerulean suit jacket and removed the grubby, taped-up tablet. He casually tossed it to me.

"Ew," I said as it flew toward me. Instead of catching it, I kicked it onto the lava rocks. "I don't want that thing anywhere near me."

"Yeah, I don't blame you. I plan to burn this suit," he said, wiping his hand on the side of his pants in disgust. "Oh, and"— he pulled out a crumpled piece of paper in his pocket and uncrumpled it: a map printout—"this belongs to you, kid."

"Thanks," my boy said in a daze, accepting it and shoving it in his pocket.

It was now shockingly, alarmingly, disturbingly clear: This man had just saved our lives.

"Why are you doing this?" I asked.

Langer took a step closer, his glacial eyes studying me. "Call it a tip for the top-notch dinner entertainment," he said with a mild smirk at Rocket Boy. "Plus, I just have a soft spot for people in trouble, especially when they're trying to do the right thing. I shouldn't. I'd be twice as rich as I am now if I didn't. But I do."

"But—" my boy started.

"There's no strings attached, by the way, and no, I didn't watch the video. I like my porn sets a bit classier. Just a personal preference." He held up his hands. "No offense."

"None taken," said my boy in a daze.

"Well," Langer added with finality, dusting off his hands with a white-hot glint in his cold blue eyes, "I'll let you guys go at it—sorry, get to it. If you ever need anything else, you know where to find me, kid." He leaned in low and murmured something in what sounded like German, something that made my boy's eyes widen under his long lashes. And to my surprise, he *responded*—in the same language.

Straightening up, Langer chuckled and clapped him on the shoulder, then turned to leave, pausing just long enough to throw us a final glance before dissipating back into the moonlight. "Stay safe," he said. "Wouldn't want to see you two end up right back here."

12

"I came as soon as I could get away," he said the second Langer was gone, holding me at arm's length, clearly examining me for injuries. "Are you—"

"I am. Nothing happened. It's okay. We're okay."

"But we—" he protested, gaze fixed darkly on where Langer had disappeared.

"Listen to me," I said, reaching up to push back a lock of his shimmering moonlit hair, something a second ago I didn't believe I'd ever do again because I didn't believe he'd ever *see* moonlight again. He relaxed into the touch ever so slightly, which gave me hope and let me breathe. "*We're okay.*"

"For now," he admitted grudgingly.

"Now is good enough," I murmured, moving toward him, exhausted and more than ready to collapse in his arms and maybe his lips, but he gestured for me to step into the shadow under the eave of the house.

I shrugged, confused.

"Camera," he explained, pointing upward. "I cased it ahead

of time to be safe, and I'll disable it as soon as I get the chance. We got lucky this time, Lou. Really lucky. But if this is going to work," he said with a resolute sigh, "we have to be more careful."

I looked closer. In the moonlight, he'd looked almost angelic; up close, though, he was clearly exhausted. He probably hadn't had a moment's rest, or maybe even a bite to eat, since I'd left him downstairs. The stress of walking the thin line between praise and a flogging—or kisses and the mines— hadn't been easy on him, either. Hell, I'd been willing to throw myself to the wolves so he wouldn't *have* to walk it anymore. But when he finally pulled me close, his expression had given way to pure enchantment. I relaxed. He was okay.

"So this is it," he breathed into my ear, his lips ghosting over my neck, composure suddenly regained.

"So do you like the dress?" I whispered shyly.

I quivered as his hands slowly, methodically slid around the open back of my dress, under the edges of the fabric, brushing the lace of my black lace panties and tracing the perimeter of my waist, exploring all the places I'd hoped they would end up when I'd slipped into that dress what felt like a million years ago.

"You know damn well I've been waiting for this moment all fucking night," he murmured.

"Well, start believing, Rocket Boy." I covered his scarred, graceful, powerful hands with mine, intertwining our fingers as they gently came to rest on my hips. "Speaking of rockets, I think Corey's planning to launch one directly at your head."

"That means it'll probably come down somewhere in Outer Mongolia, so I think I'll be fine."

I giggled, then sobered. "By the way, never, *ever* do that again, okay? You scared the shit out of me out there. I thought I was going to have to watch—well. By the way, you didn't find it worth mentioning that you speak German?"

"No less worth mentioning than that I speak French."

"What? Wait." I counted in my head, so stunned that I forgot to ask him what Langer had said. "So that makes—"

"Four," he said as if it were no big deal. "Well, five, if you count 'back to work, slave' and 'yes, sir' in Romanian."

Jesus. I scanned his face to make sure this was dark humor before proceeding. All clear.

"*Eh, bien, merde,*" I exclaimed. "*Je le parle aussi. On aurait pu converser en français tout ce temps, n'est-ce pas?*"[1]

Without warning, he effortlessly scooped me up and dipped my head low enough that my curls brushed the lava rocks, making me giggle in surprise.

"*Bien sûr, ma chérie, mais tu ne me l'as jamais demandé.*"[2]

"Let's see," I said. "Modern languages, rocket science, and camera demolition. What else? Music?"

"Actually, I used to play some piano."

And just as I was wondering how he'd managed to find multiple new ways to turn me on just *tonight*.

"Are *you* okay, though?" he asked, of all things.

I took a deep breath. It was time to reveal what I'd kept from him earlier.

"I heard the gardener threatening you the other night," I said. "And he—he cornered me at the top of the stairs. That was what started this whole thing."

"I fucking knew it," he growled. "I *knew* it. Did he hurt you? I'll fucking kill him." It's like he was trying to get ten thoughts out all at once while simultaneously looking for a sharp knife.

---

1. Well, shit. I speak it, too. You mean, we could have been conversing in French this whole time?

2. Of course, my dear, but you never asked.

"Calm down," I said, placing my hands on his heaving shoulders, not sure whether to be scared or ridiculously turned on. "Nothing happened. I'm fine. Everything's fine. He's gone now. We'll never see him again."

"*I'll s*ee him again because I'm going to track him down and strangle him with his own garden hose as soon as I get the chance. And anyone else who hurts you."

"Wait. Really?" No one had ever said that to me before. Then again, I'd never lived the kind of life where anyone would have to.

But that was the only kind of life he'd ever lived.

"Really," he said, pulling me closer, hands snaking protectively around my waist as if it were the most natural thing in the world. And somehow, it was. "I didn't get that 'dangerous' label for nothing, you know," he murmured cheekily into my ear. "Anyway, the real question is, why is this the first time you're telling me about this?"

"I just ... I didn't think it was anything you wanted me involved in."

"Well, frankly, no, it wasn't. But now that I know you know, why didn't you *tell* me? I could have warned you to stay away from him, and this whole thing never would have—"

"I *always* stayed away from him," I said, bristling slightly. "I've been dealing with him a lot longer than you have. And yes, it *would* have happened because he had a fucking video feed set up in the goddamn basement! Anyway, it doesn't matter now. What I want to know is if you ... had some kind of agreement with him." I kicked the grass, not sure I should even mention this and risk killing the moment we'd been fighting all night for and just won. "He said something about keeping your word."

"There was no agreement," he said immediately. "He tried to get me to do something for him. I refused. He wasn't happy."

He didn't mention anything about the map printout Langer

had handed him, and I decided not to, either. For some reason, I doubted I'd get a satisfactory answer. I hugged myself and stared at the lava rocks my heels were digging into. "You'd better be telling me the truth."

"Or what? You'll whip me?"

I was horrified to realize how domineering my tone had sounded—one I hadn't used with him in a long time. "Look, I'm sorry. I didn't mean that. I'm just—I'm worried about you."

"It's not your job to worry about me, Lou," he said, then added, "It's no one's job to worry about me."

I groaned. "Haven't we had this conversation before?"

He sighed and turned away. "Yeah. We have."

"Well, then you know that this isn't going to work if you're going to be like that."

"Oh, if *I'm* going to be like that?" he demanded. "What about *you*?"

"I said I'm sorry!" Then I buried my face in my hands. "Why do we always start arguing at exactly this time of night?"

To my relief, he laughed. "I'm sorry, too. And now I've made more genuine apologies in the past twenty-four hours than I have in my entire life, and you're right. We seem to do much better in the daytime. In bedrooms. And basements." He covered my hands with his and gently pried them loose from my face, and there, at last, was that beautiful smile again, right in front of my eyes, and completely, totally for me. But his expression turned serious again just as quickly, and now here we were, tempting fate and kissing all over again as if we hadn't had our first taste of each other's lips earlier that day.

But he pulled back, tucking a curl behind my ear. "From now on, no one touches you but me, yeah?" He was half-telling, half-asking.

I nodded. "But remember," I teased, "you're not allowed to touch me either."

He leaned in close, exhaling two words. "Watch me."

And he took my lips between his teeth, his mouth almost as aggressive on mine as his urge to kill the gardener had just been.

Well, shit. He was *claiming* me.

It seemed absurd, given who he was, but I still melted into his claim, letting his tongue explore the hollows of my mouth as if I were an empire to conquer. When he finally pulled back, satisfied, he nipped at my lip one more time, grazing it just enough to make me gasp for more.

"In fact, I suggest we find a way to get back there as soon as we can," he said.

"To a bedroom," I breathed, "or a basement?"

"Well, they each have their advantages." His head was back where I wanted it to be—in the crook of my neck, his hair mussed and brushing softly against my skin as he nibbled and licked his way down my jawline.

"Like what?" I said, my hand grazing down the buttons of that black dress shirt and over his belt, plunging lower, mildly terrified at what I would find. But he had already decided I needed to know, and his fingers curled around my wrist to guide me lower, then lower, until my fingertip rested over the hardness straining against his pants. And miraculously, thrillingly, I started to wonder if the moment I'd dreamed of since I'd left him in the basement might actually happen right *now*.

"Well, for starters," he said, his voice somewhere between a purr and a growl as his tongue lapped at my collarbone, "in a bedroom, we could actually lie down."

"And in a basement?" I breathed, not sure how the mere *idea* of being horizontal with him was exciting me so much.

"Less chance of the rest of the house hearing your screams of ecstasy."

"Mine?" I whispered. "What about *yours*?" I demanded, stroking him through the twill fabric. "Can't you see I'm trying to even up the score here?"

"Don't be ridiculous, young lady. It's not a competition. But I *am*"—his yawn interrupted him—"winning."

Shit. "Look at you," I scolded gently, pulling away. "You're too exhausted for sex."

"Well, we both know that's impossible," he joked.

"I'm serious! And let me guess," I continued. "You haven't eaten tonight, either."

"That's not true. I had two grapes."

"Dammit," I muttered, cursing myself. An hour ago, there had been more than enough food left. If only I'd found a way to save him one of the sopapilla cheesecakes or chili shrimp cups or whatever the hell they'd been serving. *Something.* "I'm sorry. You need *food*. I should have *brought* you something. I can—"

"I'm not your pet to feed, Lou."

I gasped at the implication. Was that really what he thought I wanted him to be? The thought of the box of pralines, still untouched in my desk drawer upstairs, flashed in my mind. "No, you're a *human being* who gets hungry like anyone else. And I—"

"It's fine," he insisted. "I'll get some leftovers from the housekeeper."

Still, I knew why he was wary. I'd been both horrified and insanely jealous of that condescending old bitch, the wife of his owner, slipping him sweets through the chain-link fence like biscuits to a caged puppy. But at the same time, there was some part of me that desperately wanted that to be *me*.

But he *didn't* want that. He'd been owned enough. Before I could think about it any further, he grabbed me and pressed himself against the side of the house, pulling me in with him. I turned my body around to look where he was looking, my back still nestled tight against him, heart pounding in time with his.

"It's Langer," he muttered. "He's headed out to the garden."

"So what? Maybe he's just admiring the landscaping. What is your problem with him, anyway?" I demanded.

"What do you mean?" He pulled back.

"He gave us the tablet. He left and made sure the gardener left, too. He *saved* us. And he didn't tell Daddy."

"That's because he doesn't care. Not about what we did, anyway. You think Max Langer, with his aged tequila and private jets and fucking ... *banana farms*, gives a fuck about me touching you? That he's like your dad? Or like Corey the Douche?"

"Well, no, but—"

"We're a bargaining chip to him, that's all. And mark my words, he's going to cash it in. Maybe not tomorrow, or the day after, but he will. And he's going to make a fuckton off it because he's not a billionaire by accident."

"What if he doesn't?"

"Come on, Lou. You're not *that* naive."

I folded my arms. "I *am* pretty naive, actually. But—think about tonight," I pointed out. "Were you not there at the dinner table tonight? Did you not hear what I heard?"

"Not only did I hear it, I believe I was saying most of it," he remarked. But his eyes softened minutely as if he *almost* wanted to believe I had a point.

"I know, and you were absolutely brilliant, so what are you so concerned about? I mean, the guy treated you like—like—"

"Like a person?" he finished. "Oh, wow, he let me look him in the eye and call him by his name. Let's give him the Nobel Peace Prize."

I buried my head in his chest, chagrined. As usual, it had

taken him seconds to completely call me out on my biases. "I'm sorry."

He laughed a little and kissed my forehead. "Don't be. You were doing it before it was cool."

"He might even find a way to get rid of slavery altogether," I said in a small voice. "He might—"

"He's not what he pretends to be," he interrupted. "Trust me on this."

"Why should I, when you won't even tell me how you know?"

He paused. "Because it's safer for you if I don't."

I gave up, for now. I knew that the notion that he'd failed to protect his mother and his sister— as if there was anything he could have done—still haunted him. It wasn't surprising he'd prefer not to add me to the list. No wonder he'd reacted violently when I'd told him about the gardener threatening me —he *was* violent. The proof was all in his file.

Still, as privileged as I felt to be on any list of people he gave a damn about, which I suspected could probably fit on a Post-it with room to spare, he had to know I didn't need it. Right? Hell, I'd come this close to throwing myself on the sword for *him*. "You can't protect me from everything, you know."

"I know," he said. "All too well."

"Even if you were free, you couldn't."

He still stared out into the darkness, at the beyond. "It wouldn't hurt."

HIM

By the time I dragged myself back to the terrace, I'd long since seen Louisa safely off to bed, assuring her I was perfectly fine and not to worry. Speaking of hidden talents, I should have mentioned acting, considering I was ravenous, my entire body ached, and I was about five seconds away from collapsing in a heap on the tile. Worst of all, it had cost me my chance to get off.

Just as frustratingly, the other slaves had devoured most of the leftovers while I was outside, leaving only some squash on a small plate the housekeeper apologetically handed me. I almost preferred nothing. I choked it down and scolded myself for being awfully picky for someone who used to subsist on gruel. But it did zero to take the edge off and I was already kicking myself for declining whatever Louisa had been about to offer.

But I was also glad I had because, from her, it would mean something. Because what I *had* with her meant something—the kind of something I didn't even have a name for yet; the kind where her tiny but steel-plated voice piping up across the dinner table was enough to make me momentarily forget that I was likely seconds away from being taken out back and flayed alive. Plus, I didn't want her thinking that from now on, she'd have to worry about my diet, my sleep habits, and my sexual satisfaction—naturally, just the third one would be more than enough.

Oh, and I didn't want her to feel betrayed when she found out everything I still hadn't told her: like that her father was probably helping Max Langer with some diabolical plan to torture slaves, that Max Langer had my sister, and that my sister thought she had joined some revolutionary movement to free us all. If Louisa knew all of that *and* heard what he'd said to me in German, maybe she'd understand why I still thought he was evil.

Nice tits, but seems like a handful. If you ever need any pointers on how to handle her ...

No wonder he and the gardener got along. Still, he'd saved us. Without him, I'd be on my way to a mine already, and

Louisa would be on her way to either ruin or slavery. And that outweighed all the crassness and misogyny in the world.

For now.

As I passed by the lounge chairs, the redhead who had been eye-fucking me earlier, whose name I'd overheard as Pauline, crooked her finger at me, the pink cocktail in her hand sloshing dangerously as she leaned back, a sly smile on her lips.

"Ma'am?"

"Come here, sweet boy," she drawled, holding out one of the chili-chocolate truffles between her purple enameled finger-nails. "I know they never feed you guys properly at these things. Go on, take it."

I froze, eyeing the treat. My stomach twisted and not just from hunger.

"Come on now, don't be shy," she cooed, waving it just inches from my face. "Kneel down and take it like a good boy."

I knew what she meant and it was demeaning as fuck, but I'd done it before, and God, what about my life—up until recently—wasn't? It was right there, the sweet cocoa aroma irresistible, the hunger unbearable, but I couldn't. There was no way.

And I wondered what Pauline would think if she knew why.

Thankfully, I still knew how to handle these bitches so they wouldn't make trouble for me. "It's *very* tempting, ma'am, don't get me wrong," I managed along with a half-smile, hoping the flattery would be just enough to shut her up, "but I'm not allowed to eat while I'm working."

Her smile turned into a smirk. "Suit yourself," she said, popping the chocolate between her rich-girl-red lips.

Back to the kitchen, where I actually dared to hope I might be done for the night. No such luck, as usual. The housekeeper sent me to bring the rest of the liquor bottles from the outdoor bar, blow out the candles, and flick off the torches and lanterns, which she hoped would gently suggest to the remaining guests to get the hell out.

The terrace had gone silent except for some terrible, tinny music coming from someone's phone and the occasional chuckle from some lounge chairs that had been pushed together in a semicircle. A few mostly male guests still sat by the pool. Cigar smoke drifted through the air.

I tried to go unnoticed as I made my way around the edge of the pool and over to the bar. I'd thought it was empty at first, but in the gloom, the orange glow of the lit end of a cigar was unmistakable.

Corey stood with his face shrouded in semi-darkness, smoke curling around his head, a livid and all-too-familiar look in his eyes. Was it too late to pretend I hadn't seen him?

"You're not a fucking rocket scientist, slave," he said, just low enough that no one but me would hear. "You're not even a person. You're a thing. You cost less than my cheapest fucking watch. And you do not humiliate me."

"No, you seem to be doing all right on your own," I replied, one of the rejoinders I'd been dying to make all night—and soon to become one of the many I'd instantly regret.

His hand shot out and grabbed my wrist over my chain bracelet, pinned it to the counter and pressed the searing end of the cigar to the center of my palm.

"Shut up," he hissed. "You fight or make a fucking sound and I'll say you attacked me. A whipping is the least of what you'll get."

I desperately shoved down the urge to throw him off. It wouldn't help. All it would do was attract attention, none of it good. I'd be in the wrong, as a slave always was, and Corey would walk away the innocent victim.

All I could do was blink and breathe against the pain: blistering at first, then strangely, eerily cool as it ate through what felt like a dozen layers of skin, moment by endless moment.

Then it was gone. He released me, leaving behind the red, throbbing mess that had become my palm.

"Next time you forget where you belong, this should help you remember."

I slumped against the countertop and cradled my hand, the pain stabbing into my flesh as if the lit end were still embedded there. All my wit and cleverness had left me. I was praying now only for the simplest of things: for Corey to leave, for cold running water to salvage what was left of my skin, for food, to rest my mind and body, and let this night finally pass into oblivion. Instead, I followed his line of sight to the full bottle of eighteen-year-old bourbon sitting on the bar; the rare, prized one that a colleague had brought Wainwright-Phillips to celebrate the deal.

He pried off the cap and took a long swig, his Adam's apple bobbing. He wiped his mouth, recapped it, and paused, a slow, cruel smirk forming on his lips. "Hey, this is good stuff." He raised his arm and smashed the entire thing on the granite countertop, tiny shards of glass and red-gold liquor flying to every corner of the terrace and into the water like amber rain. "Now it's garbage. You can think about that word while you're cleaning it up."

Weakly, I watched him plumb around in his pocket. And for some reason, like they always did, my sister's words came back to me.

All of us

Unlike me, Maeve talked about freedom. She may have called it a story, but I knew, deep down, she believed. Believed the same way she believed in white-winged horses that could fly her away. *Don't you ever think about being free, Brudderhäerz? Don't you care?* She would always scold me in idle moments.

Well, sure, I cared. I cared about *her*. As for me, like I said, freedom wouldn't hurt. But in the interest of surviving day to day, I rarely thought about it. I never expected to be free. Hell, I didn't expect to live long enough.

But other people—rich, powerful people—cared a lot. Cared about keeping us slaves, that is. Forever.

"Hey. Slave." Corey whistled at me as if to a dog.

And I did look up at him from under my exhausted eyelids because what else could I do?

But Corey said nothing. Instead, he tossed a small object on the intricate tile by my feet, where it clattered softly with a metallic sound, leaving a dark mark where it fell. "Here's something else to help you remember your place. And your sister's."

Slowly, I gaped down at the tiny, intact steel chain with its ID tag, etched with a number only slightly less familiar than my own, looking exactly how I remembered it on Maeve's slim wrist—except for the fresh blood smeared messily across the surface, drying and crusting in the grooves.

"Courtesy of Max Langer."

Wait, so *is* Max a villain or isn't he? Find out in *Never Bound:* The Unchained Book Two, coming in spring 2025. Turn to the next section for an excerpt!

And by the way, remember Louisa's childhood friend Rebekah, that walking, talking cautionary tale for getting involved with slave boys? Lou and her friends never found out what really happened in that treehouse, but now you can. *Riven,* a 20,000-word prequel novella set in both the past and the present, sets the record straight — and you can get it for free when you sign up for my newsletter. To sign up, scan the QR code or visit everlyclaire.com.

Of course, you can unsubscribe and keep the free book, but if you stick around, you'll also get ARC opportunities and give-aways, and be the first to find out about every new release before it happens. If you like dark worlds, forbidden love, and protective bad boys with a habit of getting chained up, come connect with me!

FROM CHAPTER ONE OF NEVER BOUND

HER

Who did this to you?

I noticed the blistering crater on his palm almost as soon as he entered my room on Monday, mostly because he was trying desperately—and not very gracefully—to hide it. Only one question came to mind, of course. But I didn't ask it.

Just let it go, his eyes seemed to plead when they met mine. *Nothing good can come of knowing.* And I did let it go, as much as I hated to do it. After all, it wasn't the first time someone had hurt him, and it wouldn't be the last. And why the hell was I telling myself that to make myself feel *better*?

The burn would simply join the growing list of things I couldn't ask about, like why he was still convinced Max Langer was the devil incarnate instead of the only party guest who'd treated him like a person. And where his sister was. And whether she was okay. And if she wasn't, whether saving her would in any way involve him running away and leaving me forever, just as we were finally starting to feel a little bit safe.

I didn't want to know the answer. I already *knew* the

answer. Borrowing more time didn't make the time any less borrowed.

Sunday usually meant some downtime for the slaves, and I'd been grateful for it on his behalf, though it hurt that we couldn't spend it together. However, I'd really outdone myself on Saturday, when I'd reluctantly let Juliette come over to hang by the pool. November in the Valley wasn't exactly pool weather anymore, but laying out during the heat of the day, flipping through fashion magazines—or my chemistry notes hidden inside a magazine, a certain someone would be pleased to know—was feasible. What was also feasible was choosing a laughably skimpy black-and-white string bikini I'd only ever worn on spring break—far, far away from my parents and the unceremoniously-departed gardener. And waiting until my chosen mark passed by the pool on his way to some quite-possibly-fictional chore. Of course, I let the strings casually slide off my shoulders as if I'd simply forgotten to tie them.

My only reward for all of that feasibility? Watching how fast his head swiveled. But that was more than enough—and what made it especially cute was that the poor guy probably thought he was being subtle about it.

Meanwhile, of course, I was keeping a running mental list of everything I wanted to do to him and for him as soon as we had some unstructured time. The problem was, we never had any. Even when we *weren't* being blackmailed, the only hours we ever had together were when we were supposed to be doing something else. Plus, we still had five more chapters to review before the exam and only an hour to spare for each, and if you thought sitting at the desk fighting the unbearable urge to touch each other was awkward, try sitting there knowing you *could* touch each other at any time, and why the hell weren't you doing it?

"So, I know we've gone over elimination reactions a million

times," he began professorially after he entered the room, closed the door, and sat down with no flirting, no witty comments, not even one of those seemingly ordinary looks throbbing with tension hidden meaning. What was with that? "But you also have to remember that they look a bit different when it's a modified alcohol like a methyl group, so I want to look over those with you today, and—fuck, that bikini you were wearing on Saturday could fit in a coin purse."

He barely glanced up from the book, just shook some hair off his face and gave the tiniest, coyest glance back to check my reaction.

I collapsed on the desk in relief. "I was wondering when you were going to say something." I glanced longingly at the sunburst-shaped wall clock over my bed. "Ugh, how the hell are we supposed to get by with only an hour a day for studying *and* everything else?"

"Well, luckily for you, I lived in Germany, where they know a thing or two about time management," he remarked, glancing at the clock himself before meeting my gaze with an unspoken proposal. *"Also, mach schnell, Fräulein.*[1] Are you ready for this?"

"Ready? I've only been trying to do this for the last three days. And I still prefer French."

He gave me another teasing half-smile as his hand gently took mine, guiding it the rest of the way over the fabric of his shorts and up his inner thigh. He was already hard.

"With you, it doesn't take much," he whispered in response to my little bounce of surprise. "And if you'd ever paid any attention to what was happening *under* the desk, you'd know that."

"I was trying to concentrate on chemistry, just like *you* were supposed to be," I said indignantly.

---

1. So hurry up, young lady.

"Oh, I was," he assured me. "I'm just saying, there's no reason why our approach to the material couldn't stand to be a bit more ... holistic." He glanced at the clock again and snapped his fingers. "Shit. We're behind. I should have taken it out thirty seconds ago."

I giggled as he immediately reached down and took care of that. After some adjusting under the desk—no peeking—I found my fingers curled around the hard, solid length of him. Time seemed to stand still in the silent room as I let it sink in. And he just let me cup it there, as if the weight of my fingers was, for now, just enough to make him perfectly happy. As for what came next, though?

"I—"

"Stop." He put a finger to my lips. He must have sensed something—my hesitance, my performance anxiety, my sexual imposter syndrome. "Is this your first one?"

"Well—" I blushed.

"Yes? No? Sort of?" he tried to help me along.

"Sort of."

He nodded with finality. "Okay. We can work with that."

"But I want to make it good for you."

He folded his hand—his unblistered hand—expertly over both of mine, guiding the movement of my fingers. I flexed and curled them as I brushed up and down that magnificent sculpted shaft that it would be a crime *not* to touch.

"Lou, your hand is on my dick. To me, even the *idea* of that is amazing."

That made me smile, and after he got me started, I began to drum my fingers lightly while pumping with both hands, and his entire body seemed to melt deeper into the wicker chair. "Fuck, you look beautiful like that. Do we *really* have to study today?"

I laughed and twisted lightly as I stroked, brushing my

thumb over the tip, pleased by the fluid already trickling out. My hands trailed the wetness up the shaft, encouraged by the strange, beautiful combination of contented sighs and amazed whimpers I was hearing.

"Just a bit more pressure, yeah?" he said through labored breath.

I added my other hand and meditated on the mystery of maybe—if not making up for the blister on his hand—making him feel even half as incredible as he'd made me feel the other day in the basement and pretty much always. We didn't have time to lie down—hell, we didn't really have time to do *this*—but God he looked happy and that was good enough.

"Oh, that feels so fucking perfect, Lou, you have no idea," his voice wavered.

"As good as you imagined?"

"So much better. And you were *worried?* You're fucking good at this. Just keep going."

I shifted to the edge of my chair for a better grip, hand over hand, keeping to the rhythm he was reveling in and that was making me feel ... powerful? Beautiful? Not useless? Jesus, who knew a quickie hand job could do all of that?

"I'm close," he choked out. "But I forgot—"

"On it." Like lightning, I swiveled the desk chair toward the nightstand, just close enough to grab some tissues while still keeping up the strokes. Even as he shuddered, groaned, and exploded into the tissues, my body relaxed. I balled up and tossed the evidence away while he cleanly replaced everything as if none of it had ever happened. I exhaled, cutting the strings of tension in my body. A promise fulfilled.

"What were you so worried about, young lady? You know you always earn your gold star." He motioned me forward with a blissful, contented sigh, cupping my chin and lightly kissing my forehead, my nose, and finally my lips. As he pulled back and let me fall into his golden eyes, the bedroom melted away. Even the walls of the house seemed to topple, the desert crumbled, and for a second, we stood face to face, on a hill of wavering golden grass. Somewhere where we didn't ever have to look at the clock.

"So," he said, snapping us both out of the spell. He turned his attention sheepishly back to the desk, scanning the papers and notes spread out all over it before grabbing the chemistry book and frantically flipping through pages. "Should we start studying?"

"Yeah," I said. "I mean, I guess that *is* why we're here."

HIM

It would take a very special kind of asshole to sneak onto the computer of the dirty-minded angel who had just improvised the under-the-desk hand job of my dreams — one I obviously couldn't turn down, or she'd *really* know something was wrong.

And I was about to become that asshole. But a douchebag, a cigar, and a broken bourbon bottle had made it clear that my sister's life may depend on it. And I had to believe that it did still depend on it, that I hadn't failed again. After all, she'd replied to my messages, so she had to have been alive when Corey had arrived at the party with her bracelet. That gave me hope that it wasn't too late.

But if it *was* too late, my job was to burn everything and everyone responsible for it. So sneaking onto a laptop shouldn't seem like much at all.

And it wouldn't, if it were anyone's laptop but hers.

There was some good news—other than my orgasm, that is —and that was that so far nobody had demanded to know why I'd been out by the pool all night on Friday with a mop, broom, and headlamp I'd found in a storage closet, cleaning up the liquor and trying to sweep up all the tiny broken shards from every nook and cranny, wondering why continuously splashing my face with pool water wasn't keeping me from collapsing, closing my eyes, and passing out against the bar. Which I eventually did, of course, only to jerk awake a minute later, startled and disoriented, finding nothing but a vast, silent blanket of stars looking down on me.

When I'd entered her room today, I'd stuck one hand in my pocket, clumsily trying to conceal the massive, throbbing blister, which Louisa's aloe—and nothing else — was doing its best to help. I'd accepted a gauze wrap from the housekeeper earlier, but ripped it off quickly, as it made any kind of manual labor impossible instead of merely painful. How clever of Corey to deprive me of the one and only value he thought I had.

Okay, look. The phone had no search function, okay? She told me that when she'd handed it over. And I'd have to get rid of it soon anyway. If Maeve had gotten caught—or worse—and it was somehow tracked, I couldn't have it on me. And now Louisa was out of the room, caught up in a heated phone conversation with her mom, who had called from the golf course with some incoherent emergency. The laptop was just sitting there. I already had the password. Plus, I'd pored over everything I could find about Max Langer for the past year and found nothing useful except what had gotten me here but now, at least, I had another name to research: Resi. The one who was supposedly saving us all. Typing that name into the search bar —it wasn't like it was a common name around here—was sure to give me a clue, and it would literally take two seconds. And I could delete the search history in less than that

I leaned back in the wicker chair casually, tapping a pencil against my chin, unable to make out much of the conversation from the hallway and so naturally deciding to think about Max

Langer instead. I felt further away from figuring out what the billionaire's game was than when I started, or how closely Corey was involved in it. But I was convinced that saving us from the gardener was just one short move in a long, long game. *Never assume the queen is safe just because she's standing still.*

And as for that game? Well kidnapping ambiguously-enslaved girls to experiment on them clearly hadn't worked, so he'd moved on to frightening and manipulating them into enslaving themselves. And then *that* hadn't worked, so he—

"Okay, Mom, but is there anyone —"

Grabbing the textbook, I shot up straight in the chair, then relaxed and took a deep breath as Louisa resumed pacing the hallway.

Fuck, I should just tell her. I should whip out the broken, bloody bracelet, the one weighing like a stone in my back pocket, and *show* her what happened. Throw it on the desk just like Corey had thrown it at me. *This is what your kind does.* And see how she'd react.

But I knew how she'd react. The same way she'd reacted the last time I'd reminded her what her kind did. Gasp and be horrified and offer to do anything she could to help. God damn her, this wasn't how any of this was supposed to go.

Because whatever help she could offer would lead us straight back to her father. And then where would that leave us?

With a choice. One she shouldn't have to make. One *no one* should have to make. But that was the world we were in, even if it was easy to forget while being jacked off by the smoothest, most perfectly manicured hands that had ever touched my dick.

Look, obviously, things had changed. She and I were now inhabiting an entirely different universe than the one we'd met in, one where the impossible had become possible, the untouchable had become touchable. Where strangers had become friends had become ... um, well. A universe I really couldn't bear to contemplate ever leaving, much as I wanted to be able to.

But other things hadn't changed. Some things could *never* change. And as my eyes darted between the hallway and the desk, I knew I'd have to make a decision soon. And not just about the computer.

About everything.

HER

"See you soon, Mom. Bye," I said, thoroughly embarrassed but grateful that my emergency trip to the country club to pick her up had been called off, thanks to a pitying golf league friend who happened to live in our neighborhood.

I reached for my bedroom door to throw it open, but for some reason stopped. Heart pounding, I left it ajar instead, listening for any noise coming from inside, though it was silent except for the ticking clock. I felt sick, but something told me to creep closer to peer through the crack. And when I did, I drew in a sharp breath, my stomach twisting as I spoke: "What are you doing?"

ACKNOWLEDGMENTS

While *Never Broken* is Everly's debut, it is not *my* debut. I've been writing, ghostwriting, and publishing for many years. This book had two points of origin: First, an experience ten years ago, on a vintage sailing schooner crossing the Atlantic, where two people from very different backgrounds were forced into proximity to learn from each other, and one of them had a very rich imagination and a lot of spare time to write. Second, as a longtime reader of slavery-focused fanfic and original fic, when I began to feel the way so many writers do: after endless scrolling, I never found the type of story I really wanted to read. Namely, an M/F story featuring a slave who, rather than being submissive, was an alpha romance hero in disguise. And— because I'm a classics nerd—a clever, charming con artist in the tradition of the stock slave characters in the Roman comedies of Plautus (look for more about him in *Never Bound*). Of course, those characters never got the girl, so I decided to change that.

I then shoved it aside for many years to focus on more "serious" writing more suited to my expensive MFA degree, pretty much all of which turned out to be dead ends that my heart wasn't in. At the tail end of the pandemic, struggling with mental health issues and looking for anything to give my life purpose, I dusted off the first few chapters of this book and called it *Good Slaves Never Break the Rules*. To my shock, people liked it a lot, and encouraged me to keep going. When I finished, I chose to publish it. And it did give my life purpose and explains why my first piece of advice to all writers is: Write what you want, not what you think you should. Because chances are other people want it, too.

And now that you know the rest of the story, it's time to thank those who got me from the paint room of a schooner to the moment you, wherever you are, picked up my book.

Nigel, my partner in so many things. Without you, none of this would be happening. Hell, maybe I wouldn't be happening. But beyond that, the fact that you exist lets me breathe a little easier at night. Love you lots.

My PA and proofreader, Brianne, stepped in and started organizing my life and career before I knew I even needed it, and never stopped. Spoiler alert: I really needed it.

The Ao3 and Tumblr whump and slavefic communities not only inspired me thematically but gave rise to some of my earliest fans. You would not be holding this book if they had not clicked on it first. First among equals is Kate Malden aka Little-PerilStories, who became not only my cheerleader, but my beta reader, unpaid therapist, and friend, and is the only person I know who loves boys in chains as much as I do. (The Mark of Thieves, let's go!) Special kudos also go to ThereAreNoNames-ForWhatIAm, an OG commenter and talented fellow author who stuck with me to the very end and beyond.

My beta readers, Adele, Alison, Angela, Ana, Annie, Cobalt Jade, Havilah, Love, Macabray, Micaela, Queen, Ritika, Sill, Shelby, and Shika, helped me take a 300,000-word serial story and shape it into a trilogy of honest-to-God novels with beginnings, middles, and ends.

My talented editor, Emily A. Lawrence, who spent way too much time fixing em dashes, preserved my voice perfectly, and got invested in the story even though it wasn't part of her job description.

My gifted cover designer Najla Qamber and her colleague Nada Qamber stepped in to solve my cover crisis when I was about to give up, giving this "off-market" book not one but two gorgeous works of art primed to sell.

My early Tumblr cover critiquers Anya, Emmi, Lanx, and Mallory, convinced me to get a new design and without whom you would be looking at a cover that resembled, in the words of one of them, "maybe a BDSM romcom?"

The patient folks on the Indie Authors Ascending Discord server helped as I further critiqued every single aspect of my author brand, because if I was going to publish, I was determined to do it right, dammit. And they were nice enough to only ban me once. Special kudos to fellow IAA "off-market" writer Anna Callaway. If we're ripping our hair out in frustration, at least we can do it together.

My Rule Breakers street team, a dozen or so amazing Booksta/Booktok folks, happily went above and beyond to support an author whose book they hadn't even read yet. They played a huge role in getting my name out there and made the marketing life so much easier. Many of them found me from the wonderful Dark Romance Team engagement group, which helped me gain social media traction early on.

My ARC readers—hundreds of you, too many to name. Thanks for taking a chance on a debut you probably didn't know what to make of.

Ellie at LoveNotes PR found many of my ARC readers and always responded to my frantic emails and requests.

My IRL friends Melissa, Marcelo, Amanda, and Conor support my writing and support me despite not being allowed to read this book, and no matter where in the world we meet up, are always up for a drink or ten — next year in Anegada. And of course Leslie, my home from home on the Florida coast where I no doubt wrote some of this. And for my found island family — sailing and finance folk, mostly — who don't know what the hell to make of the tortured writer in their midst who was always randomly staring off into space, but always figured I'd come out with something good one of these days. Well, here it is.

My teachers, especially Mrs. Edwards and Mrs. Wolff, have been saying for decades that I was the best writer they ever taught. Maybe someday I'll believe it.

My writing professors and classmates in my *former* writing life, after countless hours of having our work pummelled to death in undergraduate and graduate writing workshops, never thought a book like this would be the result. (Actually, knowing me, they probably did).

Too many aunts, uncles, and cousins to name, most of whom don't understand what I write, how, or why, but are always nice enough to ask me about it anyway.

Mom, Dad, David, Rachel, and Nora. I love you, and the only thing I've ever wanted to do in this life is make you proud. I hope I have.

ABOUT THE AUTHOR

Everly Claire is a full-time writer living on a palm-fringed, white-sand beach on a Caribbean island (really, you should try it!) with her partner and a couple of cats. When she's not writing, she spends her time on a boat or a beach (always with a fruity cocktail in hand), getting nerdy (and kicking ass!) at trivia night, and/or dreaming up more hot scenarios and dark twists involving protective, wounded, witty men you aren't allowed to touch (but we all know you will, anyway).

If you liked this book, a review is the single most powerful thing you can do to support me, whether it's on Amazon, Goodreads, or your social media platform of choice. You can find all my links by scanning the QR code or by visiting link-tr.ee/everlyclaire. I love to chat, so don't be shy to connect!

instagram.com/everlyclaireauthor
facebook.com/everly.claire.author
tiktok.com/@everly_claire

Made in United States
Orlando, FL
30 December 2024